THE MAYOR OF OAK STREET

Vincent Traughber Meis

A NineStar Press Publication

www.ninestarpress.com

The Mayor of Oak Street

Printed in the USA

ISBN: 978-1-64890-275-8

First Edition, June, 2021

Also available in eBook, ISBN: 978-1-64890-274-1

WARNING:

This book contains sexual content, which may only be suitable for mature readers. Depictions of addiction, child abuse, depression, drug/alcohol use/addiction, and overdose.

In the 1960s, Midwestern boy and Boy Scout, Nathan delivers newspapers and mows lawns. Nathan uses his cover to move about yards and sneak into the homes of his neighbors, uncovering their secrets.

In high school, one of the local misfits introduces him to diet pills, which help him overcome his shyness. In an amphetamine high, he meets Cindy, who he hopes will steer him along the "morally straight" path of the Boy Scout Oath he swore to.

Nathan is infatuated with a young doctor down the street, Nicholas (Dr. B), who embodies all the things his mother would love him to be. On one of his secret forays in Dr. B's house, he hides in a closet and witnesses his idol having sex with man while the wife is out of town. Dr. B's affair leads to tragedy, forcing the doctor to leave town. At college in New Orleans, Nathan meets a group of rebels and expands his drug use. Marc, a bisexual Cajun charmer becomes Nathan's first male sexual experience, but promptly leaves town.

Nathan has a chance encounter with Dr. B, who has moved to New Orleans. Dr. B is in a relationship, but still closeted. Frustrated by Dr. B's cool reaction, Nathan goes on a six-month binge of amphetamines and anonymous sex. On one night of debauchery, he overdoses and ends up in the emergency ward.

Nathan's near death rallies Dr. B and Nathan's other friends to force him into rehab. On the way home from work, Nathan witnesses the gruesome aftermath of the 1973 Up Stairs Lounge fire that devastated the gay population of New Orleans. As a result of the fire, Dr. B's live-in boyfriend leaves town, freeing Dr. B to explore his feelings for Nathan.

In memory of the victims in the arson fire at the Up Stairs Lounge in New Orleans in 1973.

One: Home Invasion

The Sangamon flows muddy and rank through the corn and soybean fields of central Illinois, giving its name to my city and the lake it fills on the south side before continuing its meander west. One of its tributaries, the even lazier and muddier Harold's Creek, ran practically up to my back door in its own journey through the woods behind the homes on Oak Street.

The afternoon sun filtered through the tall trees, warming my shoulders as I walked along the creek, imagining building a raft like I had seen my brother and his friends do a few years before. I would ride it down the creek to the Sangamon and into the Illinois, eventually reaching the Mississippi. The Mississippi would take me to New Orleans, a city memorialized in song, literature, and film as a place of wonder. It wasn't that I needed to run away like Huckleberry Finn. I hadn't yet learned to hate everything the Sangamon gave its name to. It was a boy's fantasy brought on by the heat of summer and the mesmerizingly sluggish flow of water.

I heard a branch snap deep in the woods. I often saw hobos from the nearby Wabash Line wandering in the woods, and my mother told me I needed to avoid them, but I sometimes watched them from behind a clump of bushes. My eyes darted around the area and saw nothing. I glanced at my watch. Time to go. For most kids, these were the carefree days of summer, but I had things to do. From the creek, I walked up the hill, through our backyard, and out to the street.

Mrs. Sloan's heavy oak door hung wide open while a screen kept the swarms of late summer flies and mosquitoes at bay. I put my face to the mesh in what felt like an invasion of her privacy, causing me to tingle from the top of my head down to my big toes.

"Hello? Mrs. Sloan?" I shouted into the dim interior of the hall.

No answer.

I opened the screen door haltingly and stepped inside. The door creaked shut, sounding painful in the silence of the house. I took a step, and then another. My legs shook. I peered to the right into the living room and left into the dining room. A force had taken control of me and pushed me on, my sneakers barely touching the carpet.

I went as far as the kitchen, passing two empty bedrooms on the way. Her purse sat on the yellow chrome Formica kitchen table, the keys to her Oldsmobile right next to it. Out the kitchen window, I searched for her floppy straw hat in the sunny backyard. She was neither in the garden where she often tended her vegetables nor in the lawn chair where she sometimes sat, large sunglasses on her nose and a cocktail in hand. I took note the lawn needed mowing.

Nylons hung over the bathroom shower curtain rod, hypnotically swaying in the breeze from the open window.

Though we called her Mrs. Sloan, I had never heard of a Mr. Sloan. My father once complained about entering the bathroom and finding my mother's nylons drying in plain sight. I wondered if Mrs. Sloan was sad living alone or happy she had the freedom to do what she wanted.

I should have been scared of her coming home and finding me lurking in her house, but a stronger force blocked the fear, a compelling energy moving my mind and body, making me feel impervious to danger. I continued down the hall to the living room, stopping to gaze at each of three framed needlepoint messages: "There's nothing to fear but fear itself," "A cheery smile makes life worthwhile," and "You belong among the wildflowers."

I had come to Mrs. Sloan's door in my rounds, collecting for my paper route. She was a month behind in her payments. And I rationalized my invasion of her home out of concern for her welfare. My mother once said she wouldn't be surprised to find her passed out drunk on the front lawn one day. My brother in high school sometimes came home from a night of drinking with his buddies and would collapse face down on his bed in our shared room without removing his clothes or shoes. One time, he ended up on the floor. Perhaps Mrs. Sloan had fallen like my brother. Perhaps she had fallen asleep in the bath and was at risk of drowning like I had seen on a television program.

I spent a few more minutes in the house before exiting through the front door into the calm and quiet on Oak Street. I continued up the block to do the rest of the collections. That night I drew a floor plan of her home, noting doors and windows. My brother called me a weirdo when the first thing I looked at in the Sunday paper was the page with the floor plan of a new house on the market while he went for the sports section, my father the news, and my mother the book reviews. I also scribbled notes about Mrs. Sloan's house: the color and shape of her purse, the black-and-white photo of a somber older couple in the living room, the buff-colored nylons, the approximately twelve-inch cross hanging over her bed, and the needlepoint messages.

Before I entered my teenage years, I would know my way in and out of most every house on the block without being discovered. It was the Midwest. It was the '60s. Crime happened elsewhere. In addition to delivering papers, I mowed lawns. I could cross barriers, move within fences, and befriend dogs. Access. Getting inside the house was usually the easy part.

Everybody told me my paper route and lawn-mowing jobs would be good experience though I had no idea how much I would learn about myself, about others, about life, the good and the bad. I could assume the face of the upstanding neighborhood boy, appearing at their doors to collect subscription payments, smiling and making small talk while below the surface I was another person, motivated by desires they would never understand.

The second time I entered a home was as spontaneous as the first. It was the Pruitts'. While mowing the front lawn, I noticed Mrs. Pruitt lock the front door, take her two identically dressed little girls by the hand, jump into their Ford station wagon, and drive off. When I got around to the back of the house, I spotted the kitchen door standing open, beckoning me. I turned off the mower so I would hear if the car returned. I went into the kitchen.

My mother would die rather than let our kitchen fall into such disorder; the sink filled with dirty dishes, and the kitchen table covered with open schoolbooks and scattered papers.

A half-full milk carton sat on the counter. I opened the fridge and saw a whole shelf of soda pop. I took an orange Crush and drank it as I did a quick tour of the house. Not much interesting. The rest of the house was as messy as the kitchen. I finished the soda outside, threw the bottle in the trashcan, and finished mowing the lawn. Before I went to bed that night, I drew a floor plan of their three-bedroom and put it in a folder with Mrs. Sloan's.

I thought of these intrusions as accidents, isolated incidents that wouldn't be repeated. But images of those escapades kept dancing through my head, enticing me to do it again. The rush of danger, the real possibility I might be caught, was like a drug. At the time I was still ignorant about drugs and addictions, but my body clearly knew sensations it wanted to revisit. I managed to stave off my urges for a few months. I turned twelve over the summer, and several of my customers who had heard it was my birthday tacked on a bit extra to their payments.

Lawn-mowing season came to an end as the weather turned cold, and we had our first snowfall. Soon after, I started receiving calls about paper holds for the Thanksgiving holidays. To me, they might as well have been invitations. I prayed it didn't snow as the soft whiteness would show the hard dirty prints of my boots, a trail of my activities. I had to start thinking about such things: tracks I might leave, who in the neighborhood tended to snoop out their windows, or how often people left doors unlocked, windows open.

I made a point of being friendly with the dogs on my street as I knew my extracurricular activities at houses with animals could be a problem. The Jackmans had a golden retriever. I'd received notice to put their paper on hold for five days, making me guess they weren't going to leave the dog in the house for that length of time.

When I did my collections the week before Thanksgiving, I casually mentioned to Mrs. Jackman that I had received the hold notice. People loved to give out information they didn't have to. She revealed they were going to their lake house in Arkansas. Butch was curled up at her feet. He raised his head as she took a ten out of her wallet and gave it to me. She told me to keep the change, and I thanked her profusely while I tore off her receipt.

I reached down to pet the dog. "I guess Butch is going to get a vacation too."

"Oh, yeah. He loves it down there."

Bingo, I was in. After our Thanksgiving meal, Dad and my brother watched the football game on TV while Mom cleaned up. I went to my room, saying I was going to read. Nobody thought it was odd. In my family, everybody did pretty much what he or she wanted. Normally, after a Thanksgiving meal, Dad and my brother passed out in front of the TV, and Mom curled up in a chair to read after cleaning up the kitchen. They had all had a lot of wine at dinner, including David, who my parents allowed to drink though he was only sixteen, something about him learning to drink responsibly at home keeping him from being irresponsible when he went out. I wasn't sure that was working.

I slipped out through the garage and crept into the Jackman yard. They hid a key to the back door in a place no one would *ever* think of looking—under a flowerpot. One day when I mowed the lawn, I had seen one of the kids use it when they came home from school. It was too easy.

As economically minded citizens, they had turned down the heat before going on their trip, and I felt a dark chill as I entered the house. It was overcast outside. I accidentally kicked the dog's water bowl and sent liquid all over the floor. I mopped it up with a dishtowel hanging on the oven handle. They had left a light on in the living room, a security measure, I supposed. Leave a key under the flowerpot and a light on in the living room. Not yet in high school, and I had already learned a lot of human behavior lacked basic logic. I stayed out of the living room since someone could see me from the street, then went instead to the master bedroom. They had a four-poster bed with a canopy, which made me think they had delusions of royalty. I rummaged around in a drawer of one of the bedside tables, coming upon a banana-shaped object. I flicked a switch, and it started to vibrate. My mind grappled with but could not arrive at the concept. I returned it to the drawer and hurried into another bedroom. An Etch A Sketch sat on a bed. I picked it up, drew a funny house, and dropped it on top of the comforter.

Over the holidays from Thanksgiving to New Year's, I was able to draw floor plans of four more houses and catalogue a number of details like what brand of cereal people ate and what kind of television they owned. But one house remained elusive, taunting me every time I walked by: the house of Dr. Baronian. I had never received a paper hold from them, and Mrs. Baronian always seemed to be home. On the two occasions I happened to see Mrs. Baronian leave the house, I hurried over to try the back door. It was always locked. In the evenings, the lit-up front windows stared at me, daring me to cross the threshold and uncover its secrets.

Dr. Baronian or Dr. B, as we called him, was a star in the neighborhood. His wife, Jill, seemed a little sad. Their daughter, Judy, was my age, but people said she was way out of my league—as if I had any desire to be a player. She always looked perfect and was one of the most popular girls at junior high. I couldn't say why, but I had a strong premonition that, behind the walls of the castle that held Princess Judy, an unsolved mystery brewed.

She avoided me for the most part, but when we were forced to cross paths, she seemed to see right through me. With a slight glance, she gave me the impression she knew I wasn't the boy I made out to be though I doubted she fathomed the whole story, the underlying perversity of my being. Had she, at some point, seen me staring at her father? Of course, everyone stared at Dr. B given half the chance the way Midwesterners do—the women of the neighborhood at his matinee-idol good looks and the men to make sure he didn't stare back at their wives. He didn't. And that made the husbands more suspicious.

I first became aware of the Baronians when my brother told me a family was finally moving into 432, and I should go check it out. The paper route was officially in his name back then, but I did most of the work. He gave me my fair cut. To expand our mini empire, we were always on the lookout for potential customers.

"Should I ask them if they want to take the paper?"

"Just, you know, scope it out."

I rode my bike past the house with a moving van parked out front and a short time later doubled back. Trying not to appear too nosy, I stopped at a distance from the house and straddled my bike. A woman with her hair tied in a kerchief stood by the front door and fretfully directed the movers, sometimes changing her mind at the last minute about where a piece of furniture might go. A girl about my age sat in an overstuffed chair on the front lawn, looking as if she was the one truly directing the show. She looked at me and sneered.

In the same moment as her intimidating stare made me feel I should be getting on my way, a black Porsche pulled into the driveway, and a man wearing Bermuda shorts and a Lacoste polo shirt got out. I had recently seen the movie *Goldfinger*, and the man looked like Sean Connery. He was the most handsome man I had ever seen in person.

A week or so later, I heard my parents talking about the new neighbors.

"I thought I recognized the name," said my mother. "And then it hit me. His parents are members of the country club, and I used to see him there as a teenager. When he went away to college and then med school, he was only around occasionally."

My father took an interest. "Have you met his wife?"

"I took over some cookies yesterday."

"And?"

"I don't know. She seems a bit odd. I mean, she's very nice, just...I don't know. She invited me in for coffee. We sat at the kitchen table. Everything was put away as if they'd lived there for months. At times she stared off into space, and it was up to me to keep the conversation going."

"They seem kind of young to have a daughter Nate's age."

"She said they met in college and got married right away."

"Shotgun marriage?"

"I thought the same thing. Then she confessed that the doctor isn't Judy's father. She was married before, but her husband, a medic, was killed in the Korean War. Judy was still a baby. It all makes sense because Dr. Baronian is simply too young to be her dad."

"You're saying she's quite a bit older than he is?"

"I don't know about quite a bit. I'm guessing five years or so. They lived in Chicago while he went to med school, but he always wanted to return to his hometown. She was more than happy to leave Chicago. You know, his father is a doctor too. They live out by the lake, I think."

"Sounds like you two got chummy."

"I couldn't help but think they seemed like an odd couple. He's so dashing with his sports car and good looks. And she's rather quiet and, frankly, plain, not to mention an older woman." Mom waved her hands in the air and rattled her voice at the scandal. "She's educated though."

When Mom said she recognized Dr. Baronian from the club, an eerie feeling ran through me. I had also felt something familiar about him, stronger than the impression I had simply seen him before. When I was seven, I had a traumatic near-drowning at the club pool.

I didn't have many friends growing up, and my mom always encouraged me to make new ones. She arranged for one of her friends who had a son my age to pick me up to go swimming. The kid turned out to be a real jerk. We were horsing around near the pool, and he pushed me into the deep end. I felt comfortable swimming as long as the water wasn't over my head. After the initial shock of being pushed into the water, my feet desperately sought the security of the bottom of the pool.

Despite flailing my arms, I started sinking. Panic set in. I took in gulps of water. No matter how much I kicked, a force pulled me down. The next thing I remembered was the muffled plunge of a person hitting the water and bubbles all around me. Strong arms surrounded me and pulled me to the surface. He dragged me to the edge of the pool, and I was lifted onto the concrete.

When I opened my eyes, coughing and spewing water, the lifeguard immediately turned me on my side. While he worked on getting the water out of my lungs, I stared at the hair on his feet, which I assumed to be the feet of my savior.

A crowd had gathered, and soon the mother of my failed new friendship hovered over me with furrowed brow and a tense jaw. She told me they'd called my mother, and she would be there any minute. In all the commotion, I wasn't able to thank the lifeguard for saving my life. A week later, I saw him at the pool.

"Sorry. I never got a chance to thank you for rescuing me."

The lifeguard crossed his arms and grinned. "It wasn't me. Well, I got the water out of you, but someone else dove in to get you."

"Who?"

"Some guy I see around here from time to time. Don't know his name. I think he plays tennis."

It had always been a mystery to me who saved my life until the day I overheard my mother talking about the new neighbor. It jogged a memory. As I tossed about in the water and before I went under, I saw a young man watching me from the edge of the pool. I was now certain Dr. B saved my life.

*

The doorbell rang, and I jumped up from the piano bench. "I'll get it." Any excuse to get away from Chopin was welcome. I opened the door and sucked in air. "Dr. Baronian." I was so nervous I garbled the pronunciation of his name.

He laughed saying, "Please call me Dr. B. Everybody does." They had only been in the neighborhood a few weeks, and I hadn't seen him since the day they moved in. He looked dashing in pleated khaki pants and a crisp blue Oxford cloth shirt that complimented his olive skin.

I stared at the perfect fit and tuck of his shirt while he waited expectantly on the other side of the screen. The sun shone down on him like a spotlight. A fly repeatedly buzzed against the screen, trying to get out. I realized I hadn't introduced myself. "I'm Nate."

"Yes. Your brother told me about you when he came around to collect. He said you usually deliver the papers. Was that you playing the piano?"

"Pretty bad, huh?"

"Not at all. Practice, practice, practice, though I'm sure your teacher has told you that. Is your mother home?"

"Mom," I shouted. "Dr. Baronian is at the door." This time I made sure my pronunciation was adequate.

"Just a minute. Invite him in." Her voice was muffled and seemed to come from the downstairs bathroom.

"Please come in."

He opened the screen door and stepped into the hall. He stood a couple of feet in front of me, and I didn't know what to look at, focusing at last on his hairy arms extending from his perfectly rolled up sleeves. His attention was drawn to the living room. "What kind of piano is that?"

"Uh..."

"It's a Mason and Hamlin," said my mother as she swept into the entryway and saved me from embarrassment. "My husband inherited it from his parents." I now knew why it had taken her so long to get to the door. A few minutes before she'd had curlers in her hair. She must have rushed into the bathroom to take them out when she heard the doorbell. She stuck out her hand. "I'm Jackie Landis. I had the pleasure of meeting your wife the other day, and now I'm pleased to meet you."

The doctor flashed a flawless smile. "The pleasure is all mine."

"Come on in the living room. Would you like some coffee?"

"Oh, don't go to the trouble."

"No trouble at all." She gushed like a schoolgirl. "It's already made. Cream and sugar?"

"Black is fine."

"That's the way I take it too. My husband doctors his up so much I like to say, 'Would you like some coffee with that cream and sugar?'" They both laughed like it was the funniest thing in the world. Adults could act queerly when sniffing one another out, so different from dogs that went right to it. "Nate, take Dr. Baronian over to the sofa. Maybe you can play something for him."

"I'm sure Dr. B would rather hear cats fighting."

"Oh, honey, you play nicely. You two sit down and have a chat then. I'll be right back."

We sat on opposite ends of the sofa. He kept glancing at the piano, and I searched for something to fill the awkward silence. "How do you like the neighborhood?" I asked.

"Love it. Everybody has been quite friendly. You and my daughter, Judy, must be about the same age."

Did you have to bring her into it? We were having a perfectly nice conversation. "Yes, I've seen her at school."

"Next year she'll be going to St. Mary's. What about you?"

"I'll go to Westwood."

"Here we are." My mom set a silver platter with two Haviland Schleiger cups from my grandmother's service we only used on special occasions on the coffee table. Steam rose from the dark liquid. "Oh, I'm sorry, honey. Did you want something?"

"I'll have a beer," I said.

Dr. B laughed out loud.

"Don't be ridiculous, dear. What's Dr. Baronian going to think?"

"Please call me Nick."

"Is that short for Nicholas?"

"Yes, it is."

"And your last name...?"

"I'm Armenian on my father's side."

The name, Nicholas Baronian, bounced around softly in my head. It was the most beautiful name I had ever heard. I tried it with sort of an Eastern European accent. I tried it with a French accent. I imagined it would sound wonderful in any accent in the world.

I lost track of the conversation until I heard my mother say, "Oh, you play?"

He looked down at his hands and smiled demurely. "I thought about a career in music before I decided to go to med school."

"And piano is your instrument?" She blushed slightly.

He continued with the tiniest grin on his face. "I play classical mostly. There's been a problem shipping my piano, so I've been without one since we left Chicago."

"Then you must play ours. I'm sure Nate wouldn't mind a break from his practicing."

"Well, if you insist," I said with a chuckle. "Why don't you play something right now?"

The doctor looked at my mother for her approval, and she nodded enthusiastically. "Please."

He sat down on the piano bench with his spine straight, flexed his fingers, and placed them hovering over the keys. "I'm probably a bit rusty." He stared at the sheet music I had left on the stand. He eased into the Chopin nocturne I had been trying to play, though after a few seconds I barely recognized it as the same piece. He took the simplified version and embellished it, not only with an abundance of new notes but a style and passion I could never muster. My trills never sounded like that.

Mom picked up the tray and motioned with her head I should join her in exiting the room. I guess she thought he wanted to be alone, particularly after his "rusty" comment, though it was already clear his words reeked of false modesty. As we made our exit, I glanced back to see he had, in fact, left us, already transported to another dimension.

We sat in the breakfast nook of the kitchen, smiling at the glorious sounds coming from the other room. "You could play like that someday."

I shook my head.

"Well, you could." Mothers do, at times, live in an alternate reality of hope for their children. I had no talent for the piano and knew I would never make her proud in that way. At the same time as being impressed by his playing, I had to be amused at the way he had finagled his way into our living room. He had not come to our door to pay us a social call, make friends with my mother, or, in my wildest fantasy, meet the person who delivered his newspaper. He had come for our piano, and it hadn't been necessary for him to ask to play it. We offered. It was the first time I'd become aware of how some people went through life, charming others to get what they wanted, not having to put themselves in the position of soliciting when plenty of people like us would give freely.

And yet he gave us something too—his presence, his music, and the momentary pleasure of being uplifted to a plane higher than our normal existence. In the expression on my mother's face, I observed exactly how important it was for her to not be seen as a farmer's daughter. Her whole life, from insisting on getting an education to marrying a professor to joining the country club to having a baby grand piano in the living room were strides at leaving the past behind.

She had grown up on a farm, the youngest of three daughters. She learned how to muck out a horse stall, feed pigs, and milk a cow, skills she hoped to never use once she left the farm, which she always knew she would. Until then, books took her away from the drudgery of farm life. Her father used to yell at her when he caught her reading instead of doing her chores.

She was determined to get an education even though her father railed against girls getting "too much smarts." As the two older girls had no academic aspirations, her mother put all her hope in Jacqueline, squirreling away some of the money from selling eggs and milk so she could go to college. And now I, as the next generation, would have to further that trajectory and make her proud.

We stood at the front door and watched Dr. Baronian walk down the sidewalk, tall, confident, and relaxed after his miniconcert. My mom put her hand on my shoulder, giving me the impression she hoped I would turn out like our illustrious neighbor. I hoped so too.

Two: Corncob Jelly

No one would have anticipated I would become a Boy Scout. Neither my father nor my brother had been a Scout. We didn't belong to the church where my troop met, and I certainly had enough keeping me busy with school, the paper route, and lawn mowing. My mother suggested it, most likely because she thought learning skills in the wild through camping, aquatics, and hiking would toughen me up. Even in my naïve youth, I thought it curious parents who were worried about their sons' masculinity—simply put, afraid they would be sissies— would send them out to sleep in close contact with several boys in a tent, supervised by scoutmasters who liked to get away from their wives and families and spend time running around in the woods skinny-dipping with young boys.

At the age of eleven, I agreed to go to one meeting to see what it was all about. I took to it much more than I anticipated. I wasn't sure if it was the uniforms, the structured camaraderie, or the semi-military organization into troops where you were on the inside and everyone else was out. I suppose we all have at least a little fascist in us.

The meeting began with the Pledge of Allegiance. The two leaders, laden with patches and sashes and neckerchiefs, instructed everyone in uniform to salute the flag. It was open-house night, so us "civilians" were told to put our hands on our hearts instead of saluting. The Pledge was followed by the Boy Scout Oath where all the boys held up three fingers and recited their promise to "To keep myself physically strong, mentally awake, and morally straight." Then, one Scout was chosen to lead the troop in reciting the Scout Law, the twelve characteristics a Scout should possess. Aside from the snappy uniforms with all the colorful patches—they actually had a brief uniform inspection—I wasn't particularly impressed.

At long last, we got to the promised skills instruction part of the meeting. The activity of the evening was lassoing a steer, a skill I was sure to use frequently throughout my life. The boys were given twenty-foot pieces of rope and told to make a bowline knot. A two-foot log was placed upright in the middle of the room, and everybody was given a chance to lasso it, even the new "recruits." When my chance came, I failed miserably. Apparently, steer roping wasn't in my genes.

During the breakout time, each potential new Scout was assigned a leader who would answer questions. The striking young man with curly dark hair assigned to me wore a sash with tons of colorful merit badges and another sash with a red arrow on it, signifying he was a member of the elite group of the Order of the Arrow. I asked him about the merit badges and how he got them.

He told me he earned a lot of them by documenting things he already did like coin collecting. Coin collecting, honestly? He pointed out the small circular badge with a gold coin on it. Others were more challenging, he explained, like first aid, which looked like the Red Cross symbol. I asked if there was one for lawn mowing, and he said he wasn't sure, but there was definitely a gardening badge, which he pointed out, approximately where his heart was. I considered asking if I could touch the badges, and then thought better of it. I couldn't wait to get my uniform and start collecting my own badges.

Two years later, I was a few badges short of the twenty-one required for Eagle Scout, and I was a member of the Order of the Arrow. The National Boy Scout Jamboree in Valley Forge, Pennsylvania, was that summer, and the troop leaders hoped at least one member of the troop would represent us. The trip also included a day in New York City for the 1964 World's Fair. Despite all my achievements, others were higher ranked or better liked, making me feel I didn't have a chance. As it turned out, no one else could go due to the cost or summer plans or lack of interest. It was up to me to represent my troop.

On a hot summer day a few weeks short of my thirteenth birthday, I stood in the middle of a sea of boys dressed in identical uniforms emblazoned with the brand-new National Jamboree Valley Forge patch over the right pocket and the designated troop number for our region on the left sleeve. Scouts from all over the central part of the state were gathered to board a special train to Philadelphia, a trip that would take all day and overnight. I still hadn't achieved my growth spurt, so I struggled under the weight of my duffle bag with my name and troop number spelled out in black Magic Marker across the heavy fabric. We looked like child soldiers going off to war.

Scoutmaster Jenkins, a wiry, hard-looking man with graying hair, assembled us in the corner of the station and read announcements off a clipboard. The good news was the train would arrive in a few minutes, and they had provided sleeping cars. The not-so-good news was they hadn't been able to get enough cars for each person to have his own berth. "We have to buddy up, men," he said with a chuckle.

"Oh crap," a boy next to me said in a low voice. "Have you ever seen how small a berth is? Barely big enough for one person." His name was Eric, and he was from Danville.

"I've got a list here," continued the Scoutmaster. "When you've got your buddy, come and tell me, and I'll assign you a berth."

I turned to Eric to ask him if he wanted to be my buddy, but he was already talking with another boy he seemed to know. They walked over to Jenkins and gave him their names. I looked around, and everybody appeared to be paired up, conjuring up a familiar feeling of standing on the playground alone after all the other boys had been picked for a team.

The train arrived, and we lined up. Jenkins stood at the bottom of the steps to check us off as we boarded. I reached the front of the line and told him my name.

"Who's your buddy, Landis?"

"I couldn't find one, sir."

"Guess you're stuck with me." He scribbled on his clipboard. "Berth 2A. Good thing we're both skinny." He laughed. "Next."

Nauseated, I lamented my shyness more than at any moment in my life. Of all the people around me, Jenkins was the worst choice. When everyone was choosing their partners, I should have gone up to someone, even that fat kid with glasses, and asked if he wanted to buddy up. I had never slept in the same bed with anyone, let alone a stranger older than my father.

The day progressed with box lunches, box dinners, card games, joke telling, and boyish pranks. Eric asked me who I was sharing with, and when I told him Jenkins, he laughed out loud. He promptly apologized and invited me to his compartment to hang out with them. I spent the day dreading the night.

Late in the evening, the troop leaders and scoutmasters circulated through the train, telling us it was time to go to bed. Everybody was supposed to be in his compartment by ten thirty. When I walked into mine at 10:31, Jenkins chided me. "Thought somebody threw you from the train." He was already in an undershirt and boxers. I could smell his bad breath from several feet away. The other two occupants in the top bunk laughed and made comments I couldn't hear.

I held up the toothpaste and toothbrush in my hand. "There was a line for the johns."

I had hoped against hope he would let me be on the outside. I stripped down to my underwear and T-shirt. He pointed to the inside, and I got in. It was hot in the compartment and smelled of rank feet and Jenkins's halitosis. "Goodnight, boys," said Jenkins. "Sleep tight."

I hugged the wall so that no part of me touched Jenkins. The shade was down, but a small gap at the bottom allowed me to see the lights going by, followed by long stretches of darkness. The sway of the train gradually lulled me to sleep. I was awakened by the train horn blaring and the flashing of multicolored lights out the window as if passing through a city. Jenkins's arm was draped over my chest. I tried to wriggle my body away from him, nearly impossible in the tight confines of the berth, but he seemed to get the message, removing his arm and murmuring, "Sorry."

My brain attempted to rationalize his behavior as unintentional, possibly normal considering the circumstances, and yet my heart revved up for possible fight or flight. No way was I going back to sleep. A few endless minutes went by, followed by movement. He shifted his body, so he was on his side facing me. Again, I tried to move away from him, but he thrust one arm under my side, and with the other on top, he forcefully pulled me against him. His erection pushed into my ass crack through my underwear.

"No," I said.

He immediately slapped a hand over my mouth and whispered in my ear, "Shhh. Relax." With his free hand, he crept inside my shorts. Yes, despite every fiber in my body fighting what was happening, I had a hard-on. When you're thirteen, you can get a boner looking at the rain outside your window or a bowl of cereal you're having for breakfast. It didn't mean anything, I kept telling myself. He started stroking it and rubbing his cock against my ass still through our underwear. I stared out the window at the lights going by. My stomach churned, and my breathing quickened through his nicotine-stained hand. We had been told in health education to imagine taking a cold shower when our bodies had inappropriate responses. I tried to conjure up jumping into an alpine lake in the middle of winter.

Eventually, he stopped without finishing, thank God. Perhaps he remembered two other people were in the room. He untangled his arms and turned over facing the other way.

Looking back, I question why I didn't yell out, fight him off. If I had made a scene, the two boys in the other berth would have been roused. By breakfast time, the whole train would have known what happened. And whose life would have been made unbearable? Scoutmaster Jenkins, who was there to guide us and keep us "morally straight"? Or the shy, nerdy boy?

I crawled over Jenkins, mumbling, "Bathroom." I slipped on my uniform shorts and exited the compartment. I wandered the halls, staring out the windows, feeling dirty. When I heard someone coming, I ducked into the washroom. I was barefoot, and by this time, the floor was sticky with the urine of hundreds of boys.

At around five in the morning, I went to Eric's compartment, slid the door open, and sat on the floor. Eric raised his head. "Nate, what's going on?"

"I couldn't sleep. Can I just sit here?" My voice shook, and I sniffled.

"Come here," he whispered. "You can share my bunk."

"What?"

"My friend found his own berth. Turns out there were several singles free."

I crawled into the bed and buried my face in the pillow, trying my best to stifle my crying. He laid a hand on my back. He seemed to intuit what had happened. I will never forget his kindness. For every monster in the world, there is at least one angel.

I woke up to Eric nudging me. "Hey, sleepyhead. Get up."

One of the compartment mates leaned over from the top bunk. "Who's he?"

"He got stuck with Jenkins," said Eric. "Said he had stinky breath."

"Yeah, he's kinda weird," said the other.

I stood up and stretched. "I better get back. Thanks."

Jenkins was in our compartment packing his gear. The other two boys were out. "You'd better get packed up. We'll be arriving soon."

I gathered my things, trying to stay as far away from him as I could.

"Heh, heh. I guess I thought I was in bed with my wife last night."

Does your wife have a dick? You lying bag of shit. "Is that so?" I tried to sound like I hadn't a care in the world.

"Didn't mean anything by it. Just...you know...best we keep it to ourselves."

"Sure. Don't worry." I put on my shirt and neckerchief. "By the way, I heard there were some single berths free after all."

"I'll look into that for the way back." The train slowed down as we pulled into the station. I lifted the shade to let in light. "Hurry up," he said. "We're here."

*

Eric and I sat next to each other on the bus that rolled into Valley Forge National Historic Park where George Washington and his Continental Army holed up in the winter of 1777-1778. We stopped at the Memorial Arch and looked up at Washington's words inscribed on top. "Naked and starving as they are," Eric read. "We cannot enough admire the incomparable patience and fidelity of the soldiery."

"Naked?" I chuckled.

"Have some respect. A bunch of them died of cold and starvation."

I felt the bite of his admonishment. "I didn't know."

"I'm just messing with you. It does sound funny. I doubt they mean naked like skinny-dipping naked."

"I bet they didn't have winter clothes." I couldn't help wondering if Eric and I would have the chance to go skinny-dipping sometime.

We went down into the valley where tents were already going up for the fifty thousand Scouts in attendance, nearly five times the number of Washington's Continental Army. The sun beat down on the worker boys, pounding stakes, lifting poles, unrolling canvas. Many of them were naked to the waist.

Eric and I got to be good friends over the next few days. We shared a tent and reminded each other to put cotton in our ears before we went to bed. They had put up a sign warning us beetles crawled in your ears at night, and though we laughed about it, we were religious about stuffing our ears with cotton. When we went through the obstacle course, he went ahead of me and helped pull me over the wall we had to climb. A couple of times we would see Jenkins walking toward us from a distance, and Eric would take my arm and haul me in another direction.

Each troop had to set up an exhibit of a skill related to their geographical region. One troop from Missouri showed how to make a raft with logs and rope. A troop from Oklahoma made a windmill, and one from New Mexico demonstrated how to sew leather moccasins. The skill we chose to deliver to the world was making corncob jelly. In front of our area, we put up an ugly pink banner, reading in a childish scrawl, "Unkel Bob's Korn Cob Jelly." We weren't sure who came up with the idea and the cute spelling, but we joked it was Jenkins's wife. We would boil corncobs, add pectin and sugar to the juice, and voilà, a tasty treat representing our state, which I had never in my life tried or heard of.

While Eric, Seth, and I unloaded the cob boiling pots off the truck, Seth had a brainstorm. "We should call it cornhole jelly." He guffawed like it was the funniest thing in the world.

Panic swept across Eric's face as if he was afraid I might think he had told my secret about Jenkins. Though my laughter was slightly delayed, it came out strong. "That's actually funny. That's hilarious." From that time on, the three of us always called it cornhole jelly, at least when Jenkins wasn't nearby, and each time, we had a good laugh.

That night, Eric and I sat cross-legged, our knees touching, as Anita Bryant entertained us on a huge stage with a backdrop of the Boy Scout emblem and the jamboree theme of Strengthen America's Heritage in big red letters. It was my first time seeing a famous person on stage and she sang—ironically—"Over the Rainbow." All the boys hooted and howled. Eric and I joined in. The incident with Jenkins had been forgotten, and I had a new friend.

Near the end of the week at Valley Forge, I saw a president speak live for the first time. Lyndon Baines Johnson said that in fifty years, "Man will have reached into outer space and probed the inner secrets of human life." The part about probing the inner secrets of human life stuck with me and seemed to have meaning I could only partially grasp.

As I lay in our tent at night, I longed to repeat those several hours spent in the shared bed on the train, Eric's hand on my back, the pure joy of someone literally having my back. Fear restrained me in its iron grip. I later wondered if he, too, wanted the same but was afraid to reach out, not wanting to be like Jenkins.

Three: Love through the Louvers

The spring of 1965 was endless, exactly as the groundhog had predicted. A few warm days would tease us only to have a cold spell plunge us back into dark-and-dreary winter. April brought torrential rains, and we had a freak snowstorm the first week of May. And then out of nowhere, a heat wave made the last week of school a living hell as we sat in classrooms without air conditioning, dripping sweat onto our notebooks.

When the final school day arrived, everyone sang refrains from popular songs as they cleaned out their lockers and danced instead of trudging down the halls while young lovers expressed more overt affection in anticipation of warm nights, and guys told the same jokes they had been telling all year, but now their friends laughed. No one was more pleased than me to be out for the summer. I could begin my routine of mowing lawns and scouting out houses so I could add more notes to my files and improve my architectural drawings.

The heat wave dragged on, and Mom sometimes convinced me to go to the country club and lounge with her by the pool. We took books and found chairs in the corner under umbrellas. I kept one eye peeled for a Judy sighting, which might be an indication Dr. B was on the premises. When I saw her, I would tell Mom I had to go to the bathroom and run to the changing room in hopes of catching him there. I knew he liked to play tennis at the club courts.

In late August, my bathroom trips paid off. I did in fact need to pee and was standing at the urinal when I detected the shadow of a large person step up to the urinal next to mine. I didn't have to look to know who it was. I knew his cologne well, having smelled it a couple times in his house, standing at the bathroom mirror, opening the medicine cabinet, taking out the square bottle of Aramis, and holding it under my nose.

All I knew about cologne was that my father wore Old Spice, which lived up to its silly name, and my brother occasionally splashed on menthol-y Aqua Velva before a date. But Aramis was something different and, I imagined, expensive. Its peppery smell tickled my nose and later turned into something smoky and complex.

Yes, I had found a way into the seemingly impenetrable Baronian house. One day while I was mowing the lawn, a pebble shot out and put a small crack in a basement window. It wasn't that noticeable, but as I examined the glass, I saw the latch could be easily jimmied with a knife. I had seen Mrs. B and Judy leave, and later, the doctor. I took out my pocketknife and soon found myself in the basement.

No lock on the door up to the kitchen. In the den was a cabinet with tennis trophies and lots of pictures of the doctor in high school and college. My heart thumped in my chest. I considered putting one of the small pictures in my pocket. There were so many, I doubted it would be missed, but I decided to save it for later. Now that I had a way in, a second time I had crawled in the basement window and gone to the medicine cabinet, relishing in his cologne.

With Dr. B standing next to me at the urinal, I knew it would be impossible to pee. My gonads retreated inside me, and my penis shriveled up to the size of a baby bird. Maybe he wouldn't notice me. Wrong.

"Hey there, Nathan. Been in the pool?"

I hadn't. My skin was dry to the point of being itchy. I was getting over a summer cold, and Mom said it wasn't a good idea to go in the water. I couldn't explain all that, so I simply muttered, "Yeah."

I also knew without looking he was naked, on the way to the showers. The heat radiating off his skin made me feel like I was standing next to a furnace. And then out of this furnace, a powerful stream launched, a river pounding against the white enamel, guaranteeing that I wouldn't be able to pee.

"Are your parents here?"

"Mom," I croaked, staring at the wall where the paint had peeled off in the exact shape of a phallus.

I put my withered member back in my trunks. *Don't look. Don't look. Don't look.* As I backed away, I angled my body in the opposite direction from Dr. B. His powerful stream was still audible, followed by a loud gurgling down the drain.

"You should come by next weekend to mow," he said. He shook his penis, reminding me of something my brother loved to do. With the garden hose between his legs, he would shake it up and down, sending arcs of water in my direction.

"Okay." And in order not to sound traumatized, I added, "Sunday if that works for you." I stood with my back to him, pretending to adjust the drawstring on my trunks.

He took the towel hanging over his shoulder and wrapped it around his waist "The missus is taking Judy to see her grandmother." He walked in my direction until he stood right in front of me. Beads of sweat sparkled in his chest hair. I shifted my gaze to his tennis bag sitting on the bench near the lockers behind him. I was familiar with his bag too, having once taken out a sweaty towel and smelled it.

"Is Saturday better?"

"No. Sunday's good. I'm not going with them."

The information set off a troop of fantasies, marching through my brain.

"Say hello to your mother." He strode into the shower room, threw back a curtain, and stepped into a stall.

I hurried outside, dazzled by the sun after leaving a very dark place. I turned the corner, staggering drunk from my encounter, and nearly plowed into my mother who had come to find me. My surprise caused me to let out a squawk.

"Are you okay?" she said.

"Of course." I shielded my eyes from the sun directly in my face.

"What's going on?"

"Nothing."

"It's time to go. I have to get dinner started."

I woke up Sunday morning to a light rain. The anticipation I had nourished the last few days melted into disappointment. I normally didn't mow wet grass. It was a pain, causing the cut to be less clean and the clippings to bunch up into nasty clumps under the mower. But by noon, the sun was out, and things were drying nicely. I went over to the Baronian's around three and rang the doorbell. No one answered. My spirits tumbled again. He had forgotten. I went to the side door of the garage and looked through the glass. His black Porsche 911, which I had decided was the coolest car in the world, was not there. I had often imagined riding in the front seat, top down, racing along country roads.

I turned the handle, and the door opened. Unusual. The door into the house was also unlocked. Since the women were away, he must've let security lapse. The kitchen, normally impeccably clean, was a bit of a mess. Breakfast dishes sat in the sink. Coffee had been spilled on the counter and not wiped up. The smell of fried eggs hung in the air. It looked like he had left in a rush. I went straight to the hall closet to see if his tennis bag was there. It wasn't. He must have wanted to take advantage of the improved weather. With the ladies out of town and the doctor busy on the courts, I had the house to myself.

I lingered in front of the trophy cabinet and again contemplated swiping one of the photos. Maybe on the way out. Next, I went into Judy's room. It was overwhelmingly pink—pink roses on the wallpaper, pink bedspread, pink curtains, and a pink princess phone by the bed. In the drawer on the bedside table, I found her diary, but it had a lock on it. I rummaged around looking for the key, but I decided it wasn't worth the effort.

In the master bathroom, I opened the medicine cabinet and removed the bottle of Aramis. I took off the cap and closed my eyes, recreating in my mind the scene from a few days before; the beads of sweat in his chest hair, the funny smile on his face, and the mysterious dark eyes. I was transported to a world where my arousal was okay. I made my hand into a fist and lifted the forefinger and thumb to my lips as if it were a mouth to kiss. I completely forgot where I was until I heard a door opening. I hastily replaced the cap and returned the bottle to the cabinet.

I tried not to panic. I would have to hide in the bedroom until he went into the shower. Then I could sneak out, maybe get a peek if he left the bathroom door open. The best option seemed to be the closet. It was a double closet with a his-and-hers side. I chose her side, closing the louvered door behind me. A few seconds later, I heard Dr. B's voice, followed by another male voice. Polite conversation. Comments about the house. His wife being out of town.

Sounded like he wouldn't be taking his shower any time soon, so I had to think of a new escape plan. Assuming they were in the kitchen, there was no way I could exit the bedroom and get out of the house without being seen. Their voices got louder as they approached the bedroom. I broke into a sweat, and the smells of Mrs. B's closet, a potpourri of her flowery perfume and mothballs made me ill. But the slats did allow me a good view of the room. The light flipped on as they entered.

It was late afternoon, and the curtains were atypically closed. The young man with curly auburn hair and sporting a tennis outfit looked to be a little older than my brother, possibly a student from the college. Why would he be bringing his tennis partner into the bedroom?

They stood a mere two feet from the closet door. "Relax, Jim." Dr. B put his right hand on the young man's shoulder. Jim looked down at the beige carpet as if it were of some interest.

"I should go."

The doctor raised his left hand to the opposite shoulder and began kneading the muscles. Jim rocked back slightly, his hands crossed one over the other just below his waist, shielding himself. But Dr. B held on, his right hand now snaking to the back of Jim's neck, drawing his face forward as if they might kiss.

My heart pounded so loudly it seemed impossible they wouldn't hear it. I held my breath to stop from hyperventilating.

Jim turned so Dr. B's forehead landed gently on the side of his head. With his brow, Dr. B nuzzled Jim's temples and the curls matted there by the sweat of their game. "I could give you a massage."

Jim nodded. He looked so uncomfortable, I almost felt sorry for him. At the same time, I hated him with a passion that made no sense.

In the Midwest of the '60s, affection between men was rare. I remembered one evening my father, after several holiday cocktails, came into my room and hugged me, telling me he loved me. I was so shocked I didn't appreciate the beauty of the moment until years later. So, to watch two men touching in an intimate way was astounding, much more than the stash of pornographic magazines I had found in Mr. Burnside's garage while looking for lubricating oil for the lawnmower. I was eleven at the time, and the pictures blew up my innocence. But the men in front of me were real and, I guessed, about to embark on something that would shatter my world in far more significant ways.

Jim slumped on the bed and sat with his arms between his legs. Dr. B sighed heavily. "Stay right here. I'm going to take a quick shower." He pointed at Jim like he was a dog. "Stay," he ordered as he retreated to the bathroom.

The bathroom door remained open, and the room filled with the sound of running water. Jim put his hands on his knees and stood up. He looked at the door to the hall and around the room, lingering a moment on the closet door behind which I crouched. His eyes landed on Dr. B's wallet on top of the dresser. After staring at it a moment, he grabbed it. It was thick with bills. He took a couple and slipped them into the pocket of his shorts. The water squeaked off, and Jim resumed his distraught position on the edge of the bed.

Dr. B emerged from the bathroom in a white terrycloth robe. "Man, that felt great. You're welcome to as well."

"Do you mind?" He jumped up, scooted around Dr. B into the bathroom, and closed the door. Dr. B shook his head. He turned on the radio set to a jazz station. Ella Fitzgerald came on singing, "I'm Beginning to See the Light." I only knew the song since my dad was also a fan of jazz and listened to her. He mouthed the words in a light and casual way, giving the impression this was not a new experience for him. He opened the top drawer and dropped his wallet into it without paying any attention to its contents.

Jim returned to the bedroom with a towel wrapped around his waist and what appeared to be marginally bucked-up courage. His body was athletic, and he had a mostly smooth chest with a small island of hair in the middle. He sat on the bed again, but this time lay back with his hands behind his head. Dr. B got on his knees and gingerly loosened the towel at Jim's waist and folded back each end as if he were opening a Christmas present. My whole body shook with anticipation.

Dr. B started with nibbling kisses in a circle around Jim's crotch before taking on the main course. Jim's body appeared to tense. He gasped as Dr. B took him in his mouth. The doctor's head leisurely moved down until Jim moaned with pleasure. I had heard kids say, "blow me" or "suck my dick" at school or around the neighborhood, but I had never allowed myself to visualize how the act was done or if anybody in fact did it.

At first, I thought the sounds of slurping and sucking were grotesque. I couldn't imagine participating in such a vile act. The kiss Jim avoided looked much more pleasurable to me. But clearly Dr. B was doing something that made Jim go from a skittish cat to groaning with satisfaction. I closed my eyes and put myself in Jim's place, trying to let go the way Jim had finally allowed himself to do. I kept my eyes closed, aware of the crescendo of human sounds mixing with Dave Brubeck's piano playing from the radio, building and building until it arrived at a series of pounding chords and trills.

Jim grunted, and the noises from Dr. B's mouth stopped, a disappointing anticlimactic ending. My eyes popped open right when Dr. B stood up and swiped the arm of his robe across his mouth. He turned, the robe open, his member bobbing as he walked to the bathroom. Jim lay motionless, his hands still behind his head.

In a minute, Dr. B returned with a washcloth and dabbed at Jim's crotch. "Don't worry about it," said Jim. Removing his hands from behind his head, he grabbed the two ends of the towel and wrapped it around his waist. Dr. B stepped aside, allowing Jim to stand up, hurry into the bathroom, and close the door. Now I hated him without question. I was disgusted at the way he treated Dr. B. In a short time, Jim emerged fully dressed in his sweaty tennis clothes. "Can you drive me home?"

"Let me get dressed." Dr. B dropped the robe to the floor and stood naked. With his penis now at rest, he exuded the confidence of a Greek statue. I admired him for showing no shame. To avoid looking at the doctor, Jim twisted his neck at an odd angle toward the wall like a fool.

Dr. B opened drawers and pulled out underwear and socks. He opened the closet inches away from the one I was in and took out slacks and a polo shirt.

With one leg in his trousers, Dr. B looked up at Jim. "Are you okay?"

"I need to study. Got a test tomorrow."

What an idiot.

Jim walked out of the bedroom while Dr. B finished dressing.

A short while later, I heard the door from the kitchen to the garage close. I inhaled and exhaled normally again. I left the closet and hurried to the living room window in time to see the Porsche pull out of the garage with only Dr. B visible in the driver's seat. Jim must have crouched down so he wouldn't be seen. It seemed Dr. B's confidence didn't extend to driving out of his garage with a stranger in the car. Or was it Jim who insisted on not being seen?

The experience had been both exhilarating and horrifying; exhilarating because I realized I wasn't the only one who had those feelings and horrifying that a man who had feelings for another man must abide with the likes of Jim.

When I got home, Mom was curled up on the living room sofa reading *Up the Down Staircase*.

I stared at her, wondering how long I could stand there without her noticing me. "I'd like to take tennis lessons."

She looked up from her book quizzically as if one of the characters from the novel had jumped out and stood before her. She blinked several times. "Oh. That sounds fine."

"I'll pay for it. I've got a lot of money saved up."

"You should find someone at the park courts instead of the club. It would be cheaper."

"That's what I was thinking." Although at the club I would have a chance of running into Dr. B on the courts or in the locker room, I would also run the risk of him seeing my fledgling attempts to control the racket and balls. I knew I wouldn't take to it naturally. It would be a lot of work. My brother, a track star, got the athletic talent in the family. Even after a night of drinking, he got up the next day and ran five miles through the park. I was determined to be a decent tennis player despite my late start, motivated by the thought that someday I might be on the other side of the net from Dr. B.

Mom returned to her book, and I ran upstairs. David was out with his girlfriend and wouldn't return until dinnertime. Our room had a large walk-in closet. I went in, closed the door, and pulled the cord for the ceiling light. I lowered my shorts and took the photo I had nicked out of my pocket. I fantasized giving Dr. B all the attention he deserved. In less than five minutes, I exploded. I looked down and saw that some of my spunk had landed on my brother's new sneakers. *Shit! My brother will kill me.* But that seemed to be the least of my worries. I had masturbated to the image of a man. I felt sick and alone. I vowed to stop sneaking into people's houses, but particularly Dr. B's.

The next day I signed up for tennis lessons at the park courts.

Four: Mother's Little Helper

The Baronians were witlessly accommodating in having a worktable under the basement window where I entered. One day it looked like actual work was happening on it with jars, tubes, and household chemicals: one of Judy's science projects no doubt. I had to be extra careful not to disturb anything. I had gotten pretty adept at leaving the houses exactly how I had found them, except for the occasional prank—a knickknack out of place, a clock set to the wrong time—that might cause a bit of confusion though no obvious proof someone had been there. In leaving the house, I hoisted myself up and was halfway through the window when a pair of black-and-tan saddle oxfords came into view. I raised my eyes, taking in the knee-high socks, the plaid skirt, and finally, arms crossed in front of a white blouse, Judy's high school uniform at St. Mary's.

"What are you doing?" She had a look of victory on her face as if she had been waiting for a moment to catch me in a transgression since the day we met.

I crawled the rest of the way out, sat on the ground, and hugged my knees. "A pebble from the mower hit the window." I pointed to the crack. "I was trying to figure out how to get the window out so I could take it to get repaired."

"Why didn't you just tell somebody?"

"I thought your dad might get mad as he specifically told me to be careful of the pebbles, which sometimes spill over from the gravel pathway into the yard."

"That's trespassing, you know."

"I was only examining the window from the inside."

"I think I should call the police."

She stood a few feet from me with one knee twisted in toward the other and her heel out. It reminded me of a spread in one of Mr. Burnside's girlie magazines where the girl wore a school uniform although the skirt in the photo was a lot shorter and the blouse hung open, revealing pubescent breasts. I couldn't help but chuckle.

"You think this is funny?"

"I've never seen you in your school uniform."

She came close to cracking a smile. "Well, I'm definitely telling my father."

I crossed my ankles and stood up "About the window? I'll tell him."

"I'm talking about the trespassing."

"You know, it's also a crime to falsely accuse someone of a crime. Anyway, I heard a rumor about you the other day."

She scowled and put her hands on her hips. "What rumor?"

"I'll tell you if you keep this incident to yourself."

"You're lying."

"This guy at school said he made out with you, and you let him touch your breasts."

"That's ridiculous!" She did a one-eighty and stormed away. "Let's forget the whole thing."

I watched Judy walk away and noticed how thin she looked. I remembered times in junior high when she was heavy. I commented to my mother about Judy's yo-yo weight.

"Oh, honey. She's going through puberty. A girl's body is sort of in turmoil for a while. Do we need to have that discussion?"

"No, Mom. I know what puberty is."

"You're sure?"

"Yep."

"I'm surprised you would take notice of Judy's physical changes." She chuckled. "Are you starting to be interested in girls?"

"Mom, really?"

"If you have any questions, let me know."

I appreciated Mom being open about puberty and sex, but it was the last thing I wanted to discuss with my mother. Anyway, I had my own theory about Judy's slim physique. Some of the kids at school were talking about diet pills. Danny, who sat next to me in history, said his older sister went to a doctor and got diet pills easily. She was overweight but not fat. He complained that when she took them, she turned into a chatty Cathy. Other times she would be moody, telling him to go jump in the lake for no reason.

"I had to take one myself to see what they were all about," said Danny.

I looked at him like he was crazy. "Those pills are for girls."

"No, man. It's a chemical that acts like coffee, only stronger. It made me all jittery, but it also kind of felt good. A lot of the girls at St. Mary's take them."

"How do you know?"

"That's where my sister first heard about them. She's got a friend that goes there."

The conversation made me curious about Judy, and I had to find out if she was taking the pills. At the same time, I knew it wasn't a good idea to go snooping in her house when I had only recently been caught. The winter months came, a bad time to prowl in neighbors' homes. People tended to stay home more with less chance a door or window would be left open, and they might be suspicious of a trail left by footprints in the snow. I had forgotten about the pills until early one overcast spring morning. While delivering papers, I saw Dr. B packing up Mrs. B's Ford station wagon.

I stopped my bike and handed him the paper.

"Oh, hey, Nathan."

"Going on a trip?"

"Just a couple days. Keep an eye on the house." He winked at me, and I wondered if Judy had said something about the basement window. Mrs. B came out of the house wearing a scarf and sunglasses. She got in the car without saying a word. I had heard Mom say she occasionally had to go to St. Louis for treatment of her illness. I took off on my bike before Judy came out of the house. I didn't want her to know I knew they were going out of town.

I realized she hadn't told her dad about the window when I saw the crack was still there. I was able to get in like before, though I needed to be extra careful in case Judy had set some kind of trap. Sure enough, I discovered a piece of white thread Scotch-taped to the window frame on one end and the ceiling on the other. I would have to exit by another means so I could leave the thread intact, but it would be riskier as the basement window was in the back and partially covered by a bush, making it difficult for anyone to see me.

The second bathroom was off the hall, and the drawers and medicine chest were filled with her things. I saw a box of tampons, which gave me a jolt of queasiness, and I remembered the brief conversation I'd had with my mother about puberty. The only pills I saw were Midol, and I associated them with female problems. But what if, I reasoned, she didn't want her parents to know she was taking the pills?

I felt queasy as I entered her Pepto-Bismol-pink room and carefully rummaged around in typical hiding places. I found a bottle of prescription pills in the rear of the same bedside table drawer as her diary, her drawer of secrets. The label said Obetrol. *Take 1 capsule once a day preferably a half hour before meals.* The prescribing doctor was James Biehl, M.D. At least it wasn't her father. I shook out a couple of pills and put them in my pocket.

I noticed several medical books on the floor-to-ceiling bookshelves in the living room. One was a huge tome called *Physicians' Desk Reference 1965*. I sat in one of the easy chairs by the fireplace with the heavy book on my lap, thumbing through until I found Obetrol. The description said it was indicated in cases of obesity, hence the name. It made me laugh. Judy, even at her heaviest, was no way near obese.

It was classified as a psychostimulant, and the composition had various formulas of amphetamine. Also on the shelf was a dictionary where I looked up amphetamine. It was described as a central nervous system stimulant. Danny was right. It had nothing to do with girl problems, but rather was a chemical that sped up your system. Now I had something on Judy much better than a rumor she had let some jerk touch her breasts. After what Danny had told me, I wanted to try one of the pills, but I was cautious. I put them in a box in my dresser drawer and waited for the right occasion.

One Saturday late in the summer, I had three lawns to mow. I remembered Danny saying the diet pills gave him a lot of energy, sort of like coffee but more intense. I downed one of the pills with a glass of water, seeing it as a way to help me with the work I had to do. About halfway through the first lawn, a sense of well-being came over me, making me aware of what a good job I was doing, noticing how healthy and green the grass appeared. The smell of the grass seemed particularly pungent and fresh.

Normally, I went about my business, my mind drifting off to a hundred other things: a conversation at school where I had stumbled, something I had read in a book I wanted to remember, or the forecast for the next few days, which could affect my paper deliveries. But none of that happened. My mind was completely focused. The feeling wasn't completely unfamiliar since I occasionally had that kind of buzz after drinking a couple cups of coffee, and yet, I had had no coffee that morning. The mower glided along with little effort, making me feel like

I could pick up the pace and finish the day's work early. I started thinking about increasing my business, taking on more yard work.

Before I knew it, the yard was done, filling me with a sense of pride at my accomplishment. I cleaned up enthusiastically, disposing of the cuttings not caught by the bag, wiping off the mower, normally the most annoying parts of the job. By this time of day, I usually started to get hungry, but instead of feeling a desire to eat, I was anxious to get to the next yard.

Mr. Burnside was next, and since I finished speedily with the first yard, I got to his house earlier than expected. The side door to the detached garage wasn't unlocked as it usually was when he knew I was coming. I went to the window and looked in. He must have heard me outside the door because he rushed to pull up his pants and stuff the magazines back in the cabinet. I ducked before he saw me and walked away from the garage to stand in the driveway, calculating the best way to attack the lawn. A minute later he exited the garage, flushed and nervous.

Though I wasn't one to carry on needless conversations with my clients, I launched into a long explanation why I had arrived early. I went into great detail about my morning and how wonderful it was we were getting some great weather. He eyed me suspiciously as he edged toward the house, making only cursory comments. Instead of proceeding to the garage to do my work, I found myself pursuing him as my mouth motored on. He took a step back, and I one forward.

He stopped and pointed out the obvious. "The mower is in the garage."

I smiled, and my jaw popped. "Oh, yeah."

"Come to the back door, and I'll pay you when you're finished."

"You bet."

*

The following Saturday, I approached my lawn mowing with a lot less enthusiasm. I still had one more Obetrol from Judy's stash, but I wanted to save it. Compared to the Saturday before, my mind drifted, the work was tedious, and by noon my stomach was growling. I had no work scheduled on Sunday, so I moped around the house, stuck in the throes of boredom without the slightest idea what to do about it. Mom said she was going to the club. "Who knows how many more warm days we'll have. Do you want to go with me?"

"Nah."

"Oh, come on. Don't be a spoilsport."

She was right. Summer was coming to an end. It was September, and we had returned to school. It might be fun to go to the club, and I could make the experience more interesting by taking my second Obetrol.

Mom and I settled into our usual corner, and I tackled a new book I had picked up at the library, *Dune* by Frank Herbert. A couple of hours flew by as I became immersed in the world of the desert planet Arrakis, imagining myself in the shoes of the main character, Paul Atreides. I made a connection between *melange,* the drug everyone on the planet was seeking, and Obetrol. Herbert described the drug as giving greater vitality and heightened awareness. That sounded familiar.

Entrenched in my reading, I hadn't noticed the arrival of Judy Baronian in the usual gang of four—Cindy and another girl, both in my French class, and a boy my brother and I called the private-school kid. He lived in the next block, but I had seen him roll by, his mother at the wheel of her cream-colored Cadillac Coupe de Ville and him looking out the passenger window, watching me mow lawns with a sneer of royal contempt.

In my now predictable pattern, I informed my mother I was going to the bathroom. I set off on my mini safari to the changing room in hopes of a Dr. B sighting. Normally, I avoided going anywhere near Judy's group, at times circumventing the pool in order not to walk past them. *Fuck that.* I felt good. I passed within a few feet of them and gave Judy a smug smile.

"Ça pue le jardinier," said the private-school boy loud enough for me to hear. No doubt he was trying to impress his companions by speaking French and at the same time put me down by saying I stank like a gardener. He made a quick translation, and they all laughed except Cindy.

I stopped and thought a minute. *"Le vert tu sens est le vert de l'argent que je gagne moi-même. Moi, je ne dépends pas d'un rich Daddy pour en avoir."* The green you smell is the green of money, which I earn myself and don't have to depend on a rich daddy.

Judy and the girl from my French class looked dumbfounded, not understanding a word I said but impressed I could respond with a stream of French. Cindy laughed out loud and punched the guy lightly on the arm. As I continued walking, I heard him ask her what I said.

After a fruitless trip to the locker room, I went to the poolside take-out window of the club restaurant where I ordered a Coke and french fries. Mom loved french fries, and I planned to surprise her with them even though she was sure to say, "I shouldn't eat those. They're so fattening." While waiting for my order, I turned around and saw Cindy coming up behind me.

She smiled with a little bat of her eyelashes. "That was pretty impressive. Charles goes to a posh boarding school out east and thinks he's so superior. His semester starts later, and I'll be kind of glad when he goes off to school."

"Thanks for laughing." My shyness made me stare into the darkness inside the order window, hoping they'd hurry up. Typically, I would saunter away and mumble something like "See you later." I inhaled deeply, and my whole body tingled, reminding me I didn't have to shy away. With my drug-induced confidence, I spun around, smiled, and announced with great enthusiasm, "We're in the same French class."

"You're Nate, right?" I couldn't believe she knew my name. When I hesitated, she added, "I'm Cindy."

"*Enchanté.*" I grabbed her hand and kissed it.

She giggled.

I didn't recognize myself. *What the hell was going on?* "Can I get you a Coke or something?"

"I'll take a Fresca, thanks." She wore a knee-length, gauzy, embroidered shirt from India over her swimming suit. Her blonde hair was long and straight as if it had been ironed, and she had a silver peace symbol on a chain around her neck. A lot of people at school had started calling her Hipindy. Someone had told me her parents were divorced, and she spent summers with her father in Los Angeles.

We took our drinks and the french fries and sat at a table. I glanced over at Mom with guilt for abandoning her, though she appeared engrossed in her book. I also observed Cindy's group in what appeared to be scandalous chatter. "Your friends look like they're about to shit a brick. Oops! Sorry, I shouldn't have said that."

"Oh please. I'm sure Judy will give me the third degree. You guys don't seem to get along."

"We barely know each other. She acts like I don't exist. I could care less. Why are you friends with her?"

"My mother and her father went to school together. When the Baronians moved back to town, our families started getting together, though my dad wasn't too happy about it. Not long after that, my parents got divorced. I think my mom and Dr. Baronian had something going in high school."

"Oh, really?" I hadn't intended my rejoinder be so saturated with disbelief.

She crinkled her nose. "What? You don't think my mom could handle a stud like Dr. B?"

My face flushed, and I tried to hide it with a nervous laugh. "I don't know your mom. I'm sure she's quite beautiful if you're any indication."

She looked at me guardedly. "You're a lot different than I thought you were. I can't believe we never talked before. You're funny and smart. I mean, I knew you were smart since we're the two best students in French class. I still can't get over what you said to Charles."

"A smartass doesn't deserve to be treated nicely."

"Right-o."

"Have you read *Dune* by any chance?"

"No, but I want to."

"I just started it. You can borrow it when I'm done." Of course, it was a library book, so what I said didn't make sense. I could buy a copy and give it to her as a gift, maybe dog-ear the pages to look like my copy. My mind was buzzing five steps ahead. I saw her becoming my friend, possibly my savior, allowing me to leave my abhorrent inclinations behind.

Her green eyes looked like they could sear into my brain. "What are you thinking?"

"Nothing." I drummed my fingers on the table. "I have an idea. Maybe we could study together some time."

"I'd like that. I should tell you I do have a boyfriend in California."

"I think I said study."

"*Touché.* Just want to be honest."

"Uh-oh. Here comes trouble."

Judy approached our table as if she were on a catwalk, her thinness model-like. She got to the table, and ignoring me, she stared at Cindy's Fresca and screwed up her nose.

"Charles's mom is picking us up in fifteen minutes. Are you coming with us?"

"Well, I'm not going to walk home."

"Fine."

"Hi, Judy," I said.

It took a full minute for her to rotate her head in an exaggerated arc in my direction. "Oh, hi." And then she snapped her head back to Cindy. "We'll see you out front."

"Okay. I'll be there in a minute."

When Judy left, Cindy rolled her eyes. "Duty calls. See you tomorrow in class."

"Hope I didn't get you in trouble."

"There'll be hell to pay, but it was worth it."

I was in love. She was pretty and smart with a touch of sassy. I hadn't thought about Dr. B being naked in the changing room for a full half hour.

That night, I lay awake with my brain dancing the Mashed Potato and the Funky Chicken. On one hand, I credited the drug for prying me out of my shell. I obsessed over how I could get more of it. On the other, I reasoned it was *my* mind coming up with the witticisms, *my* mouth speaking them. She seemed to like me. *Me,* not the drug. I relived every smile she cast in my direction, the two seconds she laid her hand on my arm, and the dismissive way she treated one of her best friends in front of me. Now that a connection had been made, why did I need drugs? Obetrol had been great to start the engines, but I could take it from there.

The alarm tore into the veil of sleep that had miraculously fallen upon me. I had to deliver the morning paper. I had slept no more than an hour. Mom was already up, and I asked her to make me some coffee. I barely had the strength to do the fold and tuck of the papers into neat little bundles I could throw from my bike.

As I sat on the floor stuffing the papers in my bag, Mom appeared above me with another cup of steaming coffee. "Rough night?"

"I stayed up late reading."

"I hear you. I did too." She paused as if unsure if she should continue. "I saw you made a new friend yesterday."

"Sorry."

"Sorry?"

"I went to get us a snack and promptly abandoned you."

"Don't be silly. I was happy you were talking to her. What's her name?"

"Cindy. Cindy Kramer. She's in my French class."

"Oh." She paused again as if wondering how much to pry. "You'd better get going, or you'll be late for school."

I survived the morning until third-period French class. Cindy came in right before the bell and sat next to her friend, Roberta, the third girl from the pool gathering the day before. Cindy acknowledged me by glancing over her shoulder with a slight raise of her eyebrows and a cursory smile. It was hardly an appropriate reaction upon seeing one's future boyfriend. I was plunged into despair.

I had a hard time staying awake as we plowed through a painfully boring fill-in-the-blank exercise. My chin kept creeping down toward my chest before jerking up when I caught myself. In the end I lost the battle, and my heavy lids fell shut.

"Mr. Landis, dreaming of gay Paree, are we?"

The question was like a bolt of lightning, and my eyes popped open to a classroom full of snickering students. Monsieur Renard was such a square he couldn't have meant what it sounded like.

"*Ca suffit!*" he said to quiet the room. "Continue with number *huit*, Mademoiselle Kramer."

The torturous class ended, and I gathered up my books. I followed Cindy into the hall. "Mademoiselle Kramer." I mimicked the teacher's accent. It didn't have the desired effect.

She stopped and turned with an ambivalent look on her face. "Hello, Nate."

"Do you want to have lunch together?"

"Not today. I've got an algebra test this afternoon, and I want to use the lunch hour to go over my notes."

"Oh, sure. Some other time." She hurried to catch up with her friend, Roberta. I was a puddle on the floor. *Had I imagined there might be anything between us? Had the conversation only twenty-four hours before happened? Had her friends convinced her I wasn't worth it? Was the pimple on my chin and the emergent one on my nose too ghastly to look at while eating lunch?*

I went to the office and told the secretary I was coming down with something. She appeared to be convinced by my red eyes and asked if I wanted to use the phone to call someone to come get me. I dialed the number, but before the call connected, I put my finger on the receiver button. I pretended to have a conversation with my mother.

Once outside the school, I got a burst of energy and started walking. I had no intention of going home, knowing I couldn't face my mom. Mrs. Sloan was visiting her sister in St. Louis. I didn't have to break in since she had given me a key and asked me to check on her cat.

I curled up on her sofa, annoyed by the rough upholstery, which smelled of Tabu, the nauseating perfume she wore. Her cat, with the incredibly clever name of Whiskers, formed into a fluffy ball next to me and purred loudly. I fell asleep in two minutes.

It was dark when I woke up. I ran home and tried to sneak in through the garage, but Mom heard me and stormed into my room, wiping her hands on her apron. "Where in the world have you been? I've been frantic." The freedom my parents allowed my brother and me did have its limits.

"Why?"

"Your friend, Cindy, called, asking if you were all right."

"She did?" The excitement about her call far outweighed any guilt I felt at making my mother worry.

"She said you left school at noon sick. Where did you go?"

"What time did she call?"

"I asked you a question."

"I went to the park and lay down on the hill by the duck pond. I fell asleep."

"That's so irresponsible. It gets cold when the sun goes down. You could catch your death."

"Did she say to call her back or anything?"

"Nathan, you look horrible. I want you to eat something and go straight to bed."

The next day, I didn't go to school. My body ached like I was coming down with the flu. My dad, God love him, woke up my brother and told him he had to do the paper route that morning. David was not happy about it. I slept until noon. Mom came home for lunch and heated up some chicken noodle soup for me. I ate the soup with

Ritz crackers while she sat at the table and gave me the I-told-you-so look.

"I know. It was stupid."

"Let this be a lesson. Decisions have consequences." God, how many times had I heard that?

"Cindy didn't happen to leave a number, did she?"

"No. You don't have it?"

"She gave it to me yesterday, I mean Sunday. I wrote it on a napkin and stuck it in the pocket of my trunks. Later, I stupidly jumped into the pool, and it disintegrated."

"That's not like you, Nathan. You're always so careful."

I laughed. "Yeah, must be that puberty thing."

"Okay, mister know-it-all."

I went back to bed and slept for another couple of hours, waking up right around the time school let out. I listened for the phone in hopes Cindy would call to check on me. I tried to read, but my headache was so bad the words blurred on the page.

I stayed home on Wednesday as well. No more calls from Cindy. Shortest friendship of my life. I returned to school on Thursday, though I dreaded seeing Cindy. She came into French early and approached my desk, which I used as a pillow. I still didn't feel caught up on my sleep.

"Are you sure you should be here?"

I couldn't accept she truly cared. "Thanks to your phone call, my mom found out I left school early."

"Sorry. That's why I didn't call back. I thought you might be pissed at me for spilling the beans."

I lifted my head up, making it look like it took considerable effort. "I could have died," I said in a nasally, congested voice.

"Well, I guess you've made a remarkable recovery."

"Partial recovery at best." I stared at her with my burning and no doubt bloodshot eyes.

She laughed. "I wondered if you'd like to have lunch together."

"No tests to cram for?"

"Don't be an asshole."

I didn't know why I was being such a jerk. I still felt horrible, but she was trying to be nice. Her smile tore into me. "*Je suis désolé.*"

"Apology accepted. I'll see you after class." She turned to go to her seat and stopped. "Why didn't you call *me*?"

"You know that napkin I wrote your number on? It looked like part of a paper-mache project after I went in the pool."

She returned to my desk, grabbed my hand, and wrote her number on it. "Memorize it!"

I sniffled and coughed my way through lunch.

"You could at least cover your mouth."

"You sound like my mom."

"If I was your mom, I'd tell you to go home and go to bed."

It wasn't only feeling bad with a cold made our lunch awkward. I had nothing to say. My few attempts at jokes fell flat. A few days before, she had noted my humor and intelligence, but at lunch, I felt boring and stupid. I needed a boost of confidence and wondered how I could get more of that chemical courage. Going into the Baronian house and stealing more pills from Judy was not an option.

At the same time, I had to admit Cindy didn't treat me differently from the day by the pool. She smiled and showed sympathy for my condition. The problem was not how she responded to me but how I felt about myself.

Later in the afternoon, I found Danny in the hall. I looked around to make sure no one was in earshot. "I tried one of those diet pills."

"You weren't worried they'd make you grow breasts or something?"

"Very funny. But seriously, that stuff was outta sight."

"What did you take?"

"Obetrol."

"That's the best. It's what my sister gets. You want some?"

"Yeah, definitely."

"It'll cost ya."

Five: Like a Virgin

I celebrated the beginning of my sophomore year at Westwood by moving into the downstairs bedroom David had vacated when he left for college. The room had formerly been a breezeway and was converted to a bedroom in one of my father's schemes to supplement his meager salary as an associate professor at the local university. My parents fretted over how they were going to send both of us to college, and my mother had offered to go to work, an idea she relished but my father didn't. Instead, he came up with the idea of the downstairs bedroom, which could house a foreign exchange student for which my parents would receive a stipend.

Our first exchange student was from Jamaica. David and I promptly grew fond of Beatrice, but Gran, who lived in the neighborhood and was frequently at our house, made life so miserable for our student, she had to seek other housing. Gran was diagnosed as a manic-depressive and was convinced Beatrice was going to start moving all her family over from Jamaica and take over the neighborhood. In the end, David got the converted bedroom, and I had my own room upstairs.

When David left, I convinced my mother they should turn the upstairs bedroom into a TV room since she had always complained it was a sacrilege to have the grand piano share a room with a television. The downstairs bedroom was freedom, making it easy to sneak out at night without my parents knowing. I planned to take full advantage of it in the same way my brother had.

David's departure to the University of Wisconsin on a track scholarship changed my life in other ways. I had cruised through freshman year under the protective umbrella of David's popularity and athletic stardom. As David Landis's younger brother, everyone assumed I must be cool. People asked me if I was going to try out for track. Would I be running for the student council? I didn't do any of the activities or join any of the clubs David had belonged to. I had few friends. A couple months into sophomore year, people realized my own light was dim compared to the brilliance of my brother. People looked at me suspiciously or ignored me completely. I withdrew farther into myself, living in the world of my neighborhood. Knowing about my neighbors—how they lived, what they liked, their secrets—kept me entertained. During my forays into their homes, I could, for brief periods, live in their lives. I could sit in their favorite chairs or pick up a book they were reading and thumb through a few pages, sometimes mischievously moving the bookmark.

In a small yellow house across the street and down the block lived two middle-aged women everyone in the neighborhood referred to as simply the teachers. But since I collected for the paper, I knew them by name, Miss Larson and Miss Jacobi. Though they were always polite and paid on time, they kept to themselves. I never heard my parents mention anything about them. One afternoon when they were at school, I got into the house.

I stood in the kitchen and felt an unusual chill run down my spine. Gran used to say that meant someone was walking over your grave. I stood frozen in place, staring at a cat clock on the wall with the tail ticking back and forth, except the time between ticks seemed elongated and the ticks louder than they should have been. I felt dizzy and nauseous. I turned around and walked out. That feeling stuck with me the rest of the afternoon, leaving me confused and yet curious.

As I lay in bed one night, I kept thinking about the last time I collected from the teachers and Miss Larson mentioning they wouldn't be home for the next collection because they would be taking a vacation before school started. I got up, dressed, and grabbed my flashlight.

The cover of night filled me with expectation, and the fog felt silky on my skin and softened the streetlights. I walked by Dr. B's house, dark except for the light in the den, always on late into the night. I imagined him, like me, unable to sleep, ruminating on the twists and turns of his life.

I crossed the street and doubled back to the teachers' house. I went to the shed and found the backdoor key in its usual place, hanging on a nail. I entered the kitchen, wary of the sensation that had overtaken me the last time. The only thing that engulfed me was a smell of a house closing in on itself as if the windows had never been opened, never allowing years of accumulated odors to escape. It wasn't a foul smell, only a heavy essence of older people who want little to do with the outside world.

I came to the first bedroom. The bed was made, but the room was otherwise bare, unlived in. The closet held winter jackets and boots, the drawers, sweaters and scarves. The other bedroom was quite the opposite. Family photographs and art prints lined the walls. The nightstands on either side of the bed were piled with books. On one side were biographies of Eisenhower and Winston Churchill, and books about World War II. On the other side were gothic novels, Emily Brontë and Jane Austen, as well as a couple of modern romance novels and a copy of *The Prime of Miss Jean Brody.*

I was sure most people in the neighborhood couldn't distinguish the two women. They had similar appearances—slightly overweight, glasses, short-cropped hair, drab clothing—but I now had a window into their distinct personalities. My next realization, which at first, I had tried to push into the farthest reaches of my brain, was that they were a couple. They slept together and ate together, read in bed together, and trudged through life together without anyone recognizing their union. They didn't seem unhappy. They were not two old maids. They shared a life.

The next time they asked me to mow their lawn, I did it for free. I told them I was running a special. For every five mows, they got one for free. Miss Jacobi smiled and returned her coin purse to the pocket of her smock. The following time, they paid me double.

*

Sophomore year flew by in an Obetrol haze. Danny was my supplier. His sister had decided she didn't like the effects of the diet pills and didn't care if she was fat. She preferred the money she and Danny could make from selling them, and Danny always seemed to have a large supply—Obetrol, Dexamyl, or the nasty Dexedrine, which left a horrible taste in my mouth. Obetrol was by far my favorite.

"Doesn't her doctor get suspicious?" I asked Danny.

"She goes to like five different doctors, gets scripts from each, and fills them in different pharmacies."

"Why does she need the money?"

"My parents threw her out. She got pregnant and lives with this guy on the East Side." He rubbed his finger along the skin of his arm. "He's dark skinned, darker than me."

Junior year, Danny transitioned from drug supplier to friend. I kept seeking him out for what he had to offer—sophomore year, the drug, and junior year, a high of a more lascivious sort. I spent a good part of that year lying in bed, waiting for him to rap on the window. With my eyes held open as if by a speculum, I found totems and spirit animals in the shadows and shapes of the ceiling and, from there, jumped into alternative universes where people spoke telepathically, time traveled, and sex was a free and open act. Whereas most of the guys I knew had lost their virginity, or at least claimed to have, I was still pure, a source of embarrassment for a teenage boy. And then I would remember my experience with Scoutmaster Jenkins. *No. No orgasm. No penetration. No love. Didn't count.*

Cindy had started dating Matt, a handsome, popular, student council member. I teased her, saying she needed to get back to California, or she would lose her hippie credentials. She laughed but without enthusiasm. She looked away and asked me if I'd heard The Doors album. "I think you'd like it."

"Yes, I've heard some of the cuts. I guess you're cool again."

"Thanks."

We didn't see each other much, and all those late-night phone calls of sophomore year didn't happen anymore. I was upset about her spending so much time with Matt but, at the same time, didn't blame her. What did I have to offer? I was a ghost in the halls of Westwood High. I wasn't involved in anything, on track to be one those aimless souls in the yearbook, whose name was followed by empty space—no Basketball 1,2,3,4, no Glee Club 1,3,4, not even French Club 1,2.

I still thought about Dr. B a lot and bemoaned the lost opportunities to see him when I collected for the paper or mowed his lawn. Also, in my new anti-bourgeoisie attitude, I rarely went to the club. One day, my brother was home from college and suggested we play tennis, surprising me since it was the one thing I could do better than him. I no longer took lessons but played from time to time with a girl who lived near the park courts and competed in tournaments. She could hit a powerful ball, and I loved blasting back and forth with her, especially when I was high.

Dr. B and Jim played on the next court next to us. Despite the significant distraction, I trounced my brother 6-0, 6-1. He went for a swim, and I went in the locker room where I came upon Dr. B and Jim having what appeared to be an argument, though they immediately stopped when I walked in.

"Hey Dr. B." I tried to sound casual, but my insides were doing the usual flips like every time I saw him. Instead of going to the urinal, I went in a stall where I might linger and catch some of their conversation. Their discussion continued in angry whispers, not loud enough to distinguish what they were saying. Their voices stopped, followed by the door to the outside banging shut. I flushed and exited the stall to see Dr. B staring at the spot where Jim had been, an aura of pain surrounding his body. When he felt my presence, he briskly lifted his tennis bag to his shoulder and walked out.

Danny became my partner in crime, filling the vacuum left by Cindy's time with Matt. Each time he knocked on my window, I would thank Beatrice and wish her well. I would sneak out easily and get in his Camaro. Sometimes he had a can of spray paint. I once wrote *Je ne regrette rien* on the side wall of Kroger. Danny wrote No War. Other times, we drove around with the windows down, the radio off, and feeling the night, the velvety silence of it, imagining we were the only creatures left on earth.

Once we found a house for sale on the edge of town and climbed in a window. Most of the furniture was gone, but they hadn't cleared out all the junk. As soon as we were inside the house, I got that old rush, that tingly feeling zipping from head to toe. I had, for the most part, abandoned my home invasions. A kid down the street had taken over the paper route, and I cut down on mowing lawns in the summer since I had taken a job stocking shelves at Walgreens where Danny worked. I couldn't so easily justify wandering around in a neighbor's yard. Plus, I wasn't twelve anymore where prowling inside a house would only have landed me a slap on the wrist.

Danny and I sat on the floor of the abandoned house and looked through a box of photographs with a flashlight, wondering why someone would leave so many memories behind: black-and-white photos of another era, wedding photos, family portraits, children playing in an inflatable backyard pool. In addition to the photos, the box contained a homemade birthday card to Mommy in a childish scrawl. I had never told a single soul about my prowling into other people's lives, but I had a feeling Danny would understand. As he was the bad boy and I was the square he dragged along, I wanted to impress him, show him I was an outcast too. I told him about the different ways I entered houses, the floor plans I drew, the notes I took. I left out the part about hiding in the closet and watching Dr. B and Jim have sex.

"That is far out. Landis, you are seriously demented."

"You think I ought to commit myself? I mean, I'm a menace to society."

"Me too. We could stir up some shit like they did in *One Flew Over the Cuckoo's Nest*." I had read Kesey's novel and passed it on to Danny.

We laughed and recounted our recent escapades. It made me happy to be his friend, someone who seemed equally lost in the social order. He told me he had moved to town from Chicago freshman year when his father got a job at Firestone. One winter, his family drove to Florida, and they were refused service in a small-town restaurant in Georgia.

"Why?" I said.

"The motherfucker pointed to a sign that read, No Coloreds Allowed. My father told him we were Italian, but the guy simply shook his head."

"That's a bummer. Why are people like that?"

"Girls don't want to go out with me either. They think I'm weird. In Chicago, I had plenty of girlfriends."

Maybe Danny wasn't as good-looking as a lot of the guys at school, but he had something I liked, eyes full of soul with long eyelashes and smooth brown skin from his Sicilian ancestors. "I don't think you're weird."

"Maybe I'm just ugly."

We had turned off the flashlight, but his face was lit by the streetlight coming in the window. His lips rolled into a pout. I wanted to say how beautiful he looked at that moment but caught myself. "You're..."

"What?"

"I mean I don't see why a girl wouldn't go out with you."

"You and Cindy have done it, right?"

"She's with Matt."

"Come on. Last year you guys were together all the time."

"Yeah, but..."

"Oh my God, Landis, you're a virgin! I should take you to this whorehouse on North Monroe."

"No way."

"Shit. This talk is making me horny." He grabbed his crotch and tilted his head back with a howl like it was painful.

The drumming inside me started pounding blood into my dick. I was afraid of what I might do. "It's getting late."

"Don't be a wuss. Let's jack off."

"I never…"

"What? You've never been in a circle jerk either? Good thing you found me. You got stuff to learn." He unzipped his pants and started coaxing his dick, talking to it like it was his friend. "Come on, big guy." With his free hand, he grabbed my arm and moved it so my hand would be on my crotch, now throbbing in rhythm with my beating heart. "Don't make me do it alone."

I unzipped and closed my eyes, letting the image of Dr. B and Jim start looping through my brain. It felt good as I worked my way close to the edge. But Danny started growling, making me open my eyes. He grabbed one of the photos and, with a final howl, shot all over it. He started laughing. I stared at him in shock. My hardness wilted. He tossed the photo back in the box and turned his head to give me a questioning look.

"What's the matter?"

"Nothing." I started to zip up.

"Don't you dare. We're not leaving until you shoot."

"It's okay."

"No, it's not." He got to his knees, came up behind me, and pressed his chest against my spine. He looked over my shoulder and saw that I was rising again. "Uh-huh. That a boy." His breathing was rapid, and it made me harder than ever. He bit my neck and sent a bolt of electricity up and down my body. His mouth moved to my ear. "You can do it." His words shot like fire into my brain. "Yeah, baby, come on."

Pearls shot out of me onto the wood floor and caught the light from outside. I fell back against him. He let me lean into him for thirty seconds before he unexpectedly stood up. I was rudely and swiftly unplugged from his current. He kicked the box of photos and looked at his watch. "Shit."

It was two weeks before he rapped on my window again. I had supposed it was over, whatever it was. We became regular pulling partners, never with the same intimacy as that first time and usually high in his car with the sound of crickets outside. Occasionally, he put his hand on my leg as he was about to come. Those who strive for intimacy take what we can get.

Six: Nice Moves

In the early spring of my junior year, life at Westwood progressed distant from the crises affecting the rest of the country: the Tet Offensive in Vietnam, the growing protests against the war, and the rise of Bobby Kennedy in the Democratic primaries after Johnson decide not to run. But no corner of the country was untouched by the assassination of Martin Luther King, Jr. in April and the violent aftermath. Protesters and angry mobs roamed the streets of many cities where students left class to join in the protests that in some cases led to rioting. The administrators at Westwood, desperate to avoid what had happened in other cities, hurriedly organized an assembly to honor the fallen leader and remind everyone King had believed in peaceful protest.

Black and white student leaders were lined up to speak, including Cindy's friend, Roberta, and the Black guy she was dating, Lonnie, a popular student council member and athlete. I was proud of the somber and peaceful reaction of my school but was also aware there was plenty of racism in Sangamon. My own dear Gran had frequently spoken disparagingly of Dr. King, and I dreaded hearing what she had to say about his murder.

It didn't take long for the serious mood to be displaced by the panic of the upcoming prom—who had dates and who didn't. I stood at my locker and overheard a girl ask Cindy if she was going to the prom with Matt. A rumor had been going around that their relationship was on rocky ground after Matt was seen with another girl.

"How can you talk about prom at a time like this? The country is in upheaval," said Cindy. "It's so superficial. Girls trying to look like debutantes and guys dying in stiff tuxes. Is that supposed to be fun?"

The girl, who was on the prom decorating committee, had the appearance of someone about to break down in tears. "Well, if that's what you think..."

"Anyway, it's just an excuse to go out, get drunk, and maybe have sex."

I turned around and caught Cindy's eye. She stuck her tongue out at me.

I caught up with her later in the hall. "Did you and Matt break up?"

"What's it to you?"

"I would think you would tell me. We used to talk a lot."

"Yes, it's true. I haven't wanted to talk about it."

"Would you consider going to the prom with someone else?"

Her face squeezed into a look of stupefaction. "Didn't you hear what I said about proms? I'm glad I won't be going with Matt. You were right when you said I needed to get back to California. This place drives me crazy sometimes."

"I get it. You're pissed at Matt. But I honestly don't see what prom has to do with the problems in the world. I would like to go to a prom at least once to see what it's like."

She looked at the books in her arms and then up at me. "Are you asking me to go to prom?"

"Oh, come on. It would be fun."

"You're serious? Don't take this the wrong way, Nate, but no. It has nothing to do with you. You know you're one of my best friends. I just don't want to go."

"Not even to pour a drink over Matt's head when he goes with somebody else? You know he's going to show up with someone."

That night she called me. "I've been thinking about that drink."

"Drink?"

"The one I could pour over Matt's head."

I laughed. Never underestimate the power of revenge.

"I'll go with you if you haven't already asked someone else."

"Yeah, right. Like I have so many to ask." It took a minute for her acceptance to register. "Really? You'll go?"

"Maybe we could spike the punch with LSD?"

"Oh." I fell silent.

"It was a joke!"

"I knew that."

Prom was several weeks away. I couldn't stop thinking about what Cindy said in the hall about prom being an excuse to get drunk and have sex. In my head, I was convinced it was exactly what we were going to do. I would be a virgin no longer. I could proudly crow to Danny about what I had done. He would be so proud of me. And knowing I'd had sex with a girl, he could put away any fears he might have I was queer. It was the perfect plan.

As prom night approached, Cindy remained ambivalent about the dance, but her mother was ecstatic, insisting she have a gown made, a long white satin dress with a belt of daisies. I got her a corsage of blue daisies and rented a tux with a powder-blue jacket. "I guess if we're going to do it, we might as well do it right," Cindy said.

"Did you order the LSD?"

"Don't need to. I make it in a lab in the basement."

We were good friends again, laughing and joking like old times.

One night Danny came and knocked on my window. "I can't," I whispered through the screen. "I'm crashing. Massive headache." I had been hitting the Obies hard in preparation for finals. My body felt like every nerve ending was exposed. I thought he might be angry, but he still agreed to get me some cheap champagne and helped me arrange for the motel room on prom night.

We double-dated with Lonnie and Roberta. Roberta had her own car, and Lonnie drove. They picked me up, and we went to get Cindy. Cindy's mom answered the door with such excitement, it seemed she was my date going to the prom. I presented the corsage I had bought for Cindy. "Oh, that's lovely."

A minute later, Cindy came down the stairs, and I had to admit I was struck by her beauty. Her blonde hair had a slight curl at the ends and shone in the foyer light. She wore lipstick, and I detected a new perfume.

"You'll be the most handsome couple at the ball," said Cindy's mom.

"It's not a ball, Mom. I'm not Cinderella. It's a prom. No big deal."

We walked to the car, and I opened the door for her. "I'm doing this in part for Mom. When I told her Matt and I had broken up and I wouldn't be going to the prom, I thought she was going to have a nervous breakdown. And then my prince came along." She giggled.

In the back seat of the car, we sat close. I pulled out a handkerchief and mopped my forehead. "Are you okay?" she said. "You seem nervous."

I had taken an Obie, now a common practice in social situations to combat my shyness. The underarms of my shirt were already drenched. "Nervous? Haha. It seems like we've known each other forever." I had managed to hide my drug use from her, and as far as I knew, she thought I was moody, sometimes animated to the point of being giddy, and at other times quiet and somber.

Roberta pulled a joint out of her purse and held it up for everyone to see. "I've got something for us. My brother gave it to me."

"Jesus, Berta, put it down," said Lonnie.

"Season's over, sweetie. You can have some fun."

"We don't have to announce it to the world though."

Cindy told me she had tried marijuana in Los Angeles, but I never had. In my strange way of thinking, it would be crossing into another realm. Everybody was doing uppers—housewives, overweight girls, and I was sure Danny and I weren't the only guys. They were prescription. That alone put them in a different category from pot and psychedelics. I wasn't comfortable with smoking pot, but I was desperate to not appear uncool.

We drove into the far end of the park and found an isolated place. Cindy knew I was a newbie and gave me pointers. "Take it directly into your lungs, not like a cigarette, gradually, and then hold it as long as you can. Don't take too big a hit or you'll cough it all out."

Despite the warning, I coughed like I was dying of lung cancer. We passed it around, and with practice, I got to where I could hold it in. When the joint got down to a tiny butt that burned our fingers, Lonnie popped it in his mouth.

"Did he just do what I think he did?" I said to Cindy.

"Yep, he did."

Procol Harum's "Whiter Shade of Pale" came on the radio, grabbing our attention. Lonnie stared out the window and gently nodded his head.

"This song is giving me goose bumps," said Roberta.

Cindy leaned forward and touched Roberta on the shoulder. "I love his voice." She turned to me. "Are you feeling it?"

I had no idea what I was supposed to feel. I felt the Obie but nothing more. Thoughts raced through my head, but the mellow atmosphere inhibited me from being chatty, so I kept them to myself. "Not really."

"A lot of people don't get high the first time."

The song ended. Next, we got "Strawberry Fields Forever."

Lonnie leaned his head forward. "What was that?"

Roberta sat up and looked out the window. "What?"

"I saw something run from one tree to another."

"Stop it, Lonnie. That's not funny." She rolled up her window.

"It was big and hairy."

"Let's go," said Cindy. She tried to grab my hand. It was clammy. I rubbed it on my pants before I let her take it.

"Come on, Lonnie. Start the car."

He pretended to turn the key and made a sound like a struggling engine. "Nothing's happening."

"God damn it, Lonnie. Stop messing around."

He laughed manically. When the car turned over and we pulled out of the space, everybody joined in the laughter. Each time the laughter died down, Lonnie would burst out anew. We laughed until we had tears in our eyes.

"Are you sure you don't feel anything?" Cindy asked me.

"I'm sure. I'm laughing because it's funny."

In the school gymnasium, the decorating committee had done their best to follow the theme of A Night under the Stars. We had our pictures taken in front of a blue canvas backdrop with an out-of-proportion quarter moon. Lonnie, Roberta, and Cindy giggled at everything. At first, the other students thought we were funny, but after a while, people started pointing at us. The band played a few decent covers of Motown songs, but when they tried a couple Beatles' songs, they failed miserably, and we groaned.

Lonnie was in sync with the music, moving his feet, arms and body. During one of the Motown songs, I stood beside him and tried to copy his steps. The girls stepped aside and let the two of us do a routine. The drug was obviously responsible for this new persona. If I had been sober, I would have stood quietly to the side, a wallflower wanting so bad to participate. A crowd formed around us and urged us on to more ridiculous moves. One of the chaperones, a basketball coach, headed in our direction with a purpose. The crowd parted to let him through.

"Have you kids been drinking?"

Figuring I was the most lucid, I stepped up to talk to him. "No, sir. We're only having a good time."

He looked over my shoulder at Lonnie. "If I find out you've been drinking, you're off the team next year."

I looked Mr. Grimes straight in the eye. "I swear none of us have had a drop to drink."

"Well, you're acting like idiots. Straighten up." He turned around and walked away.

I ushered the four of us off the dance floor to a corner of the room, my friends nearly choking on their laughter. "You're acting like idiots." I mocked the coach's tone. The four of us descended into a swamp of laughter.

Lonnie patted me on the back. "Thanks for handling the coach. You're the best." My emotions surged. I was part of something. One of the all-stars in the class said I was the best. My date was one of the prettiest girls in the school. I wasn't a nobody. If I hadn't done something quick, I might've broken into tears of shimmering joy.

I told Cindy I had to go to the restroom. In front of the large mirror, I splashed water on my face. I looked at my hands and saw a myriad of flesh tones moving and blending. The door of one of the stalls opened. For a second, I thought the man I saw in the mirror was Dr. B who had come to whisk me away and save me from my encounter with Cindy. In the next moment, I saw it was another one of the coaches, the only resemblance to Dr. B being that he was tall and had dark hair.

"You okay, Landis?"

"I'm fine."

"You haven't been drinking, have you?"

"No, sir."

I hurried out of the restroom and returned to my gang. "Are we done here? I'm done. Are you done?"

"I'm done," said Lonnie.

"I'm tired of people asking me if I'm drunk. I keep wanting to say, 'Not yet' though I smile and say, 'No, sir.'"

We had to stop by Danny's house to pick up the key for the motel room. At the door he invited us in, saying his parents had gone to bed. On the kitchen table, he laid out a spread for us: pretzels, Ritz crackers with Cheez Whiz, and smoked oysters swimming in a tin of oil. "I know you guys are hungry." He made the sign of putting a joint to his lips and sucking on it. "Or maybe there's a bout of pink eye going around."

Lonnie, Roberta, and Cindy attacked the food, but to me it all looked plastic, and the smell of the oysters made me nauseous. Danny noticed I wasn't partaking. "You better eat something, Landis. Got to keep your strength up." He laughed heartily, and I looked at Cindy with a nervous grin. She had oil from the oysters dripping down her chin, and I wiped it off with a napkin.

Danny brought out some peppermint Schnapps, and we had shots. I forced down some Ritz crackers without the Cheez Whiz and a couple of pretzels. After a half hour, we filed out the door, and I was the last in the line. Danny put his arm around my shoulders and whispered in my ear, "You've got this." I knew he was doing it all for me, and I felt a surge of boundless love for him. He removed his arm and gave me a pat on my butt as I walked away.

In the motel room, Danny had set up two bottles of pink champagne in ice buckets. The first thing we did was unwrap the motel glasses, pop the cork, and pour the bubbly. Lonnie held up his glass. "To a night to remember." We clinked glasses.

One by one, we went into the bathroom to rid ourselves of formal wear and get into something more comfortable. The girls had brought overnight bags as they had told their parents they were staying with friends. I told my parents I was staying with Danny. They didn't approve of him, but they were so happy I was going to the prom with Cindy, so they didn't much care where I spent the night.

Cindy came out in an oversized blue work shirt and gym shorts. Roberta wore a long T-shirt. Lonnie and I hadn't thought ahead, our male brains imagining we'd go directly from getting undressed to bed. I waited to see what he was going to do. He stripped down to an undershirt and boxers. I did the same but wore a T-shirt.

The room had two double beds and a daybed in the corner. Lonnie and Roberta claimed the bed closest to the door. As we sipped our champagne, the bed nearest the door became our universe with Roberta and Lonnie stretched out, leaning against the headboard, Cindy doing a diva sprawl across the foot of it, and me sitting in the desk chair with my feet propped on top of the comforter, distant but still connected. We talked about the people at the dance. Lonnie jumped up and mimicked me trying to copy him on the dance floor. It was all in good fun. I again brought up the coach's line, "You're acting like idiots," and we had a good laugh.

I had a hard time not staring at Lonnie's developed chest and biceps, the body of an athlete. It made me feel conscious of how thin I was, partly genetics since everyone in my family was an ectomorph, but with the uppers curbing my appetite, I had definitely entered scrawny territory. I was the guy who got sand kicked in his face in the Charles Atlas ads in the back of comic books. Cindy rested her hand on my calf and gently pulled on the leg hair. It appeared she didn't mind.

We finished the first bottle and popped open the second. I didn't usually drink and didn't like the effect it sometimes had on people. Once Danny showed up at my window drunk, and I had been afraid to ride in the car with him. We had gone out by the lake, and he tried to force me to suck him off. I refused, got out of the car, and walked home. He apologized for it later.

But in our hotel room, I saw alcohol as a means to an end. It was definitely shredding inhibitions. For a moment, I fantasized the four of us having an orgy, and I flushed at the thought of being close to Lonnie and touching his velvety brown skin. The combination of Obetrol and alcohol made me sloppy about curbing my wandering eyes, returning to Lonnie's physique time and again, drawn to the luster of his skin and the ridges of muscle that ran down his arms. The way Cindy was positioned, she couldn't see where my attention was focused, but Roberta caught me more than once. Instead of shock or anger in her eyes, I saw hints of sympathy, the shadow of a knowing smile as if we were kindred spirits. With her attraction to a Black man, she was outside the norm, if not downright rebellious, for those times. And I was desperately trying to keep myself from crossing a different Rubicon. My mutinous eyes pushed me toward disaster, and Roberta's acknowledgement sent rivers of panic up and down my spine. I downed a glass of champagne in one gulp.

About halfway through the second bottle, Lonnie and Roberta started kissing. Cindy and I took it as a sign to find our own space. The daybed on the other side of the second double bed offered more privacy. We lay down side by side and began kissing. I put my hand under her shirt and touched her breasts. We both started panting, even moaning a bit. It was actually happening. A curse was lifting from my life, allowing me to be normal.

"Hey, keep it down over there," said Roberta with a snorty laugh. They switched off the lamp, throwing the room into darkness.

With my tongue, I searched inside Cindy's mouth. I rolled on top of her, and my erection sought a home between her legs. I was ready. She was ready. I just didn't know what to do. Was I supposed to remove her panties or was she? Should we get completely naked? How did the bra snap work?

In the next moment, a rumbling instantly became an eruption inside of me. An acidy gurgle surged up into my throat. "Oh, oh, oh," I groaned.

"Man, he's a fast shooter," said Lonnie.

Cindy stopped her rapid breathing. "What is it?"

I jumped up and ran into the bathroom to commune with the toilet bowl, spewing pretzels, Ritz crackers, and an acerbic pink liquid that burned my throat. It felt like my guts were turning inside out. I hugged the bowl, dry heaving. After a few minutes I stood up and looked in the mirror. I had splotches of vomit on my T-shirt. After turning on the water, I first washed my mouth out, not getting rid of the horrible taste, and then dabbed at my T-shirt. I took a couple of deep breaths. I thought I was okay and was anxious to get back to the task at hand. The chance to be normal was awaiting me.

I opened the door and stepped into the room, dark and completely silent like it had been evacuated. I padded over the rough carpet back to Cindy. She barely seemed to be breathing.

"Sorry," I said.

"You're okay now?"

"Yeah." The second I was prone, the room commenced to spin again. "Maybe not." I bounded to the bathroom for a new round of dry heaves. My body shuddered, and my head pounded. I couldn't stop retching. Clearly, I was dying. I would die a virgin. I could hear whispering outside the door, and I imagined it was angels coming to take me away. I lay down on the tiles and curled into a ball.

Cindy knocked on the door. "Can I come in?"

"No."

She came in anyway. She got me off the floor and sat me on the toilet. She ran a washcloth under the faucet and wiped my face, then cleaned the bitter drool from my chin.

"I'm so sorry," I said.

"It happens." She kept the cloth on my forehead. Tears streamed down my face. "It's no big deal."

"I'm sorry. I'm so sorry."

"A night to remember."

I laughed through my tears.

I was eternally grateful that Cindy, Roberta, and Lonnie never said a word to anybody about my breakdown in the motel room. The topic at school the next week was how wild we were at the dance. Everyone assumed we had been plastered. My stature at school shot up.

Seven: He's Musical

Cindy called to say she was free to see *Rosemary's Baby* on Saturday night. Her plans with Judy had been cancelled when Judy and her mom decided to visit the grandparents. Instead of feeling excited about seeing the movie Cindy and I had been talking about for a long time, my mind immediately went to Dr. B.

With Jill and Judy out of town, the doctor might revert to his old habits. I knew he still had a regular tennis date with Jim on Saturday afternoons. I wasn't up on how their relationship was progressing as I had cooled it with my home prowling, telling myself I was growing out of it. It didn't mean I had completely abandoned my compulsion for secretly wandering the halls of people's lives.

Six months before, I had snuck in to watch Dr. B and Jim from my perch in the closet. Same scenario: the girls out of town, tennis date with Jim followed by the after party. For better or worse, Jim appeared to be more relaxed, not that he participated much, but he no longer flinched every time Dr. B's touched him.

I lay on my bed trying to read, but the thought of spying on Dr. B and Jim if only for that momentary view of Dr. B naked, led to me reading the same page over and over without processing the words. Your brain goes to great lengths, telling you how inappropriate and dangerous compulsions are, but sense memories keep pumping you up with the message of one more time. One more time becomes that song you can't get out of your head.

Around two in the afternoon, I went through the woods behind Dr. B's house and looked in the garage. No car, but the door was locked. When I went to the basement window behind the bush, I noticed the window had been repaired and a new, more secure lock had been installed. I accepted my fate and returned home to get my bike, thinking I might ride over to Cindy's even though I was going to see her that night. Despite our disastrous prom night, we continued spending a lot of time together, and most people assumed we were an item. We hadn't attempted to sleep together again and avoided talking about it. She claimed to be done with boyfriends until she went to college.

As soon as I returned to my house, I saw Dr. B's Porsche go by. He had a passenger in the front, most likely Jim, but they went by so fast, I wasn't sure. I debated about going to Cindy's, but after some time, I got on my bike and started down the block. I screeched to a halt when I got to the Baronians' and saw Mrs. B's car in the driveway. With the garage door closed, I gathered Dr. B's Porsche was already inside and she had pulled in behind, making me wonder if she had parked down the street, watching and waiting for the moment to catch her husband. I dropped my bike on the front lawn and ran toward the house. I had to warn Dr. B or find an excuse to engage Mrs. B before she got inside. My sole purpose in life at that moment was to save Dr. B from discovery.

The side door to the garage was open. As I approached, I heard Dr. B shout, "No, Jill!" It was followed by a loud crack, and then "Oh, God" from Jim. The loud bang ripped through the fabric of tranquility that covered Oak Street, scattering birds from a nearby tree and shaking the ground under my feet.

I entered the garage as if stepping into a poster from a crime drama, a frozen moment that draws you in, first to the young man lying on the hard gray cement, the red fanning out from his head like a halo, then to the woman standing over him, her arm hanging away from her body at an odd angle as if not part of it, a gun barely attached to her fingers, about to clatter to the ground. A second man extends his hand in disbelief, the realization on his face that he was seconds short of stopping a cataclysmic string of events.

Dr. B had no problem removing the gun from her hand. "Jill, go in the house." He spoke forcefully, but without anger. She followed his command, expressionless. Dr. B squatted down and checked Jim's pulse. "Jim, can you hear me? Open your eyes, Jim. Please." He took off his shirt and put it on the head wound. He looked up and saw me standing right inside the door, his eyes expressing a multitude of emotions from grief to embarrassment to hopelessness.

"You shouldn't be here."

"What can I do?"

"Go in the house and call 9-1-1. Ask them to send an ambulance. Tell them someone has been shot. No details. And then you need to leave."

Inside the house, Jill sat at the kitchen table with her hands spread on the Formica. Her face was freckled with blood. She looked up, though she didn't seem to recognize who I was. She watched me as I made the call without appearing to comprehend what was happening.

I went back to the garage. "An ambulance is on the way. They started to ask me questions and wanted me to stay on the line. I hung up. Is he...?"

"He's still alive. You did the right thing. I'm going to ask you to do one more thing. I want you to drive my wife over to my sister's. It's a few blocks away. You can drive, right?"

"Yes, but why?"

"My wife was not here. You were not here. It was an accident. I will call my sister and tell her to expect you."

"You can't take the blame. It's not your fault."

His face communicated a lifetime of guilt. "But it is. Please do as I tell you." The please was so desperate, it shook me as if I was watching the fall of greatness, the destruction of an empire.

He went in the house and got Jill. She walked stiffly, a robot. We took her out the side door and got her in the car. Dr. B and I locked eyes for a moment, barely a second before a wall came down between us. "Thank you. I have to attend to Jim." He handed me a slip of paper with his sister's address on it.

"The prints," I said as he turned to go.

"What?"

"On the gun."

"Right." And he was gone.

It had started to rain, and as I put the car in reverse, it started to pour. Lightning flashed in the sky. Somebody up there was looking out for us as the storm meant it would be unlikely anyone would be on the street to see us.

An eerie silence settled on the car as Mrs. B stared at the hands in her lap. I kept my eyes on the road. I drove guardedly, shaky hands gripping the wheel. Each block seemed eternal.

Dr. B's sister stood on the porch when I eased into her driveway. She came down the stairs, and I rolled down the window. She acted surprisingly calm. "I'll take over. Thank you."

I got out and she got in. She made a zipping sign over her lips. "Not a word."

"Of course."

I walked back to Oak Street in the pouring rain with the feeling that the world had changed not only for the figures in the movie poster, but for me, Judy, and anyone whose life Dr. B touched.

*

The two men standing in the foyer with my mother, I immediately surmised, were neither door-to-door salesmen nor colleagues of hers from the university. They held matching brown fedoras in their hands, and raindrops spotted their trench coats, making them appear they had just left the set of *The Detectives*, though neither of them looked anything like Robert Taylor. Both had a doughy appearance as if out of the same mold, although the older one with cracked lips, facial creases, and a ruddy complexion showed signs of being left in the oven too long.

My mother had a startled look on her face, looking as though she was unsure if she should have let these rough creatures into the house, and if she closed her eyes they might go away. She took a deep breath. "These men would like to ask some questions. Let's all go into the living room."

The older man introduced himself as Detective Gunn—I had to stifle a snicker—and said the other was Detective Smith. We all shook hands, and the detectives sat on the sofa: my mother in an armchair, and I on an antique chair that tended to creak. The detectives put their hats on the coffee table, and Smith removed a small notebook and a stubby pencil from an inside pocket of his coat. My mother hadn't invited them to remove their coats. I stared at the spots of rain on the upholstery.

I had no doubt what they were there to talk about. The shooting at Dr. B's had stirred up the neighborhood, causing unaccustomed interactions, disturbing presumptions. Rumors jetted from house to house. A young man nobody knew was dead, and a gun had been involved. Apparently, Dr. B had taken responsibility. Only four people alive actually knew what had happened, and two of us weren't supposed to have been there. I was curious why the detectives wanted to talk to me.

The detective with the ruddy face asked the questions. "I suppose you've heard what happened. We're talking to people who might have some information. It's a formality."

My mom jumped in. "We don't know anything. I mean we've heard what happened like everybody else, but beyond that..."

"Well, we have some specific questions for Nathan."

"Like what?" said Mom with protective anger creeping into her voice.

"It's okay, Mom. I'm happy to answer any questions."

The detective looked me right in the eye. "You know Dr. Baronian, is that right?"

"Oh, yeah. I used to deliver their paper and still mow their lawn from time to time."

"And what about Judy Baronian? You must know her too. You're about the same age."

"Sure. We go to different high schools, but..."

"You're friendly?"

"I wouldn't exactly say that. We have a good friend in common." As soon as I said it, I regretted it. No need to drag Cindy into it.

"And what's the friend's name?"

I glanced at Mom, and she nodded.

"Cindy Kramer."

Detective Smith wrote it down.

"Really, Detective. What's this all about?" Mom said.

"Ma'am, please bear with me. Right now, we are calling this incident an accident, but we have to rule out all the possibilities." He turned back to me. "Son, do you know James Beard?"

"Well, how would he...?"

"Please, ma'am. I would like to hear from Nate. It's okay if I call you Nate, right?"

"Sure. No, I don't know Mr. Beard."

Detective Smith extracted a photo from his pocket and handed it to Gunn who handed it to me. "Look carefully. Do you recognize him?"

"No, doesn't look familiar." The photo was a professional portrait, possibly for a yearbook. It was disturbing to see it. I imagined him with his smug expression, lying on the bed, waiting for Dr. B to service him. Inside, I was in knots, but outside, I was cool. I was Obetrolling. The drug made me focused and appear surprisingly calm though the chair had started creaking a bit. I handed the picture back to Gunn.

Gunn looked at the picture again and shook his head. "Apparently, he's a tennis buddy of Dr. Baronian. Do you play tennis?"

"A little. I've taken a few lessons."

"Why's that?"

"It's a great sport."

"Have you ever played with Dr. Baronian?"

"No. He's out of my league. I'm barely a beginner."

"Detective Gunn," said my mother in a raised voice. "What does any of this have to do with my son?"

He ignored Mom's question. "But you and the doctor have a good relationship?"

"I respect him a lot. He's always treated me well, you know, when I collected for the paper and mowed the lawn."

My mom stood up. "I'm calling Nate's father. I would like him to be here."

"That's quite all right. We only have a few more questions."

When Mom was out of the room, he lowered his voice. "Miss Baronian seems to think you more than respect her father. That you admire him. That you like to hang around the house. That you feel particularly friendly with the doctor. Now, I have to admit the doctor is impressive. He's good-looking, an excellent tennis player, and, from what I hear, musical." His eyes sparkled as if pleased with his cleverness.

I sat motionless with a slight grin on my face, staring right back at him. I gave no indication he was getting to me. "What did she tell you exactly?"

He hesitated. We locked eyes. He had the experience of an investigator. But I had Obetrol. He was not going to win. It came to me in a flash what had happened. Judy had tried to implicate me to save her father. She must have told them I was jealous of Jim's relationship with Dr. B, but I wondered how much she honestly knew about Jim and her dad. "I shouldn't say this, but Judy does have a reputation as a liar." My mother returned to the room and stood next to me. "She's always hated me. I don't know why."

Gunn continued. "Where were you the day before yesterday around three o'clock in the afternoon?"

Mom's face contorted. "This is outrageous!"

"I only ask because I understand you're often out and about with the lawn mowing, etcetera. Maybe you saw something, heard something."

"I was home reading in my room. I read a lot."

The detective looked at my mother.

"I was at work. I work at the university. I sometimes have to go in on Saturdays. But if my son says he was home, he was home."

Gunn stood up, and Smith hastily followed the cue. I got to my feet as well.

"Thank you, Nate, for being so forthcoming with your answers." And to my mother, "Sorry for bothering you. Thank you for your time." They picked up their hats, and Gunn dropped a card on the table. "There's my number if you think of anything else."

When the men had left, Mom slumped into the armchair. "What is going on, Nate? Why did you tell that man Judy hates you?"

I sat on the sofa. "It seems that Judy said some stuff about me."

"What kind of stuff?"

"I'm sure she's upset about her father and saying crazy things."

"Like what, Nathan?"

"Ridiculous things. All those questions about what kind of relationship I had with Dr. B and if I knew that guy who died must have derived from something Judy told the detective."

"Did he tell you that?"

"In so many words. I'm guessing most of it. She's grasping at anything that might take blame away from her father."

"Oh my God. They can't suspect you were involved."

"No, no, no. Don't worry, Mom. Cindy told me Judy is acting completely bonkers right now. After talking to me, I'm sure the detectives could discern who's telling the truth. I think they left quite satisfied."

Her mouth hung open. She didn't seem satisfied. "When your father gets home, we'll tell him it was no big deal. That they are talking to everyone in the neighborhood. He doesn't have to know exactly what kinds of questions they were asking."

"Sure, Mom. Don't worry about it."

"I'd better start dinner."

At dinner Mom and I put on our best faces and attempted to defuse Dad's inquiries. "But you sounded so upset on the phone."

"I thought they were rude, and I didn't like having them in our house. I guess they were only doing their job."

"The whole thing seems so bizarre," said Dad. "Where was Jill when...?"

He directed his question at Mom, but I answered. "She and Judy were out of town visiting Mrs. B's parents."

Dad laughed. "I guess I should have asked the Mayor of Oak Street." Dad had started calling me that because every time they had a conversation at dinner about something in the neighborhood, I would chime in with what I knew. "What do you think happened, Nate? I mean, a gun? Nick Baronian doesn't seem like the kind of person who would be messing around with a gun."

"Gun accidents happen all the time. Americans love their guns."

Mom wiggled in her seat. "Can we talk about something else?"

"I feel so bad for Jill...and Judy of course. Not to mention all the rumors going around."

"Ben, please!"

"Sorry, honey. This salisbury steak is great by the way."

After dinner I told them I was going to ride my bike over to Cindy's house.

"I wish you wouldn't go out."

"Jackie, let the boy go. We can't let this thing interfere with our normal lives."

*

Cindy and I sat on her front stoop. The rain had stopped, and the sun hung on the horizon ready to make its descent.

"I just had two detectives at my house asking me questions."

"That's weird. What kind of questions?"

"I guess Judy told the cops some things about me. Have you talked to her? Do you know what she told them?"

"We talked for a few minutes this morning, but she didn't say anything about that. She mostly talked about her mom being a total mess."

"I should also tell you the police might contact you."

"What? Why me?"

"They kept asking me if I was friends with Judy and if we got along. I said we weren't close, but we had a good friend in common. Then they asked for your name. I have a feeling she told them some bad stuff about me, even trying to implicate me in some way."

"That makes no sense..." And then her head jerked slightly as if two train cars coupled in her brain. "Wait. Did you know that guy?"

"James Beard?"

"How do you know his name?"

"The police told me."

"Everybody's saying it's weird that when his wife and daughter are out of town, he invites his tennis partner over to the house, and the tennis partner ends up dead."

"Of course people are going to gossip in this town. I can't wait to get out of here."

"I know what you're saying. I'll probably go to college in California. But I have to say I heard my mom talking on the phone, and apparently, it's not the first time people are floating rumors about Dr. B. Last year, he came back from vacation sporting a beard."

A James Beard, I wondered?

"People thought it was weird," she said.

"And a beard means what?"

"I don't know."

We both fell silent. I wasn't sure how deep to go into this conversation, and I had the feeling Cindy wanted to drop it as well. But I was still kind of high from the Obetrol, and silence wasn't normally part of the territory. "Aren't you going to ask me what else the police wanted to know?"

"Do you want to tell me?"

"It got pretty intense when my mom left the room. The detective implied that I had a special admiration for Dr. B, insinuating an infatuation. It must have been based on things Judy told them, which is strange. If she wants to send the police in that direction, it will only fan the fires of those rumors you were talking about."

Cindy was dumbstruck. Her golden hair caught the last light of the day and swayed with the breeze. I had opened the proverbial can of worms. To continue in this conversation would alter our relationship, though it was becoming more and more obvious that we weren't headed for romance even if both of us were in denial, hoping romance might still be an option.

I couldn't stand her silence. "Are you going to say something?"

"I suppose a lot of people have fallen for Dr. B. He is pretty impressive."

"That's what the detective said."

"I have to be honest. I've wondered if you were attracted to girls."

Now I was the one compelled to act dumbstruck though I was fully aware her question might be coming. "What? Because we didn't make it on prom night? I disappointed you?"

"Don't be an ass. Your friendship has made living here and the breakup with Matt tolerable. If you don't have those kinds of feelings for me, I understand." She stopped to let out a bitter chuckle. "History repeats itself. You know why Chad and I broke up?"

I groaned. "You're kidding. His name was Chad? The California boyfriend?"

"You're an asshole sometimes."

"Sorry."

"He said he was having feelings for his roommate. He's already in college, and I guess he's experimenting."

"That sucks."

"I think that's an inappropriate comment." We both laughed.

"*Je suce, tu suce, il suce, nous sucons,*" I said through my laughter.

"That should be our new mantra: I suck, you suck, he sucks, we suck."

"I suck, you suck, he sucks, we suck," we shouted together.

"Next year is going to be a bitch at school," I said.

"I don't even want to think about it. But when things get bad, we know what to say."

"I suck, you suck, he sucks, we suck," we shouted again.

Cindy's mom opened the front door. "What in the world? Keep it down."

"Sorry, Mrs. Kramer." After the door closed, I whispered, "We should say it in French."

I rested my head on Cindy's shoulder. "I'm so going to need you next year when all the shit comes out."

"I know. We'll take care of each other. Poor Judy is going to have it tougher than any of us."

As I walked home in the dark, I regretted not telling Cindy everything I knew about Dr. B and Jim and Mrs. B. I would have loved to share those secrets and all the ones I carried about my street, but even Cindy, who I had just learned had an amazing capacity for acceptance, probably couldn't handle the deep stuff.

Eight: Burn, Baby, Burn

I lay in bed, waiting for Mom and Dad to leave for the university. I had slept poorly, obsessed with the image of Gunn and Smith breaking down our door, rifling through my room and finding my folder with five years' worth of floor plans, notes, and character sketches of my constituents, the people of Oak Street. I had to get rid of all of it.

We had a large barrel behind the house we used to burn leaves in. I took some lighter fluid from the garage and a pack of matches, put the pages in the barrel, doused them with fluid, and watched them burn, watched a big part of my life burn, watched my sins go up in smoke as if they never happened. I wasn't religious, but I found myself promising a supreme being I would be good if Dr. B and I survived the crisis without too much damage. Undoubtedly, there would be some. I stirred the ashes with a stick, making sure every page was consumed.

An hour later, I went to the police station and asked to speak to Detective Gunn. He invited me into his office and offered me a seat on the other side of his desk piled high with folders and loose papers. My folder could have ended up mixed in with those on his desk.

"Mr. Landis, I didn't expect to see you so soon."

"Only wondered how the investigation was going."

Gunn chuckled. "Now, I may not be as smart as you, but I doubt you came all the way down here to ask me how things were going. And I'm sure you know I couldn't tell you that anyway. Do you have something to tell me?"

"Based on the questions you were asking me yesterday, I got the feeling you were a bit skeptical of Dr. Baronian's version of the story."

"I'm not at liberty to say. Why don't you tell me what you have, and we stop this little dance around the maypole?"

In addition to worrying about my files, I had, during my sleepless night, gone over and over what I was about to do. I felt bad for Mrs. B, but even if they had a hard time disproving Dr. B's version of the shooting, they still might try to get him on involuntary manslaughter. On the other hand, if I told what I knew, they would look for a motive in her actions. Either one would make him a pariah in the community. But if they could prove Mrs. B pulled the trigger, it should keep him out of prison. "I lied to you yesterday."

His only reaction was slightly raised eyebrows. "Uh-huh."

"I wasn't home all afternoon on Saturday. I was out and about, as you say, riding my bike. I rode by the Baronian's and saw Mrs. B's...uh... Mrs. Baronian's car in the driveway. I thought that was strange since I knew she and Judy were out of town."

"How did you know that?" He picked up a ballpoint pen off his desk and started clicking it.

Telling half-truths is as problematic as telling complete lies. The story has to be tight. I had spent a good part of the night coming up with something that made sense. "My father doesn't call me Mayor of Oak Street for nothing. I know what's going on in the neighborhood. I hear things. I see things. And besides, my friend Cindy had told me she couldn't go to a movie on Saturday night due to plans she had with Judy. A short time later, she called me back and said Judy was going out of town with her mom, so she was free." At least some of the story was true, and Cindy would verify it.

"And did you hear anything while riding your bike?"

"I heard a loud pop. I thought it was a car backfiring over on Main Street."

"What time was that?"

"Right around three o'clock."

"What do you know about Mrs. Baronian?"

"I know she has mental problems. My mom tried to be friends with her when they first moved in but found her difficult. My grandmother was diagnosed with manic-depressive disorder, and my mom recognized a lot of the same symptoms in Mrs. Baronian. I also heard she checked herself into County Hospital Saturday night."

"As the mayor, weren't you inclined to investigate when you saw Mrs. Baronian's car in the driveway, knowing she was supposed to be out of town, and then hearing a loud noise that could be a gunshot?"

"No. None of my business. I figured she and Judy came back early for some reason. And like I said, the noise could have been anything. I had never heard a gunshot before. A short time later, I rode by the house again, and the car wasn't there. The ambulance and police cars arrived soon after. Did you ask Judy if she was with her mother that afternoon?"

"I can't tell you that."

"You didn't ask."

"All right, smarty pants, you want to take over the investigation?"

"Didn't you say you wanted to cover all the possibilities? I'm simply trying to help."

Gunn stopped clicking the pen and threw it on the desk. "Maybe you're simply trying to protect your friend, Dr. Baronian."

"You mean protect him from himself?"

"And the motive if it was the wife?"

"That's not for me to say." I smiled. We both knew the motive. I stood up. "I won't take up any more of your time."

"Have you considered that if I'm able to verify what you say, it could be more damaging to the doctor than his accident story?"

"The truth can be painful."

"Oh, brother!"

I got to the door and turned around. "One more thing. There's a lady across the street from the Baronian's, Mrs. Sloan. If I'm the mayor, she's the secretary. There's rarely a car door closing on the street that doesn't bring her to the front window. If she's sober, that is. She might be able to confirm if Mrs. Baronian's car was in the driveway."

*

Mom called me to the phone with a worried look on her face. "It's that detective." Detective Gunn wanted me to come in and see him. I assumed he needed me to make a formal statement I had seen Mrs. B's car in the driveway at the time of the shooting.

As soon as I sat down in front of him, he started clicking his pen, making me feel nervous that things might not be as simple as I thought. He also had a hunger in his face and a sparkle in his eyes like he was about to pounce. "I guess we won't be needing your statement or for you to testify if it goes to trial."

Based on the information I had given him, they questioned Judy and interviewed Mrs. B. She admitted to shooting James Beard. The gun was registered to Mrs. B's father, a gun collector. Dr. B was let go. Dr. Baronian, Senior got the best lawyer in town to create an insanity plea for Mrs. B. It was all in the *Herald*, including the information an unnamed neighbor had seen Mrs. B's car in the driveway at the time of the shooting.

"Why not?"

"We got a statement from Mrs. Sloan."

"Okay, so she saw the car too."

His pen started clicking faster, and he couldn't contain himself. "And more."

It had taken less than a minute for us to get Mrs. B in the car. It was raining and visibility was limited. I specifically looked at Mrs. Sloan's window to see if she might be watching. I didn't see her, and even if she had been lurking in the shadows, it would have been difficult for her to see me. Looking back at my last conversation with Gunn, suggesting he contact Mrs. Sloan hadn't been such a good idea since I had a pretty good idea where this conversation was going. One of the downsides of uppers is that you can't shut up when you should. That day I had been pleased I was able to come up with a story that changed the course of Gunn's investigation but kept myself out of any direct involvement.

"More?" I said.

"She told us she saw a young man helping Dr. Baronian get Mrs. Baronian in the passenger seat, and then the young man drove the car."

"Was she able to identify that person? It was pouring rain, you know. Bad visibility."

He stopped clicking his pen and laid it carefully on top of a pile of papers. He folded his hands next to the pen and leaned forward. "Hmm. I guess we could take fingerprints off the steering wheel in Mrs. Baronian's car. Or you could tell me the parts of the story that you left out. The truth would be nice." Delight enlivened his face with a ruddy glow.

"I didn't actually see her shoot him. When I saw her car, I was inclined, as you said, to investigate—"

"Or warn somebody?"

"My natural curiosity. I went around to the side door of the garage. It was open. She stood over Mr. Beard holding the gun. The doctor asked me to call 9-1-1. And then asked me to drive her over to...uh..."

"We know you took her to Dr. Baronian's sister's house. My goodness, the truth is hard to come by these days. You lied. Dr. Baronian lied. His sister lied. Judy lied. And now everybody else has flipped their stories to something more or less resembling the truth, including you. Isn't it wonderful everybody is trying to protect the doctor's reputation? But no need to worry. The senior Dr. Baronian has a lot of influence in this town. In an agreement with the DA, no motive for Mrs. Baronian's actions will be discussed at the hearing, at least beyond her being a little off her rocker. They might suggest she thought the stranger the doctor invited over for an innocent beer after their tennis game was a prowler. After her confession, I was told to back off. That's okay. I suppose the rumor mill will do its grind toward justice. Don't imagine the good doctor will be hanging around in this 'town without pity' very long." He laughed. "But I do want to say to you seriously, son, you're young and have your life all in front of you. Don't make the same mistakes as Dr. Baronian. His goose is cooked, but yours isn't."

My gut reaction was to make a snide comment or say I had no idea what he was talking about. Fortunately, I wasn't high that day, so it was easier to hold my tongue. I also realized his concern for me was genuine, and the authorities were going to keep me out of it. I wasn't in trouble for lying or being an accomplice to covering up a crime. I had to count my blessings and be humble. "Thanks for your advice."

*

It was sure to go down as one of the momentous days of my life. At least, that's what it felt like at the time. In the morning, a police detective had begun the conversation calling me out for lying and ended with the implied message that my proclivities didn't have to end up with a wife shooting my secret lover.

In the afternoon, the doorbell rang. I answered it, and Dr. B stood on the other side of the screen. I hadn't seen him since the day of the shooting. Mom came up behind me in a flash.

"Hi, Jackie. Would it be all right if I talked to Nathan?"

"This is not a good time."

I turned around to my mom. "Why not?"

She looked past me, giving Dr. B a hard stare. "Nate has been through a lot lately."

"Mom, I'm not a child. If you won't invite him in, I'll go out. You can't stop me."

"You should listen to your mother." Dr. B started to back away.

I opened the screen and stepped outside. "I won't leave the porch."

She stood at the door as if she planned to chaperone.

"Mom, please. Close the door. We'll be right here."

She closed the door without saying a word.

The porch wasn't large enough to have chairs, so we sat on the ledges, which bordered the steps that went down to the sidewalk.

"How are you doing?" said Dr. B.

My whole body ached. I needed about twenty-four hours of uninterrupted sleep after a several-day binge. "I'm fine. More importantly, how are you?"

He looked like I felt: bags under his eyes, unshaven, and a deep sadness in his eyes. "I didn't come here to talk about me. I wanted to thank you for what you did. At first,

I was angry. We had agreed on a story, and you went behind my back."

"Respectfully, Dr. B, your story didn't make sense. An accident? Even if they believed it, you likely would have gone to jail."

"Better me locked up than Jill."

"That's not your decision. The person who commits the crime is the one who should be punished."

"You have a lot to learn about the world."

"That might be true, but what you're saying is bullshit."

He was taken aback by the harshness of my words, my irritated tone. He started to protest, but I cut him off and softened my voice. "I know about you and Jim."

"You believe what everybody is saying?"

"I believe my eyes." I was so close to telling him about the closet, but I couldn't. I didn't want him to see me as a freak. "There was something about the way you looked at him, spoke to him as he lay on the ground, the sadness on your face, the tenderness in the way you touched him." To a certain extent, I was bullshitting, but it had the desired effect. He was both wowed and embarrassed.

"I don't know what to say. You don't find me repugnant?" It broke my heart to see this big, strong, cultured, educated man beaten. He had tears in his eyes. I wondered if I was the first person to show any sympathy, the only one who didn't look at him with disgust.

"If I found you repugnant, I would have to find myself the same."

My words seemed to shatter what was left of his composure. "Don't say that, Nathan. Please. I want a better life for you. Look at the mess I've made. And on top of that, if I thought I had any influence on you in the wrong way, I don't know what I'd do. You're a good person."

"You're a good person. What I am has nothing to do with you." To be honest, I wasn't sure of that, though it seemed like the right thing to say.

"You scare me, Nathan. You're so smart and aware and sensitive. You don't know how cruel the world can be."

"I'm learning." I wanted to hold him badly, needed to hold him. My body shook. I think he picked up on it, maybe wanted the same.

"I should go." He stood up and started for the street.

"Don't go," I whispered.

Halfway to the street, he turned around. His expression had changed. He had assumed his neighbor-down-the-street face. "I'm putting the house on the market. It's doubtful I'll see you again. I wish you all the best."

My tears flowed. I couldn't stop them. If we had been in a movie in some distant future or on another planet, I would have run after him, told him I loved him. Instead, I sat there choking on my sadness.

I couldn't go back inside and let my mom see me drowning in my emotions. I walked around the front of the house and picked bagworms off the evergreen bushes with one hand while wiping my eyes with the other. With the bagworms in hand, I went out to the street, threw them in the gutter, and stomped on them. A grotesque wormy substance oozed out of the pods. The noise of a car down the street caused me to turn my head toward Dr. B's house. Soon there would be a For Sale sign in the front yard. Some lovely young couple with several kids would likely buy it. He would sell life insurance, and she would be a housewife. They would have no appreciation for the ghosts of the house, the pain that lingered within its walls: Mrs. B's diminishing ability to deal with reality, Dr. B's struggle with what he could not change, my budding love for someone who could not return it, and Jim's demise due to his addiction to the pleasure Dr. B gave him.

*

I hopped on my bike and rode downtown to a record store called Music Town I had heard a new song on WLS by The Doors, "Hello I Love You," and I wanted to get the 45. A few kids from my school were also shopping for records. I noticed them staring at me, making comments and laughing. I bought the record and hurriedly exited the store without having the chance to check out other new songs on the charts.

It was obvious what Gunn had said about the rumor mill and Dr. B applied to me as well. Everyone in Dr. B's orbit got sucked into the scandal, and what Judy had reported to the police about my supposed obsession with Dr. B started making the rounds. She must have told other people besides Gunn in her inexplicable desire to destroy me.

My parents and I had a torturous dinner conversation I will never forget. Dad and I sat awkwardly as Mom served the food. The casserole had burned on the top. She served peas, which she knew I hated. We picked at our food in silence. Mom put down her fork. "Did Dr. Baronian ever try to—?"

"He never touched me," I shouted. I was crashing from several days of an Obetrol high, and my nerves felt like they were on fire.

"Calm down, buddy. Your mother and I are concerned."

"I can't believe you two have jumped right on the rumor bandwagon. I thought you liked Dr. Baronian."

"I don't give a hoot about Dr. Baronian except where it concerns my son. Your dad and I are worried about you. You're so irritable at times, so moody. High school can be daunting. We know that. But something else seems to be going on."

"I don't think Dr. B is being treated fairly. Mrs. B is the crazy one. She's the one that did it."

"Nate, you're missing the point," said Dad. "It was a horrible tragedy for the Baronians, and we're sorry about that. And we could see that you admired the doctor. Hell, everybody liked him. And yes, Mrs. Baronian had obvious mental problems. But something made her snap. And frankly, the rumors about Dr. Baronian didn't begin with the shooting."

"Because he's different? Because he plays piano? You always taught me not to pay attention to rumors and gossip, that a person's character is what matters." I was a bit disingenuous as I had firsthand knowledge that the rumors were, in fact, true.

My mother, momentarily stymied by my argument, rallied quickly. "Again, we're not judging Dr. Baronian. We only want to make sure you're not making any decisions you might regret later in life. What did he say to you when he came by today?"

"What? He was here at the house?" My father sounded outraged. "You let him in?"

"No, Dad, she did not let him in. I went out and talked to him on the front porch. Why shouldn't I?"

"About what?"

"He wanted to thank me for the statement I gave to the police about seeing Mrs. B's car in the driveway. He never asked me nor wanted me to do it. He said he thought it was better he got locked up rather than his wife. And you don't have to worry anymore. He's leaving the neighborhood and most likely the town. He's putting the house on the market."

Dad shook his head. "He made a mess of his life."

"He knows that."

Nine: Somebody to Love

Senior year at Westwood was predictably a nightmare, and I got through it thanks to Cindy, drugs, and music. On my last birthday, Cindy had given me the Jefferson Airplane album, *Surrealistic Pillow.*

She presented the album to me with a mile-wide grin. "I heard 'Somebody to Love' on the radio, and I thought you'd like it."

I started listening to the album nonstop. Every song was fantastic. I recognized Grace Slick wasn't a great singer technically, but her low, powerful voice could set your insides on fire. Some songs you like, some make your body move, some compel you to sing along. "Somebody to Love" was in the category of touching my soul, making me want to weep and shout for joy at the same time. Since my own voice seemed to be wandering around in a wasteland, undeveloped and changing, I needed her voice to sing out in anger and protest and frustration and longing.

Grace's voice helped to drown out the scandal of Dr. B. I was, at the very least, guilty by association. In the minds of some, I was a dedicated member of the doctor's homo den of iniquity. When I walked down the hall alone at school, I would get jostled, called queer and faggot, have books knocked out of my hands.

Cindy and Roberta would walk with me whenever they could, but some of their friends started giving them a hard time. Cindy didn't care, having pretty much dropped out of the social scene, anticipating her escape to California, but Roberta was more sensitive. She had her own battles to fight with racism occasionally raising its ugly head even though Lonnie was extremely popular as class president and a quarterback on the football team.

A couple of times, Lonnie saw guys harassing me and told them to knock it off, but in the end, he had to play sports with the same boys who bothered me. Maintaining team spirit had to take precedence over being my defender.

I tried my best to not give any indications of my misery to my parents, but I could tell by their expressions they knew. They must have had so many questions they wanted to ask, questions that would get us into painful territory. And advice they wanted to give though they didn't know how. They let out a sigh of relief when the Baronian house sold, and a family astonishingly similar to the one I had predicted moved in. I had withdrawn from the affairs of the neighborhood and stripped myself of the title of Mayor of Oak Street.

One day, walking home from school, I ran into Miss Larson and Miss Jacobi. It was rare to see them out, particularly together.

"How are you doing, Nathan?" said Miss Jacobi with a kindly smile.

"Oh, you know, I'm nervous about college, where to apply and all that."

"What school are you thinking about?"

"Tulane in New Orleans, but I'm looking at others."

"Now, isn't that an interesting choice?" Miss Larson scrunched her shoulders and looked at me sideways as if I had announced I was going to do something nasty like visit a brothel.

She directed her gaze at the house across the street. "I see we have some new neighbors. I guess things will be getting back to normal."

"Normal?" I said.

The two women looked at each other. Miss Jacobi chuckled. "What is normal?"

"We've been thinking about you," said Miss Larson. "Hoping you're okay."

I felt a tightness in my chest and the irritating sensation behind my eyes before my ducts produced tears. "I just...just... hope I can get in a good college." In reality, I didn't care where I went as long as it was away.

"You will be fine, my dear," said Miss Jacobi. "You have a brave soul like Winston Churchill."

"I was thinking Mr. Darcy," said Miss Larson.

"Oh, heavens, Mildred, this is hardly Regency England."

My sinking emotions of a few minutes before were uplifted by their light and endearing exchange, and I chuckled to myself, realizing the mystery of who read what was solved. I suffered a pang of guilt for having invaded their privacy. I didn't know how to control my dark side. At the same time, I told myself I wasn't an evil person. I didn't hurt people or tell the secrets I had discovered.

Miss Jacobi let out big sigh. "We're sorry you're not delivering our paper anymore. You were always so polite and did a great job mowing the lawn. The new boy is...well..."

Miss Larson took over. "He doesn't have the same profundity behind his eyes, the romantic aloofness that seems to help you through life. We know you are a noble character at heart."

"There you go with your Mr. Darcy," said Miss Jacobi.

I'm not noble. I broke into your house. I wandered about and touched your things. There is something wrong with me. "It's been nice talking to you. I have to go. My mom is expecting me to help her with something."

"I hope we see you before you go off to college. If not, best of luck to you."

I watched them walk down the street. In a better universe, they would have been holding hands.

I thought of my grandmother alone in a nursing home, talking to people no one else could see. When we went to visit, she would call my mother by the name of one of her sisters. She had no one with whom to share her life or discuss books.

The decision to put her in a home had been agonizing for my mother. Neighbors had started coming to our door with tales of Gran's antics. Mrs. Burnside said she saw her walking through the park talking to herself. She stopped to ask if she was okay, and Gran told her to go to hell and lifted her sweater, exposing her bare breasts. Gran's next-door neighbor told us she had heard loud weeping, so she knocked on her door. Gran didn't answer. The weeping stopped, but she said she detected a foul odor.

My mother knew she had to act, but she procrastinated. One day, she got a call that Gran had fallen in the park, twisted her ankle, and bloodied her head. At the emergency room, the nurse took Mom aside and whispered that Gran was wearing seven slips, one over the other, but no dress. She wore a long winter coat over the slips. They patched her up, but they wanted to keep her for a couple days of observation.

That weekend Mom asked David to come home, and the three of us went to Gran's house. It was knee-deep in clutter and garbage from front to back. She had taken to buying things through the mail: gadgets, health food products, shampoo, and cooking utensils, much of it still in its original packaging. Magazines and newspapers were piled up in no particular order. Clothes and shoes were everywhere. But the thing that got to all of us, bringing my mother to tears, was the stench. A box of rat poison sat on the kitchen table, and we soon came upon the rotting carcasses of rats and mice.

My mother had taken a handkerchief out of her pocket to dry her eyes but now held it over her nose. "I'm so sorry you boys have to see this."

"We should hire someone to clean up," said David.

"I don't want anyone to see this. Plus, there might be valuable things amongst the junk—her jewelry, some pieces of her china, silver serving dishes, and whatnot. Forgive me for asking you boys to help me go through things."

Before going home to get work clothes, bandanas, boxes, shovels, and rakes, we took a moment to examine the backyard garden where weeds had taken over. It was a sad sign things had reached a crucial level; when Gran could no longer garden, her tenuous connection to reality had slipped away. I felt partly to blame. In the past year, she had called me multiple times to help her pick and shuck corn, build a cage to put over the lettuce so the rabbits wouldn't eat it all, or dig shallow ditches between the rows so the water would get to the roots. I started telling her no. I didn't have the time. I had to study. The truth was I had music to listen to, daydreaming to engage in, and drugs to take. I couldn't be bothered with trying to help Gran maintain a grip.

Later that day, as we raked and shoveled, picking out treasures from the rubbish, I stopped to look at my mom. Her hair was tied up in a scarf, and she wore a pair of my father's faded trousers, rolled up and cinched at the waist with an old belt, and a paint-splattered work shirt my father had used when he ventured into one of his rare household-improvement projects. She was bent over, raking trash onto some old bedding too stained and moldy to save. It made me sad to see her looking exactly like the farm girl she had spent the last twenty years of her life trying to escape. She put her hand on her lower back, straightened up, and produced a nearly inaudible groan.

"Mom, why don't you take a break?" I said.

"Thanks, honey, but I'm all right." She looked at me with tenderness. I smiled back, her innocent, sweet boy. It was a few weeks before the neighborhood blew up with the Baronian affair. I didn't know then it would be a long time before she looked at me in the same way.

*

Cindy and I were both in honors French. I called to ask about a translation we were working on; at least, that was the excuse I gave. I had been thinking a lot about Dr. B, missing him. I could no longer walk by his house at night and see the lamp lit in the den.

"Have you heard anything from Judy?" I knew she had gone to live with her maternal grandparents in a town not far from the state hospital. She would be able to visit her mother often. The court had assigned Mrs. B to a secure mental health facility where she would have to spend at least the next seven years.

"Like you're really interested in what's going on with Judy."

"That's the problem with good friends. They always know what you're thinking."

"Kind of scary, isn't it? I got your number, Landis. No, I don't know anything about the doctor. He was supposed to contact Judy when he got settled. Last I heard, he hadn't. He's left town. I can tell you that."

"That much I figured."

"What would you do? Write him a letter?"

"No. I don't know."

"Things'll get a lot better when we both go off to college."

"Two-thousand-eight-hundred-and-eighty hours till we graduate."

"That's not helpful."

"I nearly went over to Dr. B's sister's house the other day."

"Don't, Nate. That's crazy. She probably wouldn't tell you anything."

"I only want to know if he's all right."

"You'll forget all about him when you get to college. We both need a change of scene. You'll see. Why did you choose Tulane anyway?"

"I read this funny description in the *Real Guide to U.S. Colleges*. Sounds like my cup of tea." I still had the book on my desk and opened it up. "Let me read it to you. 'It's hard to believe Tulane can maintain its reputation as the Harvard of the South when distractions abound. Music, debauchery, and a legal drinking age of eighteen, not to mention Mardi Gras season, make studying a challenge. Tulane must be one of the only schools in the country that gives you a four-day weekend to whoop it up before Ash Wednesday crashes upon you. The student body covers the spectrum from ROTC fanatics to pseudo-hippies with 4.0 GPAs. And with most of New Orleans below sea level, you're constantly drenched in sweat, feeling like you might be snorkeling through the Great Barrier Reef, considering the number of colorful and possibly scary characters you encounter wherever you go, particularly in the French Quarter.'"

"I hope you didn't read that to your parents."

"They told me I could go anywhere I got accepted. I think they will be content if I get into any school with a decent reputation. They also seem to understand I need to get away from this town after all that's happened. My mom returned to work in part to provide me with a good education. I hope I don't screw it up."

I honestly planned to cut down on the drugs and get serious. I wanted to keep studying French and maybe go to business school. I could work for a company with an office in Paris, write poetry on the side. At least that was the *idée du jour*. The next day I would fantasize being an international weapons trader, selling to countries trying to overthrow their dictators.

Cutting down on drugs would have to wait. I had to get through senior year without having a nervous breakdown, and working with Danny at Walgreens, I made sure I had a regular supply. I had moved from stock clerk to cashier, and Danny had become an assistant manager. He was a year ahead of me and had already graduated. He scheduled himself to work the pharmacy cash register as much as possible and got to be friendly with the pharmacists. He learned all the names of medicines and knew the regular customers.

He had a number of tricks for siphoning off pills. When the pharmacists were backed up, they would let him count pills and put them in the bottles, which was most likely illegal. As he counted pills, a few would end up in his pocket. By the end of the day, he would have a stash of uppers, including my favorite Obies, as well as the downers like Seconal and Valium to help us sleep. I would offer to pay him, but he usually gave them to me for free. It was unbelievable how many women and teenage girls came in for diet pills, making sure Danny had a chance to pocket pills on a regular basis.

Danny had started dating a girl from the East Side, and he avoided being alone with me, never coming to my window at night anymore. He kept saying that Cindy and I should double date with him and his girlfriend.

"She's not my girlfriend," I told him.

"You are hopeless, Landis. You need to get laid."

I couldn't have agreed more. At times, I looked at Cindy and thought, why not? I had a strong feeling for her that might be called love, though I was still confused about what the word meant. After that night in the motel room, the thought of touching her in a sexual way would leave me confused, and confusion led to inaction. One day I came upon the magic word—bisexual.

Some of the novels I read had bisexual characters. I had read Gore Vidal's *The City and the Pillar* and James Baldwin's *Giovanni's Room.* I was fascinated by the concept of free-flowing genders in *The Left Hand of Darkness* by Ursula Le Guin. If great writers wrote bisexual characters, the concept couldn't be too disgusting. Maybe if I got out and experienced the world, I would find other people like me who didn't conform. I had my hopes on New Orleans.

*

My brother came home from Madison more often than usual my senior year, most likely prompted by my parents, to spend time with me, talk to me about college and other things I might have on my mind. He would suggest we go play tennis, knowing it made me feel good to beat him. He would wake me up early in the morning to go running and keep badgering me until I got up. I would start out okay but lose steam way before he did.

We spent a lot more time talking about the state of the world than any problems I might be having. After three years at the University of Wisconsin, he was full of new ideas. He talked about the absurdity of the war. He worried about getting drafted when he finished school and told me he was considering going to Canada.

The first time I noticed a political awakening was when he came home in the summer of 1968. He was excited about the candidacy of Bobby Kennedy, particularly his stance against the war in Vietnam. He hadn't been home a week before he woke me up in the middle of the night after being out with friends and told me Kennedy had been shot. We turned on the radio and listened for news. When he was declared dead the next day, David was devastated, and we remembered JFK's assassination a few years before when the whole family had watched the funeral on TV, and our parents had wept. I realized my most formative years took place between Kennedy assassinations, the murder of JFK around the time Dr. B moved into our neighborhood and Bobby's death that fateful summer Mrs. B shot Jim. With Martin Luther King's assassination a few months before, we both acknowledged something sinister was happening in our country.

After Bobby's death, David became more openly against the war. He let his hair grow as long as his coaches would allow. He started talking about being a draft dodger if he got his notice.

He also told me about his girlfriend, Lola. "She's smart and reads like you. I bet you'd like her."

"You should invite her home."

"I will. Her mother is Brazilian and father American. From her mother's side, she has darkish skin. I guess Mom and Dad would be cool with that. Poor Gran wouldn't like it, but she barely recognizes us anymore. And what about you? Are you and Cindy still dating?"

"The only real date we had was prom. We hang out." David had asked me several times about prom night and pressed me for details. I did my best to change the subject. Since I refused to tell him anything, he most likely assumed I was still a virgin.

David and I went to visit Gran, and she greeted us with a big, "Hello, David." She looked at me. "Is that your friend?"

Her main caregiver was a large Black woman named Millie who had just given her a sponge bath. She looked at me and winked.

"Oh, come on, Gran. You remember Nate. My brother? Your grandson?"

She started to laugh. We weren't sure if she was laughing at her forgetfulness or the absurdity of me being her grandson.

I later took Millie aside. "Does Gran treat you all right?"

"She cantankerous, but I don't pay her no mind. Sometimes I stand behind her and brush her hair. She can't see me, so she relax. She start purring like a cat."

"Thank you so much for putting up with her."

The Earth is a giant house of ironies. On a planet that is three-quarters water, people die of thirst. We fight wars to gain peace. And after all Gran's racist rants about the Blacks taking over, the person who gave her comfort at the end of her life was a Black woman.

On the night before I left for college, a few people came over for a going away party. Danny gave me a Walgreens bag.

"It's kind of a gag gift, a bottle of aspirin for the headaches you'll get from all your studying." Later, I opened the bottle and found an assortment of pills, including lots of Obetrol.

Cindy gave me a poster. "Something to decorate your dorm room." It was a picture of Grace Slick in what looked like a Boy Scout uniform shirt sitting next to Janis Joplin in a fur hat.

Roberta gave me a pen-and-pencil set. "This is from Lonnie too. He couldn't make it but said to wish you all the best."

And that was the grand finale to my high school years.

Ten: The Big Easy

The Tulane campus was inundated with freshmen like me in uncomfortable clothes our parents had demanded we wear to make a good first impression. Mothers showed expressions of bewilderment that their children were in college and would soon be leaving them to fend for themselves. The new freshmen distanced themselves from their precollege lives by walking either a few paces ahead or a few behind their parents.

I had achieved my childhood fantasy of going to New Orleans, though it wasn't on a raft down the river as I had first imagined. I was eager to be on my own and away from Sangamon and told my parents the train would be fine, but they insisted on driving me, a trip that took two days with a stopover in Memphis. My mother kept saying it was a parent's duty to see a child safely accommodated in his new home away from home. I had the feeling that as much as getting me settled, they were excited about spending time in a city they hadn't visited since shortly after they were married, conjuring up those carefree early years before they had children.

By the time Dad and I carried my bags up to the second floor—Mom following along with a care package of homemade cookies and bags of snacks—we were all drenched in sweat. We were used to humidity in the summer, but this seemed something else, making us feel that we truly were underwater. I stopped on the landing to take off the summer sport jacket Mom had bought me for the trip. I had large cones of sweat under each arm.

"Did you put on deodorant this morning?" my mother asked.

"I might have forgotten." In addition to the sweat stains, I smelled of adolescent angst.

"In this climate, you have to be particularly careful about personal hygiene."

"I know, Mom." I couldn't wait for them to leave and let me begin the next phase of my life.

The door was open to my new room. High on the list of trepidations about starting college was who would be my roommate. I prayed it wasn't a football jock or an ROTC enthusiast who would object to my Grace Slick and peace posters. I was pleased to see he looked like neither of those. He had longish hair and a face so soft and smooth, he looked incapable of growing a beard. He wore a loose-fitting V-neck shirt that looked more like a blouse, cutoff jean shorts, and sandals. From behind, people might have taken him for a girl.

I introduced myself and my parents. My mother tensed up as she shook his hand. His name was Kevin, and he was from Maryland.

My father asked him what he planned to study, and he said he hadn't decided on a major yet but planned to do some liberal arts courses as well as art courses like ceramics and printmaking.

"They teach that here?"

"My dad's a history professor at the college back home," I explained.

"I loved my history courses in high school," said Kevin.

"I'm thinking about studying psychology," I said.

Mom knitted her brow. "I thought you were going to study business."

Business sounded so conservative. I didn't want my new roommate to think I was straitlaced. "Maybe anthropology. I haven't decided yet. It's only the first semester."

"Well, I hope you study something useful."

"I think psychology is useful considering all the crazy people in the world." Mom got a pained look on her face. "I didn't mean Gran...or...or... Mrs. Baronian. I was thinking of the people that want to send young men to fight in a war a million miles away that's none of our business."

"Okay, Nate," said my dad. "I don't think you want to bore your roommate with your political ideas right after you've met. Your mom and I will go down and take a walk around the campus and let you get unpacked. We'll meet at the car in about an hour."

Kevin looked out the door to make sure my parents were out of range. "I agree with you. It's a stupid war. If I had said that in front of my dad, he might have smacked me. I'm a military brat, grew up all over the place."

"I'm going to let my hair grow like yours."

A few hours later, I sat with my parents in the elegant dining room of Galatoire's, surrounded by waiters in tuxedos. It was the fanciest place I had ever been, and I wondered if my parents had known what they were getting into. Dad looked at the prices and cleared his throat, looking at Mom over the top of his menu. She shrugged. The offerings included a lot of seafood and fish dishes. Growing up in a meat-and-potatoes family, I had never developed a taste for seafood. I asked Dad if I could order a steak.

"Son, you can order whatever you want. This might be your last good meal for a while."

Mom picked at her Salad Maison. "You know, if you're unhappy with your roommate, you can always request a change. I checked with the house office."

"Really, Mom. You didn't."

"He looks like kind of a hippie."

"And the problem with that is..."

"We don't want you to come under the wrong influences. You seemed to change your major right on the spot."

"Jackie, let's enjoy our meal. God knows we're paying enough for it."

"The point I'm trying to make is that the people you meet at college and the choices you make can change the course of your life."

"You're making assumptions about him based on the way he looks. Everybody in here is dressed up because the restaurant requires it. Does that make them good people? Half the men are cheating on their wives, cheating on their taxes, and cheating in business."

"All right, Nate. That's enough," said Dad. "We get the point. Can we just have a quiet meal and not talk about anything controversial?"

"Look. Here's the food." The waiter set a Shrimp Étouffée in front of Mom. She stared at the plate, perplexed, as if she wasn't sure what she had ordered.

*

Countless hours of the fall semester, I sat on the steps of the Student Union, relishing in the contentment of being far from home, listening to the conversations of people going up and down the wide stairway, watching people cross the quadrangle dodging Frisbees. The assortment of students swirling about me was as diverse as the description I had read in the guide, from frat boys to jocks to debutantes in jeans to young people playing hippie on their fathers' dime.

One group, which proudly owned the label the Freaks, included a wild-haired girl in long skirts who carried a balloon with her everywhere she went; a spry young man in overalls, no shirt, and a head of blond Afro curls; a girl who frequently dressed as a court jester; a chubby boy who seemed to own a vast collection of tie-dyed T-shirts; and a Twiggy lookalike who wore miniskirts and combat boots. I wondered if they got tired of playing their roles around the clock.

Kevin and I sometimes joined the Frisbee players. With practice, I became part of the gang who could, in a good throw with the wind in the right direction, send the spinning disc from one end of the quadrangle to the other. As I rarely played tennis anymore, it was the only exercise I got aside from running to class when I got up late.

Since my parents made sacrifices for me to go to a private university, I felt an obligation to maintain my grades, not to mention I needed the deferment to avoid the draft. With the supply of uppers Danny gave me, I would cram for tests, write papers that received high marks, often surprising professors, who due to my complete silence during class discussions, must have assumed I had nothing to say or was always too stoned to open my mouth.

My English professor told us to write an essay expressing an opinion we thought the teacher wouldn't agree with. I wrote on the legitimacy of nonstandard forms of English. He gave me an A and wrote a note. "Maybe one day you'll stop hiding behind that hair and share your views with your classmates." My hair was now parted in the middle and often hung down, covering my eyes.

In truth, I did attend class high a lot. Kevin and I, along with a group of guys in our dorm, smoked pot and listened to music. One of the guys from Florida showed us a flyer a friend had sent him about a pop festival in West Palm Beach near his hometown. It was going to be even better than Woodstock, he claimed, since The Rolling Stones were part of the lineup. We speculated on the possibility of a festival that would compare with Woodstock though none of us had been there.

"Is Jefferson Airplane on the bill?" I asked.

"Oh yeah. And Janis Joplin, Sly and the Family Stone, The Byrds, Steppenwolf, a bunch of others."

Kevin grabbed the flyer. "Look, it says Johnny Winter is going to be there." He was a blues fan. Johnny Winters and Muddy Waters were gods to him.

"When is it?" I asked.

"Over Thanksgiving weekend."

Kevin turned to me. "We should go."

"How would we get there?"

"Hitchhike."

"Are you serious?" I had never hitchhiked before. The idea sounded exciting and dangerous.

"It's over eight hundred miles!" said the guy from Florida.

"I hitched from Maryland to Ohio once," said Kevin. "Got a ride from a trucker who took me all the way. All I had to do was talk to him to keep him awake."

"Don't take offense," said a guy in a Georgia drawl. "But looking the way you guys do, I would not recommend hitching across the Florida panhandle. They've got more rednecks per square mile than anyplace in the country."

Both Kevin and I now had hair grazing our shoulders. Kevin waved him off. "You're paranoid. People on the road are nice."

Mom sent me a package with my sleeping bag and a few camping items from my Boy Scout days. We told our parents we were going camping on the beach in Pensacola for Thanksgiving. Though my parents weren't thrilled I was going with Kevin, I gave them credit for not spending a lot of time trying to convince me not to go. We filled our packs with boxes of macaroni and cheese, dried fruit, cookies, and cans of tuna fish.

A little after noon on Wednesday, we headed out with the idea we would get as far as we could by nightfall. Thursday we would go the rest of the way. The music was scheduled to begin on Friday. We had no tickets but didn't worry about it. We were armed with the notion that music and the peace movement were in the process of changing our society forever, and by participating in the festival, we would be part of a new age.

A student going home for the holidays took us as far as Pensacola. We stared out the window in awe of the remnants of one of the worst hurricane seasons ever. Widespread damage was evident along the Gulf Coast with ruined beaches, downed palm trees, and boarded-up hotels. After he dropped us off next to an abandoned gas station missing a roof, we followed the coast highway so we could sleep on the beach when night came. Another couple of rides took us beyond Panama City. We sat by the road as cars went by with children's faces at the windows staring at us as if we were from another planet. The sun had begun to go down when an officer from the Air Force base picked us up and took us as far as a campground outside Apalachicola where he told us we could camp.

We made a fire, and I heated up water in my official Boy Scout mess kit and added a box of macaroni and cheese. To round out the menu, we each had a quarter of a muffuletta sandwich. Then we spread out our sleeping bags and looked at the stars.

"You don't have any hard feelings about Susan, do you?" said Kevin. Despite people's first impressions of Kevin, he was a womanizer. He had dated several girls since the beginning of the year. The last couple weeks, it had been Susan. Susan had been interested in me first, but when I didn't respond with the enthusiasm she anticipated, she took up with Kevin. She looked like a model, a taller and thinner version of Cindy, and I was surprised she was attracted to either of us. I didn't care that she ended up with Kevin because I knew it wouldn't have worked out. I didn't feel what I was supposed to feel.

"No hard feelings at all. I think you're a better match for her."

"You still have someone back home, right?"

"She's going to school in California, so I doubt it will continue. I mean, we'll always be friends." In the recesses of my mind, I still held the belief it was possible for me to find the right girl. Challenging that belief was the fact that I still fantasized about Dr. B when I masturbated.

"You'll find someone."

Clouds moved in and covered the stars. I felt a chill as the temperature continued to drop. I burrowed down into my bag. It was a beautiful moment to be lying next to Kevin under the night sky, off on an adventure, anticipating a better future. I felt a warm contentment. What I did not feel was an urge to touch Kevin. In a short time, we had developed a strong bond, and yet I had no desire to take that to some kind of intimacy. Maybe there was hope for me.

The next morning, we ate some cookies and got on the road. Car after car passed us by, people again staring at us and occasionally flipping us the bird. After a couple of hours, a pickup stopped. We didn't like the look of the two guys, but we were desperate. The driver had an opossum face with a flattop haircut. The passenger was hairy with a beer belly and wavy black hair that covered his ears.

"One of y'all ride up front. The other in back," said the driver. Kevin hopped in the bed of the truck with our backpacks, leaving me to ride between the two men who smelled of beer, possibly from a liquid breakfast or from a binge that had begun the week before. Beer Belly popped a can and gave it to me.

"No thanks."

"What? You too good to drink with us?"

"No. It's early."

They laughed. "Fuckin' pussy."

I took the can of Dixie and started sipping on it. For the next twenty minutes, I had to defend my existence as a long-haired student, a Yankee, a human being, choosing my words carefully. I found myself regurgitating some of the arguments from my Tulane History professor, a man from Mississippi who lectured us on how the Civil War, which he called the War of Northern Aggression, was justified and how the South got a raw deal during Reconstruction. I had been skeptical about what he taught us. Little did I know he was preparing me for this moment.

"Damn right! Bunch a faggots came down here and gave the coloreds our land."

At one point, I turned around to show the beer to Kevin and make an agonizing face that he was being left out of a particularly troubling conversation. He sat with his hair whipping in the wind, enjoying the scenery, oblivious to what I was going through.

The driver snorted. "You worried about your girlfriend?"

"Doesn't seem fair I'm up here drinking a beer."

The driver took a beer from under his feet and threw it over his shoulder out the window. It landed in the bed of the truck, causing Kevin to start. The driver howled with laughter. I turned around and again tried to communicate with more animated facial expressions that we might be in some deep shit. Kevin grabbed the can and stared at it like it had fallen from the sky. At times, I felt Kevin didn't need drugs. He was a natural space cadet, not picking up on my anxiety in the least.

"You know what we do with queers in the South, don't you?" said the hairy one. He opened the glove compartment, pulled out a pistol, and rubbed the nozzle of the gun against his cheek. It was the second time in my life I had seen a pistol up close, and the last time didn't end well. I thought how devastated my parents would be when they heard my body had been found on the side of the road in the scrub pines of the Florida panhandle. I wondered if Dr. B would ever hear of it and if he would feel sad.

"They shot this one guy up the butt hole," said Flattop.

"Yeah, after they stuck something else up there."

I stared at the tall skinny pine trees lined up like soldiers on either side of the road. My heart pounded in my chest. The windshield was splattered with bugs. I was in a horror film.

"Our college friend has gone kinda quiet," said Flattop.

My mind clicked like a camera taking multiple shots of a crime scene, looking for that one detail to solve the case. "Look, we have long hair because we're in a rock band, and that's what people want. We both have girlfriends." I kept a picture from prom in my wallet. With shaking hands, I took it out and showed them. "That's my girlfriend, Cindy."

Beer Belly cooed. "I'd like to get me some of that. Bout making me horny."

"Let me have a look," said Flattop. "Fine piece of ass."

I had to think of something fast. "Can we stop for a piss?"

"What? You getting hard too?" His belly jiggled as he laughed.

"Damn, I gotta piss too," said Flattop. He pulled the truck to the side of the road, and we got out. They danced over to the edge of a ditch and barely got out their dicks before they were peeing. I ran back to Kevin. He was still enjoying the scenery. "Get the fuck out of the truck. Grab our packs. Run!" He sat a moment, looking confused. "Kevin. Move!"

We ran down the middle of the road in the direction we had come. There wasn't much traffic, but each time a car came, we waved our hands for them to stop. They swerved around us and sped off. Any minute Belly and Flattop were going to turn around and come after us. After about a mile of running as fast as we could with our packs, we managed to get a car to stop. A family, dressed in their Sunday finest, looked like they were on the way to Thanksgiving dinner at Grandma's.

"God bless you." I tried to control my speeding heart. I must have sounded like a madman. "So sorry to stop you like this, but we were riding with some drunk men, and they threatened us with a gun. Could you possibly give us a ride to the next town?"

The wife rolled up the window, so it was only open a couple of inches. "Oh, dear. Not sure we feel comfortable with that."

"We understand," said Kevin. He seemed to have returned to the world of the living after our run, even had the brass to put on a Southern accent. "We may not look like it, but we're good Christians. We truly feared for our lives. I said my prayers, and y'all came along. And on this Thanksgiving Day, we would be eternally grateful if you helped us get on our way so we can make it home to our families."

The woman turned to her husband. "What do you think, Pa?"

The man looked in the rearview mirror. "Bessie, come up here and ride with your Ma. We can take you as far as Crawfordville. Where are you going?"

We hesitated a moment. "Tallahassee," I blurted out.

"That's up the road a piece from where we're going."

We got in the back seat with the boy, who was about ten years old, and rested the backpacks on our laps. I smiled at him, and he looked away. A minute later, he returned to gawking as if the opportunity to see something out of the ordinary was too good to pass up.

"You should report them yahoos to the police when you get to Crawfordville."

"We might do that," I said.

"My daddy's in the military," said Kevin. "He taught us to respect guns and not go waving them about, scaring people."

The wife nodded her head. "That's God's truth."

We said goodbye to our Crawfordville friends and within a few minutes got a ride to Tallahassee from a salesman who talked nonstop on the half-hour drive. Outside Tallahassee, an eggplant VW van stopped. As soon as they opened the side door, I knew they were going to the festival. "Thank you, Jesus!" I yelled, and everybody laughed. There were already four people in the van, but no one seemed to mind being crowded.

"I can't believe you guys are hitching through the panhandle," said the driver. "How's it been?"

I groaned. "Don't ask."

We drove eight hours straight to the edge of the Palm Beach International Speedway where traffic was backed up for miles. Since they had tickets and we didn't, we got out to walk and, hopefully, discover a way to get in. The flyer said they wouldn't be selling tickets at the venue.

Eleven: Muddy Waters

Kevin and I tramped along a narrow path between cars lined up to get into the raceway and ditches filled with dark water, greeting and high-fiving people sitting in their cars with music blaring and marijuana smoke drifting out the windows. It was dark and cooler than we had expected for South Florida. A light rain had begun to fall, causing us to stop and pull our ponchos out of our packs.

We asked people along the way about tickets, and though no one had any extras, several of them confirmed there wouldn't be any sold at the entrance. When we got close to the gate, a guy overheard us requesting tickets and pulled us aside. "I've got a couple."

"Are they real?" We had been warned about counterfeit tickets.

He pulled a plastic bag out of his pocket with tickets inside and pointed out the features that made them authentic. "I'm selling them for twenty-five. That's only five over face value. A lot of people are selling them for thirty or more."

Kevin and I looked at each other. Neither of us had brought a lot of cash.

"If you don't have the bread, I can show you how to get in without a ticket for ten bucks. But you have to swim across a canal." He laughed. "Rumor has it the sheriff, dead set against this festival, filled the canal with alligators to stop people. Been across five times and ain't seen a gator yet." His clothes were soaking wet, but it was hard to tell if it was from the rain or swimming the canal.

"Let's pay the twenty-five," I said to Kevin. "We've come this far."

We exhaled with relief when we got through the gate with our slightly damp tickets and immediately felt overwhelmed by what surrounded us. I was struck by the contrast to the last time I was camping with thousands of people. The Jamboree had been like a military camp, neat rows of tents organized in sections. The festival was chaos, a refugee camp surrounded by mud, cars and vans randomly parked, tents scattered and improperly set up, looking as if a light wind would topple them.

It had been raining all week, and the large numbers of unprepared attendees stretched out on blankets and tarps thrown down over the mud. Some huddled around fires, the flames casting a desperate light on their faces. Everyone's hair hung unkempt and damp as if they had just gotten out of the shower. A young man passed by with a blue blanket over his head, his angelic features conjuring images of the Virgin Mary.

"When I said the other night my ideal concert would be Johnny Winter and Muddy Waters together, this is not what I had in mind," Kevin said.

"We need to make friends with someone with a tent. I heard a guy say it might rain all weekend."

"Keep an eye out for our friends in the eggplant VW. Didn't they say they had a tent?"

We wandered around to see if we could find drier areas to camp in case we were stuck in the open. Walking down close to the stage where they were still in the process of setting up, we found the toilets and facilities for washing and looked at food options. We thought of the flyer our friend in the dorm had shown us, boasting of "over three hundred toilets, a hundred wash basins, finest concessions with fair prices, a hundred drinking fountains."

If the fifty thousand people they'd predicted showed up, it hardly seemed sufficient. The brochure had also claimed, "finest grass and picnic tables." The finest grass was all buried in mud, and all the picnic tables had been claimed, mostly by people trying to stay dry under them. The rain fell harder, but we were determined to have a good time. Here and there, people with battery-powered radios danced in the mud or under tarps they had rigged up. Clouds of marijuana smoke hung in the thick air. People sold drugs openly. No, it was not like the Jamboree or like anything I had seen in my life. It was a new world.

Despite arriving the night before the music actually began, we found no good spots to claim as our own, no places where you didn't sink into the muck up to your ankles. We headed back to the main gate in hopes of spotting the VW with our friends as they entered. It was another half hour before the van came into view, and we followed them to the place they were directed to, sheepishly standing outside the van as the four of them piled out.

"Friends!" said Klaus, the driver. "Glad you got in."

They didn't have a tent but a large tarp they attached to the roof of the van and extended out. They told us we were welcome to sleep under it. Klaus's girlfriend, Ingrid, stayed with the van while the rest of us went foraging for wood and any dry paper or cardboard we could use to start a fire.

We combined our food with what Klaus, Ingrid, Sukie, and John had brought and cooked a meal on their Coleman stove. As the only Boy Scout, lighting the campfire fell to me, a difficult task with the wet wood. We stayed up late talking and, at some point before sunrise, tumbled into a restless sleep with people still partying nearby and the rain intermittently pattering on the tarp above us.

The music on Friday started with Iron Butterfly. The rain continued. We moved up closer for Country Joe and the Fish and King Crimson. In the evening, Kevin got to see his beloved Johnny Winter. We staked out a space near the stage with our new friends, and this time no one stayed at the van to watch things. At a festival focusing on peace, love, and music, we reasoned we could put our trust in the universe.

It was crowded, bodies pressed together, smelling damp and sour. Joints were passed around. The announcer said Johnny would be on stage in a couple minutes. I looked at Kevin and pointed at the stage. "Johnny Winter." I pointed at the large puddle we were standing next to. "Muddy Waters."

I had never seen Kevin so stoned. He started chanting, "Johnny Winter! Muddy Waters!" pointing like I had. A buzz started circulating that Muddy Waters was going to show up to play with Johnny.

"Kevin, look what you've done."

"You started it."

A minute later, Johnny was on stage, his long, white hair blowing in the wind as he launched into his hard and fast picking. The music was new to me, and I wasn't sure I liked it, but Kevin was mesmerized, eyes wide, face beaming.

On Saturday, I got up after another night of little sleep and took an Obetrol just because. I spent hours wandering around by myself, looking at people, hearing the various performers from a distance, and moving closer to the huge stage if I liked something I heard. Sly and the Family Stone did a great set. I also heard the Byrds, enjoying their harmonies and the psychedelic references in the lyrics. It was my first time seeing live music by major groups I had heard on the radio and on records, and the experience was beyond what I could have imagined, the power of the musicians bolstered by the energy of the crowd, feeding on one another, lifting everyone up.

Kevin and I joined up later for Janis Joplin. She swigged Southern Comfort and crooned into the microphone, wild hair hiding her face. When she sang, "Summertime," I felt like my heart was going to break. Near the end of her set, Johnny Winter and Vanilla Fudge joined Janis on stage. She staggered amongst her musician friends and kept offering Johnny the bottle. Despite her drunkenness, there were brilliant moments, and we felt we were viewing a unique moment in history.

Kevin kept eyeing a girl near us who swayed with the music. In an instant, she disappeared. When the set ended, he went off to find her. He never ceased to amaze me with his gentle male predator guise. Once, when he and I were at Der Rathskeller, Tulane's pub in the Student Union designed to resemble a German *biergarten*, I asked him how he was so successful with girls.

He lifted his eyebrows up and down. "It's all in the stare."

"How's that?"

"It has to be forceful and smooth at the same time. Watch this."

Two girls were sitting a few tables away. Kevin turned slightly so he had a clear line of sight. He tilted his head faintly and beamed in on one of the girls. After a short time, she looked over at us. Kevin didn't smile or waver. She turned to her friend and said something, making the friend look over at us. I felt embarrassed, but Kevin maintained his gaze. The girl looked back at him and made a face while Kevin eased into a coy smile. Within seconds, he stood up and walked over to her table. That was the girl he dated before Susan.

I stumbled, sloshed through mud, and teetered on narrow boards that had been laid across the worst puddles. I spotted a curly-headed boy wrapped in a comforter sitting on the roof of an old, battered pickup. His legs hung over the back of the cab, his bare feet sticking out from his frayed jeans. His feet were so dirty they looked as if they had been painted black.

I stared, forceful and smooth, and got his attention. He looked away and then back at me. He seemed to pat the seat next to him, though I might have imagined it in my state of near oblivion brought on by the amphetamines, countless hits on joints, and swigs of alcohol from bottles passed around. He took a joint from behind his ear and showed it to me. I climbed up on the bed and tried to hoist myself up to the roof. I kept slipping. He grabbed my arm and pulled me up. That moment of having our arms connected, feeling his strength, electricity shot through my muscles and a shiver coursed through me.

He lit the joint. "It's strong. Be careful."

We smoked without exchanging a word. No introductions.

After a few tokes, he snubbed it out on the roof of the truck. Someone was playing on stage in the distance, but I didn't know who. I wanted to ask him, and yet I had forgotten how to form words. The rain stopped, and smoke from a hundred fires rippled the soggy air. I drew a deep breath and was struck by the sensation I was taking in the toxicity of the whole world: acrid smoke, unwashed bodies, overflowing toilets, and gases rising from the swampy earth.

And then I felt the truck begin to move through the crowd, and I shook with fear we might crash into tents, cars, or possibly the stage. I put my hands on either side of me to hold on. The clouds overhead cleared and let the moon shine through, showering us with odd particles of blue light. I thought for a moment I was back at Valley Forge, Eric sitting next to me. I had the strongest desire to throw my arms around him.

I angled my head in millimeter increments and saw it wasn't Eric, but a stranger, whose eyes flashed on and off like blinkers. Perhaps I had been transported to the original Valley Forge, the ragtag Continental army trying to stay warm around fires, soldiers fighting against the empire, wrapped in blankets and barefoot. The truck started rolling and bucking, filling me with a fear of falling off. I must have produced some primal utterance as this companion or soldier or creature from another time gave me a look of horror. His lips were blue.

"Hey, man. Are you okay?"

"The truck is moving."

"No, it's not. The brake is on and everything."

I thought he was lying to me. "Down. Help me."

He jumped to the bed of the truck and took my arm as I slid down. I threw off his support and moved to the edge away from him. "You want some water or something? I've got some in the truck."

"No. I need to go." I had no idea where. I half-crawled, half fell over the side of the truck.

As I lay on the ground, he stood looking down at me with fiery, devil eyes. I grabbed the side of the truck and pulled myself up. I retreated from him, still locked in his trance.

"Hey, wait. Let me help you."

I staggered in the direction of a group of people around a fire. I tried to run, but I couldn't. The mud pulled me down with a sucking sound and felt like quicksand. Ahead was a narrow board over a puddle, lit up by the moon like an emergency path to safety. I stepped on the wood, and it became a diving board, bouncing up and down, attempting to toss me in the dark water. Dr. B wouldn't be there to save me. Halfway across the bouncing board, the world around me turned to melting chocolate, the music warbled in and out, and I stumbled. Blackness.

I woke up on a cot in the medical tent. It was light outside. A hammer pounded inside my head. A tube was attached to my arm, and I followed it up to a bag of fluid. A woman in a medical vest came over. "How are you doing?" She lifted my eyelids and shined a tiny light in my eyes.

"How long have I been here?"

"Five or six hours. Can you sit up? Very, very carefully." She put her arm under my back and supported me.

I sat on the edge of the cot, my head spinning. "I'm dizzy."

"That's normal. Do you know what happened?"

"After I smoked a joint with this guy, the world started getting crazy. I guess I passed out."

"Some people found you in the mud and brought you here. A good chance the joint was laced. There's some pot mixed with PCP going around."

"What's that?"

"A horse tranquilizer. Are you here with anybody?"

"A friend. We hooked up with some people that have a van."

"We just about sent you to the hospital, but your vitals were okay. Let me take them again. I can remove the IV, and you can be on your way."

I found our encampment and Kevin sitting under the tarp with the girl he had been chasing the night before. He jumped up. "Where have you been? God, you look like hell."

"Medical tent. Almost died." I figured I'd milk it for all it was worth. Since he hadn't come looking for me, I wanted him to feel guilty.

"You're shitting me, right?"

"Apparently, I passed out face down in the mud." I touched my face and felt a patch of caked mud.

"Are you going to be all right? Should we go home?"

"Home?"

"I mean school."

"Are you kidding? Miss the Airplane? No way."

Klaus let me sleep in the rear of the van most of the day. Kevin managed to find a soggy ham and cheese sandwich for me to eat. The "finest" food concessions were out of food. We were down to one can of tuna fish, and we were trying to save it.

"Guess what?" said Kevin. "I saw a car with a Tulane decal on it. They can give us a ride back, but they're diehard Stones fans and won't leave until they've heard them. Nobody knows when or if they'll show up. I suppose Monday classes are a wash."

Around eight, Klaus and the gang packed up and left. A couple of them had to work on Monday, and they planned to drive through the night. Jefferson Airplane came on after midnight. I attempted to get close to the stage, but I didn't have the energy. I told Kevin and his friend to go ahead while I huddled in my poncho at a distance with most of the clothes I had brought layered on my body, sitting on an overturned milk crate someone had left behind. A girl walked by and offered me a joint, but I shook my head.

The second song they played was "Somebody to Love." Despite being exhausted, cold, hungry, and alone, the song brought me to my feet. I let it fill me, move my body as I danced around the milk crate, desperately afraid someone might try to steal it and take away the possibility of sitting down on a dry place. I mouthed the words along with Grace, but by the end of the song, I shouted the lyrics. At the same time, a hopelessness deep inside made me doubt I would ever find somebody to love.

I was brought to my feet again when the haunting bass guitar riff ushered in "White Rabbit." Every time I heard the song, I imagined the pill that made me larger was Obetrol, and the one that made me small was a downer that reduced my world to sleep.

After Jefferson Airplane, I met up with Kevin, and we found the two guys from Tulane, sticking with them for fear of losing our ride. We braved the cold, intermittent rain and a mounting desperation until four in the morning when the Stones finally came on. Only a few thousand fans remained to hear the opening song, "Jumpin' Jack Flash." Even the ardent fans had a hard time getting energized. It was the coldest night yet, and people burned everything that could be burned, including dismantling the portable toilets and setting them on fire.

The sun came up as we got on the road. We drove in silence for about six hours until the driver pulled over at a rest stop. Everybody else slept, but since my flop in the mud and my long lazy afternoon left me exhausted but not sleepy, I stared out the window and let the memories of the last few days march through my head.

*

We trudged into the dorm well after dark. Kevin had multiple messages from his parents, and I had a couple from mine. Brian from across the hall came in and started laughing.

"Where have you been? Mud wrestling? Kevin, please fucking phone your parents. They're driving me crazy, calling every hour. Your mom is hysterical."

Kevin had promised to call Sunday night when he returned. When they couldn't get ahold of him, they somehow got my parents' number and called them, causing them to panic. Kevin got a long lecture over the phone while my parents gave up after a few lines, the main theme being they had warned me about Kevin. I explained I had equal responsibility in what happened. I tried my best not to sound fuzzy, but my head was anything but clear. As I lay in bed that night, each time I closed my eyes, dark creepy things flashed on the back of my eyelids. I feared I might have sustained permanent damage to my brain.

Twelve: Dying Young and Old

By the time I got home for Christmas, my parents seemed to have forgotten the Thanksgiving incident and were much more interested in talking about Cindy. When I said she would be home for the holidays, they expressed an overenthusiastic desire to see her and insisted I invite her for dinner. Mom asked me several times if Cindy and I had been in contact and how it felt to be so far away from each other.

I had missed Cindy a lot but thought it better to downplay my feelings so as not to get Mom's hopes up. As traumatized freshmen overwhelmed by new impressions, Cindy and I had written back and forth regularly. By November, the letters had gotten shorter and less frequent. I deliberately didn't write after getting back from West Palm Beach. It seemed a better idea to talk to her in person about what happened.

I walked around the old neighborhood on a bitter cold evening, feeling more than ever like a stranger in town. Lights were on in houses, but shades were drawn to keep out winter. Leafless trees raked the night sky, and dirty snow formed a crust atop dormant grass. It felt like years since I had left Sangamon to venture out into the world, and Oak Street seemed drab and lifeless compared to New Orleans. In order to feel less like a ghost, I needed to connect with someone. Cindy wasn't home yet, but Danny had sent me a postcard, saying he was living with his girlfriend, giving me an address.

A girl I didn't recognize answered the door with, "Whaddaya want?"

She seemed a miserable wretch, though I had a habit of rushing to judgment when first meeting people. It was hard not to when her appearance was slovenly, her hair disheveled. She had a gaunt look and vacant eyes.

"I'm looking for Danny. We went to school together. He gave me this address."

"He's sleeping." It was four in the afternoon.

From the interior of the house I heard, "Who is it, babe?"

"Nobody." Strike two. I was a nobody. She started to close the door.

"Hey, Danny," I shouted.

In seconds, he was at the door, throwing it open wide, smiling ear to ear. The girl slunk toward the back of the house. "Well, look at you. You've got your freak on. Come on in here." He took my arm and pulled me into the house. I had a feeling he wanted to hug me but held back. He couldn't, however, hide his excitement at seeing me. "Goddamn, Landis. You look good." The warmth of his response pleased me while his appearance hit me like a punch in the gut. His buzz cut and bony face made him look like a concentration camp escapee. He wore a wool peacoat despite the electric heater at full blast giving the living room and his face a searing orange glow. He looked like a captain, years at sea, facing a red sky in the morning warning.

He sat down next to me on the sofa. Since he had his coat on, I kept mine on in solidarity. The room was oppressive in its general disorder and its smoky, excessive warmth. The coffee table ashtrays overflowed with cigarette butts. The green shag carpet held enough food droppings to be a feast for whatever creatures might share the house with them.

Danny lit up a Kool. "Want one?"

"No, thanks."

"Sorry about Clare. She's only trying to protect me."

I'm sure she could scare invading monsters from Mars. "No problem. How long have you guys been together?"

"Couple months. She took me in after I lost my job. My parents threw me out."

"Walgreens fired you?"

"They let me go. It was either that or turn me over to the police. I guess they suspected something, and one day they made me empty my pockets at the end of a shift. We had a good run though, didn't we?" He slapped my leg.

"I guess I won't be going there to ask for a job in the summer."

"Not a good idea. They asked me if anyone else was involved in my little schemes, and of course, I said no." He looked away and stared at the heater, making me wonder about the truth of his statement. "What the hell have you been doing? How's college?"

"Nothing like here, I'll tell you that. I went to a pop festival in Florida. I saw the Stones, Jefferson Airplane, The Byrds, Janis, Johnny Winter, everybody was there."

"Fuckin' a, man. You got to see your lady, Grace Slick." He let out a chuckle full of sexual innuendo. "You're living the dream. Far out." He snubbed out his cigarette and lit another one. "Hey, you want to smoke a joint? I've got some good shit."

"No. We're going over to visit my grandma later. That place is so depressing when you're stoned. But if you've got any to sell, I could get some for later." If he was dealing as I suspected, I could help him out with some cash.

His face tensed, and a spark of paranoia danced across his eyeballs as if he wondered for a split second if this might be a setup. And then he let it go. "No, man. I'll give you some. You're my friend. But if you know somebody who's cool and wants to score...got to pay the bills, you know."

"Be careful, Danny. I don't want to visit you in jail."

His face softened, and his eyes watered. His nerves were shot, and emotions bounced around inside him. "But you would, wouldn't you? You're that kind of friend. You're one of the few decent people to come out of this town."

Clare stood in the doorway, waiting for Danny to notice her. "You said you were going to take me to Kroger. We got nothing to eat."

I stood up. "I've got to go anyway." I immediately started to sweat, bathed in the greater warmth in the upper half of the room. I lowered my voice. "You don't happen to have any..." I hated myself that he might think it was the only reason I had stopped by.

He shook his head. "Sorry."

"That's cool. It was great to see you. I'll be around another week or so."

"Come by again. I want to hear more about the festival."

I walked out the door knowing I wouldn't likely see him again this trip, maybe not ever. His appearance, as well as his living in squalor, frightened me.

Mom, Dad, and I had a simple Christmas dinner. David had gone to his girlfriend's in Milwaukee for the holidays. I helped my mom clean up though she kept telling me I didn't have to. When my parents were comfortably installed in front of the TV, I called Cindy.

"Cindy's picking me up, and we're going out."

"On Christmas?" said Mom in a hurt voice. Dad gave her a funny look. "Okay, honey. Have fun."

"Do you need any money?"

"No, thanks, Dad."

Cindy and I sat in her mom's car in the park smoking a joint from the pot Danny gave me. I told her about getting together with Danny and the dire straits he was in.

"Stay away from that house. The police are probably watching it. I imagine the girlfriend was paranoid for a reason."

"And I just thought she was being a bitch. I'm a terrible person."

"No, you're not. You were good to go and visit him. Not sure he deserves your loyalty."

"Meaning?"

"He didn't always treat you the best."

"Different friendships offer different things. There was a time when he made me feel a little less like a weirdo."

"Nate, you need to love yourself more."

"And then I'll find someone to love me, right? Isn't that what they say out there in Cal-ee-for-ni-ya?"

"Don't make fun. I say it because being down on yourself all the time is exhausting."

"I know. There were times at the festival, despite the rain and cold and dubious sanitary conditions and shitty food and my six hours in the med tent, I was part of something inclusive, part of a movement for peace, love, and understanding, as cliché as that sounds."

"I think I'd settle for peace and understanding. The love part is tough."

"You're not dating anyone?"

"Not at the moment. And you?"

"Nope."

"I'm curious about that guy at the festival, the one who later turned into the devil. What made you approach him?"

"I was high out of my mind."

"That's not an answer."

"You want honesty? Don't laugh. He looked like a young Dr. Baronian."

"Oh, Nate," she groaned. "I wish you could get that man out of your head. It's not healthy. And before you ask, no, I don't have any information about his whereabouts.

Judy won't talk to me. It seems my friendship with you makes it impossible to continue my friendship with her."

"I don't want you to have to choose between her and me."

"She made the choice. But back to the guy. Why did he turn into the devil? Did he say something or do anything to you?"

"No. He had an aura of softness about him. But after smoking that joint—the medic said it was probably laced with PCP—I was completely out of my mind. It wasn't his fault he fell into the nightmare of my tortured past. I thought about looking for him the next day and apologizing."

"Why didn't you?"

"Fear. Fear I would like him, and he would reject me. Fear he wasn't so attractive and didn't look anything like Dr. B when I wasn't on drugs. Fear he wouldn't talk to me because of the way I had behaved. Fear I would truly like him, and he would tell me he had a girl at home."

"I sometimes wonder how you get through the day."

"It's because I have friends like you. You know I love you." It flew out like a bird escaping its cage. I never said that to anyone, not even my mom, at least not since I was about six.

Cindy turned her head in my direction like an owl.

"You know what I mean."

"Like a sister?"

"Never had a sister."

"Like a best friend?"

"I don't know, Cindy. Yeah, I guess. You've been everything a best friend should be."

"Sorry. I should simply accept it, huh? What you said was beautiful. We're all so programmed to be suspicious. You're going to make someone so happy one day. I don't know if it will be a man, a woman, or an orangutan, but someone."

"Hmm. I hadn't considered bestiality."

"Dogs are the best."

"Oh my God! You did not say that."

"I'm not talking about that, you pervert. They're kind and loyal…"

"Trustworthy, helpful, courteous, obedient, cheerful, thrifty, brave, clean, and reverent."

"What?"

"The twelve points of Boy Scout law. We used to recite them at every meeting." I palmed my forehead. "Now I get it. Boy Scout law is modeled after dog behavior."

We both laughed so hard the car shook.

Cindy made choking sounds as she tried to control her laughter. "Not sure about the thrifty part." And our laughter took off again.

We calmed down and tried to catch our breath. Cindy looked in the rearview mirror. "Jesus! I think a cop car is coming." She started the engine and turned on the heat full blast to defog the windows and air out the car. "Roll down your window."

She put the car in reverse, and the other vehicle slowed down a few feet behind us. It was clearly a police car. "Go," I said.

"I can't see until the windshield is clear." She stuck her head out the window and waved to the officers. "Merry Christmas," she shouted.

They waved back and drove on. Nothing more than a couple of white kids having some alone time on Christmas. How nice.

*

The following spring, I got a call from Mom to tell me Gran had died. Heart failure. I took a long weekend and flew home for the funeral. Mom did her best to portray the grieving daughter, but I could tell deep down she was relieved. They'd had a complicated history, and yet Gran had done everything she could, hiding money and defying her husband, so that Mom would be the first in her family to go to college. Since Mom's sisters had always resented her for her education and escape from farm culture, and Mom didn't like being reminded of her roots, David and I grew up barely knowing our aunts, uncles, and cousins.

The funeral was at the Presbyterian Church in the town near the farm, and the reception was in the church basement. Mom, Dad, David, and I were surrounded by hostile relatives, trying to be civil. Mom had begged me to cut my hair before the funeral, but I refused. Everybody looked at my brother and me like we were aliens, and we had made things worse by smoking a joint before the funeral. We kept making derogatory comments about our relatives and suppressing giggles. Dad pulled us aside and begged us to get through the ordeal without causing a scene.

When I talked to my cousins, I made sure to mention I had been to a freaky pop festival and seen the Rolling

Stones and Jefferson Airplane. The most common question they asked me was if people got naked.

"Oh yeah. I've never seen so many bare breasts and butts in my life." I wanted to say flopping dicks, but I didn't want to give my aunts a coronary.

I went by Danny's that evening despite Cindy's warning. I had been worried about him and wanted to make sure he was okay. No car was in the driveway, and the windows were bare. I put my face to the glass and saw the house was empty. I turned around and looked at the gray sky with a sense of dread. I drove to Danny's sister's house.

Beth answered the door, holding a beautiful boy I guessed to be about three years old. "Hi. You're Nate, right? I suppose you're here about Danny. Come on in."

I had vague recollections of the one night Cindy and I had gone with Danny to the house. I recognized the sofa covered with an Indian bedspread. The coffee table, which had been a board atop cinder blocks, had now been replaced with a glass-topped metal one. I recognized the turntable where they had played The Doors, my first introduction to the band. Beth put the boy down and told him to go play with some blocks sitting in the corner.

"Please sit down. Would you like some coffee?" She began to organize things on the coffee table: a wooden box with inlay, magazines, coloring books, and a box of crayons.

"That's very kind, but no thanks."

She sat, alternately looking at her hands and glancing at her son playing with the blocks. Lighter skinned than Danny with dirty blonde hair, she had never lost the weight that had originally precipitated the diet pills. Thanks to her and Danny, I used to always have a supply.

"I went by the house where I visited him at Christmas, and it was empty."

Her nervousness changed to surprise. "So, you don't know?"

I closed my eyes for a minute, preparing myself for the inevitable. "Know what?"

She gazed at her son and lowered her voice. "He passed about a month ago. He was not well." She briskly wiped away a tear, glancing again at her son.

"He didn't look well when I saw him last. What was it exactly?"

"I'm not going to lie to you. You were his friend. He OD'd."

"What's your son's name?"

"Jonathan." The boy looked at his mom.

"Does he understand what we're talking about?"

"He's okay. I doubt he understands. Danny was doing meth, sometimes shooting it. Then barbs to come down. It was the barbs that did it. He choked on his own vomit. I tried to get him away from that woman, even told him he should come stay with us. But my husband didn't want somebody with a drug history around our son. I don't blame him. It's sad because Danny loved Jonathan so much. My parents refused to discuss Danny, let alone try to help him. My father said he was dead to him. It was like he died twice."

"I'm sorry. He didn't deserve that."

"I don't know why Danny kept hooking up with the wrong girls. He was better than that. He liked you a lot, talked about you all the time."

She took me by surprise, and I wondered what she was implying, how much she knew. "When I first started high school, I felt lost, and he was nice to me."

"Not long before he died, he told me you had come to see him. It made him real happy. He said he should have treated you better. I didn't know what he meant. If he did anything to hurt you, it wasn't to be mean. I can assure you, he respected you and was quite fond of you."

Being fond of someone wasn't a typical way to describe a feeling between two men. I could only assume what she wanted to say is that he loved me. It brought up more emotion than I was prepared for, and I found myself fighting tears. "I should have kept in touch more."

She started crying as well. "I thought I was over it, but I guess not."

"Don't cry, Mama," said Jonathan.

"Come over here, baby, and give your mama a hug." He padded across the room and crawled into her arms, still holding a block in one hand. "Isn't he the most beautiful thing in the world?" His skin was light brown, and he had a head of auburn curls and blue eyes like his mother but a broad nose from his father.

"I've always thought mixed-race kids were the most beautiful. Have your parents accepted him?"

She held Jonathan tighter and shrugged. "They've met him. They refused to meet my husband though. Maybe they'll come around some day."

"I hope so. It's their loss."

"I'm not proud of everything I've done, you know, dropping out of school, the diet pill thing, but my husband is a good man, and he loves Jonathan more than any man could. I don't regret that one iota."

"I wish he were here, so I could say hello."

"He'll be home soon. He works at Caterpillar." Jonathan crawled out of Beth's arms, found a place on the couch between us, and stared at me. I smiled at him, and he smiled with a certain way of moving his mouth, reminding me of Danny.

"Daddy home?"

"Not yet, sweetie. But soon."

"I've got to get back. I'm only in town for the weekend."

"What brings you home?"

"My grandma died. I'm here for the funeral."

"My condolences. Sorry you have to deal with Danny's death on top of everything else."

"Gran always said bad news came in threes. I'd better be on my guard."

"I sure hope not."

When I got home, my parents and David were in the middle of an argument. He had managed to keep from my parents that his grades had fallen so low he had lost his scholarship at the end of his junior year. He hadn't registered for spring classes and was working in a grocery store to survive. I came in on the part where he explained he had moved in with his girlfriend on a communal farm outside of Madison. The irony of the last bit of information hit my mother so hard, I thought she might collapse.

"A farm?" she said through bitter tears. "Your whole life I've tried to instill in you the importance of education, and you want to throw it away."

"It doesn't mean I won't finish school at some point. Just not right now. There was too much pressure. Lola and I are worried about the state of the world."

"Did she drop out too?" asked Dad.

"She graduated. She's working on a research project with one of her professors on integrated circuit computers."

"You couldn't tough it out one more year?" said Mom. "What about the draft?"

"I'll deal with it."

David had already told me all the news the night before. He and Lola were planning on going to Canada if he got his notice. We talked about how horrible Nixon was and the coming revolution if something didn't change. We both vowed not to participate in an unjust war. I already had the incentive to stay in school to keep my deferment, but now the pressure was even greater. I didn't think Mom could handle both of her sons dropping out.

It was a time of turmoil in the country, but that turmoil brought David and me closer than we had ever been. I admired him for his stance and hoped he wouldn't have to leave the country, especially now that we had finally gotten to be friends.

Shortly after I returned to school, we got news of the massacre of four student protesters at Kent State University by the National Guard. Kevin and I joined a demonstration on the quadrangle where an effigy of Richard Nixon was burned. Along with several hundred students, we marched to Newcomb Hall to demand the flag be lowered to half-mast. A counterprotest by a conservative student organization created a scuffle around the flagpole, but eventually, the flag was lowered. Our demonstration was relatively peaceful, but I worried about David. Madison was a much more radical place, and we all expected more violence against campus protestors around the country.

Thirteen: A Taste of Sherry

In the fall of 1970, I returned to parking my butt on the hard steps of the Student Union, watching the world go by. It was a few weeks into the semester, and I had recently declared my major as psychology in a decision based on a desire to understand people rather than a well-thought-out career plan.

The immediate subjects of my analysis were the Freaks, who had returned this year in a slightly modified configuration. The guys had longer hair, the balloon girl no longer carried a balloon, and the waif, who used to dress as a harlequin, had replaced the outfit with an oversized T-shirt and extremely short shorts. They had joined an activity sponsored by the Friday Afternoon Club, which involved using thick chunks of colored chalk to decorate the sidewalk in front of the union. A couple of them worked on a rainbow while others created a mandala.

I still hadn't spoken to a single one of them, though Kevin was friendly with the balloon girl who was in his ceramics class. For a while I had been entertaining the notion I wanted to get to know her. She stopped her work on the mandala and glanced up at me, making me contemplate joining the chalk brigade.

"They're just people." The voice from a higher step hit me in the back of my head, making me realize the comment had been made for my benefit. "Nothing particularly special about them."

I turned around to identify the source. She nodded with her chin in the direction of the Freaks. A certain bitterness in her voice made me wonder if she had been rejected by them. She, too, had adopted the hippie look, wearing faded bell-bottom jeans and a Mexican peasant blouse. Her feet were bare, and her thick hair was in disarray, framing a face that still held the scars of a traumatic bout of teenage acne.

"I can't argue with that. I do like observing people though."

"I've seen you here on the steps a lot, staring at them like they're rock stars."

The fact that someone would spend her time watching me watch other people was disturbing. I twisted my body in her direction. "I think you're in my Psych 101 lecture."

"Yep. The prof is the most boring teacher I've ever had. We'd be better off doing the reading and skipping the lecture. So far, he mostly regurgitates what's in the book."

"What's your name?"

"Sherry. Come sit up here. Unless I'm bothering you."

I scooted up a couple of steps to sit next to her. "I'm Nate."

"I pretty near didn't return this year. Not sure college is my thing." Her accent was particularly strong, a combination of southern and country hick, unlike any I'd heard.

"Where are you from?"

"Hah! Even other people from the South can't place my accent. I'm from northern Mississippi."

"Where do you think I'm from?"

"Nowhereland." She laughed heartily. The first time you hear someone laugh you can tell a lot about a person. I liked hers, deep and unrestrained.

"Thanks a lot."

"I guess I should say Anywhereland. You've got that middle-of-the-country general English that allows you to blend in anywhere. I assume your identity has roots in your interior complexity rather than exterior factors."

"I have no idea what you just said. You're making shit up."

"You got me. Can't help it. Sorry if I rubbed you the wrong way."

"No. Don't worry about it." In her bizarre come on, I had the impression she might be the one to end my drought. Though I occasionally thought about having sex with a girl, if only to pass that milestone in my life, I had put no effort into it.

Shyness still plagued me. Since Danny's death, I had vowed to cool it with the uppers. Without the social boost they gave me, I defaulted to my pattern of withdrawing into myself. I had nothing to say while at the same time I believed most of what people said in conversation was either useless drivel or bullshit to achieve some purpose.

"What *are* you thinking? It's as if you're hankering to say something, but it won't come out."

"Do you actually think we can understand people by studying psychology?"

"You can observe patterns of behavior and modify it, I guess, but understand it? I doubt it."

"I'm also taking some anthropology courses. Seems more verifiable. I'm intrigued by the fact that a common artifact from a culture provides a window into that society, what they think, what they believe."

"What are future generations going to think of us when they find Frisbees and colored chalk and McDonald's hamburger containers?"

"Or electric can openers and hula hoops?"

"Just a bunch of lazy bums that wanted to be entertained. Since the world is going to hell, we might as well have fun. Should we join the mandala group?"

Sherry introduced me to Meredith, the balloon girl, and asked if we could join them. Several of the others said hi to her, destroying my speculation she had been rejected by the group. After a few minutes of polite conversation, it seemed more likely she was, like me, a lone wolf who didn't enjoy traveling in packs.

"You're one of the Frisbee players, aren't you?" said Meredith. "You guys are really good. Last time I tried at the beach, it wobbled into the ocean on the second throw and got lost in the surf."

"There's often too much wind at the beach. That's why the quad is perfect."

"I would still screw it up." She smiled at me shyly and went back to work on the mandala. Her hands and arms were covered with colorful chalk. "It's an eight-point Buddhist mandala," she explained. "The tree in the middle represents the mind of Buddha."

Those who had been working on the sidewalk for some time expressed the need to get up and move. Sherry proposed a bike ride through Audubon Park to the levee for sunset. I had bought a cheap one-speed—all you needed in the flat bottom of a bowl that is New Orleans— and the others had bikes or knew where they could borrow one.

Ricky with the blond Afro, Sherry, Meredith, and I pedaled along the Audubon Park Trail that skirted the park, marveling in the Spanish moss that dripped from the muscular live oak trees like stringy manes of tangled hair, catching the golden light of late afternoon and swaying listlessly in the gentle breeze. As we got near Magazine Street, Ricky picked up the pace. "Why so fast?" yelled Meredith.

Ricky held up his camera. "Want to get some pictures before dark." On the other side of Magazine, we continued on River Drive along the edge of the zoo. Bathed in sweat, we crossed over the railroad tracks and arrived at an observation point on the levee overlooking the muddy Father of Waters.

"Come on," said Ricky. We locked up the bikes to the railing, weaving several locks and chains through the wheels. Ricky led us to a path that went down the river side of the levee to a flat grassy area that looked to be part of the park. "This is called the batture, the land between the river and the levee. Here it's an extension of the park, so it's kept up. I want to show you another side of the batture." Our scout waved us forward.

We walked the length of the green area until we arrived at a chain-link fence. Ricky showed us where to crawl through a break in the fence, which led us into a wooded area, wild and thick with bushes though a trail weaved through it. After a few minutes, we came upon a cluster of shacks on stilts, looking like they had been pieced together with driftwood and salvaged materials, perched above the banks of the river with raised wooden walkways leading to each house. They seemed abandoned until we noticed a thin trail of smoke coming from the chimney of one of them.

A Black man in his fifties came out on the porch of the shack where there was smoke and gave us a hard stare, cradling a walking stick in his arms that could double as a club.

Ricky waved at the man. "Hello, friend. We're here to see Marilu."

The man jerked his head sideways in the direction of the next house before he turned, scratched the head of a goat tethered to the railing of the porch, and disappeared into the darkness of his cabin. We had ventured not only to the edge of the river but to the edge of the world. *Who were these people? Why did they choose to live on the river?*

"Do the people who live here own the houses?" asked Sherry.

"It's government land, so I guess you could call them squatters. They construct the homes from whatever floats to the banks of the river. Marilu says the guy next door built his house a long time ago."

At the end of the walkway to Marilu's, a cowbell was attached to a post, and a stick on a rope dangled next to it. Ricky, already snapping pictures, instructed Meredith to strike the bell three times. A dog started barking and came out on the porch. It was a medium-sized mutt with a ferocious bark. "That's Nacho," said Ricky.

We heard, "Shush, Nacho," as Marilu appeared on the porch with her hair tied up in a scarf, wearing a man's shirt and a long colorful skirt. She waved and told us to come in. "Watch your step."

Ricky pointed to the several missing planks as he led us to the porch. Marilu, who I guessed to be only a couple years older than us, seemed to be friendly with Meredith as well as Ricky, but kissed all of us on each cheek. Pots of herbs lined the porch. I recognized oregano, thyme, and parsley from my grandmother's garden, while the rest were strange to me. In a rectangular wooden flat, she grew what looked like lawn grass carefully cut to the same height. I stared at it, thinking of the grass I used to mow.

Marilu saw me looking at the grass. "That's wheat grass. You juice it to make an excellent tonic."

I leaned down, took a sprig, and tasted it. As I did, I looked through the spaces between the floorboards and saw the river below, lapping at the bank. It made me dizzy, the sensation of being neither on land nor water, suspended in the air by a few planks of wood.

"We could sit out here, but the skeeters would eat us alive, especially if you're not used to them." Her Chicago accent seemed incongruous with her country persona.

Inside she lit lemony-smelling candles and a kerosene lamp though it was still light outside. On shelves were jars of dried herbs, beans, and grains. The table in the center of the room consisted of a plank of wood on two sawhorses, and on it sat a painted ceramic bowl of ripening bananas, peaches, and mango. In the corner,

Nacho stared at us from a blanket he had formed into a den, following our every movement with a turn of his head. Through an open door, you could see into the other room where a low pallet bed was covered with a patchwork spread.

"I'll make some tea." She had a one-burner camp stove for cooking, but an old wood-burning stove sat on a metal plate next to it. She filled a pan with water from a jug and mixed herbs to put in a fine net bag. I smelled mint but couldn't identify the others.

While the water heated up, she told us she'd moved into the abandoned shack with a boyfriend. A lot of the furniture had been left behind, but they picked up other pieces from the street. Sherry and I sat on a rough bench while Ricky and Meredith occupied low, rough-hewn stools. Marilu sat on a wooden armchair with cushions spilling their stuffing.

She poured the tea into a collection of mismatched chipped cups and added honey. "We felt ostracized when we first moved in, but after a while, we won the trust of the neighbors."

"Yeah, it looked like the guy next door was ready to club us," said Sherry.

"Joseph is very protective of me. I'm alone here now. My boyfriend split a couple months ago, and I don't think he's coming back. If you love them, set them free." Her sparse chuckle didn't sound like she believed it. "Joseph lives with his son, who isn't right in the head—not dangerous, just simple. Sometimes he brings me flowers."

"How do you get water?" asked Sherry as we were about to taste the infusion.

Marilu shrugged. "From the river."

We all stared into our cups of steaming tea.

She surprised us by bursting into laughter. Up to that point, she had been serious and told her story in an unemotional monotone. "I'm kidding. I collect rainwater in barrels for washing, but I haul in drinking water. I can fill bottles in the park. I also have a friend who lets me take a shower at her apartment."

While Ricky moved about the house shooting photos, Marilu told us what it was like to live on the river, the sounds, the smells, the spiritual feeling of hovering over the water that drains a good part of the United States. He came back into the room, put the lens cap on, and strapped the camera across his chest. "I think we'd better head back before it gets completely dark."

"You'll miss the frog symphony," said Marilu. "One of the best things about this place is that it comes alive at night. All kinds of creatures."

Meredith shivered. "Now I *really* think we need to go."

It was dark and much cooler with a light breeze coming off the river by the time we unlocked the bicycles. A huge freighter with twinkling lights glided silently past, and we listened to the wake slopping on the batture.

*

Sherry and I found ourselves joining our lone-wolf statuses into a duo without actually giving up any independence. That is to say we spent a lot of time together as platonic friends. Kevin was my roommate in the dorm for the second year though I rarely saw him due to his constant activities, time in the ceramics lab, and sleeping over at his girlfriend's.

Sherry and I often took late night trips to Café du Monde for beignets and chicory coffee or spend a late afternoon in St. Louis Cemetery, a popular spot since the movie *Easy Rider* had come out the year before. We tried to recognize all the spots where Dennis Hopper, Peter Fonda, and their lady friends cavorted through the cemetery on LSD.

Closer to campus, we often had breakfast at the Camellia Grill on Carrollton or sauntered through the Garden District, trying to decide which was our favorite house. The comfort we felt with each other was unspoken. Sometimes we talked about the state of the world, and at others we spend long periods of time saying nothing. Occasionally, we fell into criticizing cliques like the Freaks who often had a gang mentality and tended to be suspicious of everyone outside. But if the Freaks invited us on an outing, we jumped at the chance. One place they liked to go was a remote beach on the Pearl River, accessible only by car.

Marc, who frequently ran with the group though he wasn't a student, had an old Buick LeSabre. On a splendid fall day, Ricky, Meredith, Sherry, Betsy, Marc, and I piled in Marc's car for the hour-and-a-half trip to the river. We parked the car on the side of the road in a wilderness area and hiked through scrub pine and bushes to a place Marc told us you rarely saw other people. We heard a rustling in a bush, and a creature promptly darted across the path.

Betsy screamed. "What was that?"

"It's an armadillo. Cool, huh? They won't hurt you, no." Marc had the local Cajun accent and a tiger tattooed on his forearm: two things that made me feel like I had with Danny. I was frolicking with danger.

After a mile and a half, we came to a break in the trees and saw the river, green and flowing so gently it seemed still, and if you stared at it for any amount of time, you would become hypnotized. "This here's the Mississippi side, but over dere is Louisiana. This point in the river is only about ten miles from where it flow into the Gulf of Mexico, so there's lots of sandbars, which make nice beaches when the wada is low." We spread out blankets on the sand and unloaded the baskets of food we had brought to satisfy the munchies after the several joints we had smoked in the car.

Sherry shook out a couple of tablets from a small envelope and held them out to me in the palm of her hand. "Before you eat, you might want to try one of these." Thanks to Danny, I had a familiarity with a lot of the prescription pills people took recreationally, but I didn't recognize them. I had also been trying to limit my drug use recently to pot and a few Obetrols when I had to write a paper or study for a test. I was still freaked out about Danny's death, and we had only recently heard of Jimi Hendrix's demise, which people blamed on a cycle of uppers followed by barbiturates. The detail of choking on his own vomit sounded hauntingly similar to Danny's death.

"You're looking at it like I just offered you heroin. It's only a Quaalude."

"What's that?"

"It's what the student health service is giving out these days to try and keep us freaks off smack."

"You're kidding, right?"

"It's weird. All you do is go in and say you're stressed about your schoolwork and not sleeping. They'll give you a ten-day supply, that is if you only take one a day and don't give them away to your friends."

"So, it's a downer?"

"It's kind of a sedative, but it makes you feel so good you don't want to go to sleep."

"Good how?"

"It actually gives me a burst of energy due to the sensations. You can get all tingly. And it lowers inhibitions like alcohol, but it won't make you as obnoxious as your retard uncle on moonshine. I can't explain it to you. You have to try it for yourself. Are you in?"

I took one and washed it down with warm Coke. We ate po'boys and fruit, pretzels, cookies, and then chips. I lay back with my hands behind my head and looked at the fluffy clouds drifting across the pale-blue sky.

About a half hour later, I noticed a tingling in my hands and feet. At first, I thought my hands had gone numb from my head resting on them, but it was my feet as well and my lips and tongue.

"Um. This is weird," I said.

"Ah-hah. You're feeling it."

"Big time." It was strange to feel a sense of well-being similar to uppers from something that was basically a relaxant.

Marc stood up. "I'm going in the wada." I loved how he pronounced water. I loved everything about the way he talked, the way he moved with comfort in his body, his way of being both childish and masculine at the same time. He took off all his clothes and dove in the river. It thrilled me to look at his beautifully defined body. My inhibitions had slipped away, and I made no attempt to curb my stare. Ricky, Meredith, and Betsy followed him into the river. Sherry gave me a look that said, "I will if you will."

When we were camping in Scouts, we would sometimes go skinny-dipping but never in mixed company. I had never seen a woman naked in real life, but I refused to let my natural shyness stop me.

"Let's go," I said.

We took off our clothes and joined the others in the cool, green water. It felt silky on my skin. The river was only up to our chests at the deepest, and the silty bottom squished between our toes. The women's breasts bobbed on the surface of the water, from Sherry's ample ones to Betsy's small boyish chest.

Meredith had the idea that we should all form a circle holding hands. I had Sherry on one side and Marc on the other. This was a test, I thought. Whose hand felt better?

"Now," said Meredith. "Send a wave of energy around the circle counterclockwise. Nate, you start."

I squeezed Sherry's hand, and a few moments later the energy came back through Marc with ten times the force. Boing! That wasn't a fair test.

"Now clockwise. Marc, you start."

The power was strong when it came around to me through Sherry, and I sent it to Marc. He jerked and turned to look at me. "Wow!"

Meredith, our caller, told us to move in closer and put hands on shoulders. Having Marc's arm on my shoulders was pure euphoria. The Quaalude clearly enhanced the sense of touch. I rested my hand on the nape of his neck, losing it in the curly mop of his hair. He caressed the back of my head, sending rivers of joy up and down my spine. I turned to Sherry and smiled, not wanting her to feel left out, wondering if she had any idea what was going on inside me. She returned my smile, leaned her head toward mine, and kissed me on the lips.

"Thank you." I defaulted to the idea if you're at a loss for words, say something polite.

"Thank you?"

"Okay, everybody," said Meredith. "Lean back and float. Stay connected. Kick your legs in the center."

Betsy giggled. "Water ballet!"

"Wish I was in a tree with my camera," said Ricky.

Meredith pointed at a nearby oak. "Well."

Ricky broke out of the circle, ran to the shore, and got his camera. He threw on a pair of shorts and climbed into the oak. We reformed the circle.

"Keep kicking," he said. "Oh my god, it's beautiful." The camera clicked, clicked, clicked.

"Hey, everybody. This is amazing, but I have to tell you, there's a snake in the water coming down river."

Betsy screeched, breaking out of the circle and scrambling toward the shore. The rest of us followed close behind, arms flailing, dicks flopping, and breasts bouncing. We fell on the blankets screaming and laughing.

Ricky was still in the tree, snapping pictures as we lined up on the blankets. Sherry ran her hand up and down my arm. I closed my eyes and imagined it was Marc, knowing full well he had ended up on the opposite end of the line.

*

Marc dropped us off at campus. He excused himself, saying he had to go home. I turned to look as he drove away, imagining a fishing line unreeling with the hook piercing my heart and pulling it along. As we walked across the campus, the sense of the circle breaking up was ridiculously saddening as members of the group drifted off on different paths. Sherry invited me to her room. I didn't want to be alone. We had already been naked together, so removing our clothes was no big deal.

We laughed and relished in the sensations of touch. The drug, the communal sharing of a beautiful place still fresh in my memory, sun warmth lingering on my skin, and Sherry's perfect amount of aggressiveness made me forget where we were heading. I had a completely normal erection. There was no reason not to. She told me she wanted to be on top. It was all the same to me since I had never done it in any position.

I had heard of guys climaxing after about five seconds their first time, and I fully expected that to happen, even welcomed it. But the drug allowed me to stay on the edge for much longer, and I hoped Sherry got some pleasure out of it. After I came, I remained hard and she continued to ride. Then she stopped.

"Hello. I'm still here."

I opened my eyes and deflated at the same moment. Had I done something wrong? I knew women were also supposed to have orgasms though I had no idea what that meant.

"Sorry," I said.

She rolled off me, and we both contemplated the acoustic ceiling tiles with small craters, making them look like the surface of the moon. "I had been thinking about that all afternoon," she said.

Did women think about sex all the time too? I had always believed women were more romantic. Did she mean our encounter was nothing more than sex? I should have been pleased. A woman who is out to snag a husband wouldn't say something like that. "You drugged me so you could seduce me." I laughed.

"Hmm." She patted my hand as if she might be telling me it was time to leave. She let out a sigh. "Do you honestly like girls?"

Here we go again. I didn't expect we would get there so speedily. She didn't know that after years of anticipation, I had climbed the mountain and entered the promised land. And if the promised land wasn't quite what I had expected, it was a rite of passage in a young man's life, and I didn't want to lose the feeling of accomplishment. But I had to play my role of being offended. "Did we not just have sex?"

"You had your eyes closed the whole time."

"I didn't."

"You did. Was it Marc you were fantasizing about?"

"Now wait..."

"It's fine. No problem. It's only fair that I should know."

It hit me hard. The signs had been there for a long time. I couldn't fake it. "If you must know, it was not Marc. I guess it could have been, but it was somebody else."

"Have you had sex with a guy?"

"Do we have to talk about this now?" I got up and put on my underwear.

"That sounds like a no. I can take you by Marc's house some time."

"No! He's not...I said I didn't want to talk about it."

"I have a feeling he can go either way."

"I'm hungry. Are you hungry?"

She snickered in the joy of torturing me. "All right. I know the perfect place. Don't you fret, honey child." She got up, grabbed her clothes, and went into the bathroom she shared with three other roommates. She didn't seem to care if someone figured she had just had sex.

Fourteen: The Quarter

The St. Charles streetcar rocked on the old rails past mansions lit up behind cut-glass front doors. I blathered on about the palatial homes and elegant architecture until Sherry put me in my place.

"Rich people." She sneered. "The ancestors of these people were more than likely slave owners. I ought to take you to some of the neighborhoods where people, the descendants of those slaves, have a hard time putting food on the table."

Sherry was right, of course, but I was sorry she had to walk around with so much anger. I tried to summon an expression of concern to my face, but all I truly wanted was to savor the first few hours of my nonvirgin status and look at the pretty houses. Call me superficial.

We got off the streetcar and walked across Canal Street. "Where are we going?"

"You'll see." Her wry smile made me suspicious.

We headed down Bourbon Street, launching ourselves into the revelers gearing up for a Friday night at one of the biggest street parties on the planet. The city government had recently declared it a pedestrian mall after seven p.m., so drunks who previously had difficulty maneuvering the narrow sidewalks and precipitous curbs could now weave and stumble down the center of the street, spilling drinks from large plastic cups. Giant posters outside bars boasted of nearly naked girls and drink specials while open windows and doors allowed glimpses into the seedy interiors. One large window offered a young, scantily clad woman on a swing going in and out, beckoning men to enter. From other windows, Dixieland jazz spilled out onto the streets. All our senses were bombarded from each direction, the intensity increasing as we delved deeper into the center of the quarter, the complete opposite of the sensory input earlier in the day—the gentle, joyful, sensual foray into nature, the river flowing lazily, the birds breaking into song.

"I don't know how much more of this I can take," I said.

"It's not pretty, but we're turning soon." I was surprised she didn't make some comment, linking the debauchery to the collapse of modern American society.

At St. Peter Street, we turned and entered a restaurant called The Fatted Calf. The only seats available were at the counter. The waiter, wearing an American flag bandana to hold his wavy hair in place, sashayed by and dropped two menus in front of us. The burgers on the menu were named after characters from *Gone with the Wind*.

After passing by several more times, delivering orders, picking up dishes, and twice winking at me, the waiter stopped and leaned forward. "What can I do you for?"

Sherry laughed and ordered a Rhett Butler. He turned to me. "And you, hon?"

"I guess I'll have a Rhett as well."

"Ooh, you two and Rhett. A delicious three-way."

"You only live once," said Sherry.

A scream rang out over the roar of conversation in the crowded restaurant. We turned to look at a table of four men, laughing hysterically as the screamer fanned himself with his hand. Some scandalous news had apparently been shared, and the screamer was having a hard time handling the rising heat it provoked.

"Interesting place," I said.

"I thought you'd like it."

"I didn't say I liked it. But if the burgers are good..." I considered it insensitive to cast me into the lion's den so shortly after "proving my manhood." As soon as I had passed one test, she changed the parameters and transitioned seamlessly from being my savior to being my tormentor. I remembered the mischievous twinkle in her eye when she said she knew exactly the place for us to eat. It was obviously her intention to bring me to a place frequented by homosexuals and see how I would react.

The waiter arrived with our plates. "Here you go, sugar." He put the plate in front of me. "The cook prepared it especially for you." I looked up and saw the cook, a handsome Black man with a moustache, staring at me from the other side of the pickup window. He tilted his head and gave me a big smile that cut through me like a knife.

With a momentary gaze, he had summed me up, labeled me as one of them. I wasn't like them. I would rather die than draw attention to myself by screaming in a crowded restaurant. I stared at the burger and fries with the absurd notion that if I ate it, I would be transformed, inducted into a secret society.

Sherry scooped up her burger. "This looks good."

"I'm not that hungry."

"What? A minute ago, you were starving."

"Why did you bring me here?"

"Honey pie, you need to loosen up. Life is full of possibilities."

"Easy for you to say."

"You think my life is easy? Being forced into a debutante ball when I was fifteen, making an entrance on my daddy's arm as if he was putting me on the auction block for a good marriage, and knowing inside I didn't want any of that shit? When you're a freak in a small town, everybody has eyes on you like you're a wild animal, trying to escape from a cage. You know when I lost my virginity? I was twelve. I was raped by an older cousin I couldn't denounce because he was a local hero of the football team, and where I'm from, sugar, that's everything. My parents were overjoyed when I decided to come to Tulane." She stopped to let out a hardy laugh. "They still thought of H. Sophie Newcomb College as a school for white Southern Christian women. But I knew New Orleans was full of outcasts like me, and I couldn't wait to get here. I planned to make friends with an array of people who would horrify my parents."

"It's one thing dressing like a hippie and not living the way your parents want, but it's quite another thing being a sexual deviant. I saw firsthand how it can destroy your life. The finest person I've ever met—educated, sophisticated, talented—was brought to his knees by the exceptional people of my hometown."

"That's what I'm saying. It's the fault of the society, not the individual. We have to change it. Being here, surrounded by free spirits, is a blessing. If you only want to be another brick in the wall, go back to your hometown and marry your childhood sweetheart, have two kids, and buy a house with a picket fence. But you're never gonna escape what you are. Now eat your burger. It's getting cold."

The nearby table again filled the restaurant with a burst of cackling joy, though I still saw it as a spectacle, a forced celebration reserved for safe spaces. I bit into the hamburger, and the juice ran down my chin. Once more, I felt someone watching me. The cook now smiled apologetically, seeming to pick up on my discomfort in the surroundings. I gave him a thumbs-up to let him know the burger was good. I wiped my mouth with a napkin, and he blew me a kiss.

We left the restaurant, walked back to Bourbon, and turned right. A few blocks down, Sherry pointed out a bar called Café Lafitte in Exile as a place where homosexuals went. "I don't remember signing up for the gay tour of the quarter."

She cackled, and we continued walking to Esplanade Avenue, then turned left in the direction of City Park. Once under the majestic arms of the live oak trees, I felt a hushed sense of mystery, a welcome change from the boisterous French Quarter. Creole mansions were on either side, many tumbling into disrepair. Palmetto bugs darted across the sidewalk in front of us, and the smell of jasmine tickled my senses. My shoulders relaxed, and my step became lighter.

After a few more blocks, Sherry stopped in front of a two-story house where vines looked poised to return the front yard to jungle and rusting metal posts seemed inadequate to hold up the second-floor balcony. A broken upstairs window was patched with cardboard. "This is where Marc lives."

"You are not going to let up, are you?"

"I'm only pointing it out. Not saying we need to stop and say hello. He lives with a whole passel of roommates. Did you want to stop?"

I thought of Marc's hand on the back of my neck, the sparks it sent through my body, the awakening of desire.

"No, I want to walk." I wanted to keep walking until I exhausted my body. I wanted to fall into a deep sleep without dreams.

We walked another hour in near silence and then caught a bus back to campus where she took the path to her dorm and I to mine. We parted without a hug or a kiss, only a simple goodnight.

I was surprised to see the light on in our room, a sign Kevin was spending a rare night in the dorm. I had hoped to be alone. I wasn't ready to talk about what had happened that day, but I had no choice but to share some of it, the trip to the Pearl River, swimming naked in the green water, eating in a peculiar restaurant in the quarter.

"I wish I had gone. Susan and I had another fight."

"I thought something must have happened for you to be back here."

"She says I'm selfish, and we always have to do what I want. We've had that argument a thousand times. She says I'm always looking at other girls."

The part about looking at other girls I had noticed and wondered how Susan felt about it. I was sure he hadn't told her about the girl in West Palm Beach who he had exchanged numbers with and called several times, or the girl at home in Maryland, or I don't know how many others.

"Marriage is a dying institution," he said.

"Does she want to get married?"

"She's never said that, but sometimes I wonder. I've got this friend at home who I think is gay. I bet he has all the sex he wants and doesn't have to worry about someone trying to trap him into marriage."

"How do you know?"

"That he's gay? It's so obvious. I've got nothing against it. But, come on, you can tell."

"Yeah, I guess." I wasn't sure how to steer through the murky waters of that conversation. Why did he bring up his gay friend? He had never hinted he thought I was gay, but if he believed it was so easy to tell, maybe he didn't say anything so as not to embarrass me.

"Is Sherry your girlfriend now?"

"Not really."

"But you've had sex with her, right?"

Maybe I did want to talk about it. Maybe I wanted us to be two guys telling stories of conquest. For once in my life, I wanted to feel normal. I smiled in a way that gave it away.

"You old dog, you. You have."

"Yeah. I don't think it's going to continue though."

"Why? Because you don't love her? Don't you know a man reaches his prime sexually at eighteen? It's all downhill from here. You'd better enjoy it now."

"Are you having sex with other girls besides Susan?"

"Don't tell her, okay? I can't be pinned down to one person."

"I think you should tell her that."

"You know, Nate, you're a little square."

"If that means being honest, I guess so. But don't worry, I won't tell."

"By the way, did you hear the news?"

Phrased like that, I knew bad news was coming, and I particularly didn't want to hear bad news at that moment. "What?"

"Janis Joplin died. Heroin overdose."

"No. Fuck. Jimi last month and now Janis."

"I'm glad we got to see her last year."

Danny, Jimi, and Janis lost in the same year to drugs, a year that was far from over.

*

I started going to the quarter by myself, sometimes late at night. I walked past the gay bar Sherry had pointed out on Bourbon but never considered going in. I sauntered down St. Peter and lingered in front of the Fatted Calf, looking in the window. The same waiter pranced up and down the counter, flirting with customers. The cook put a plate on the pickup window and looked in my direction. I ducked away and moved on. I would occasionally catch furtive glances from men on the street, which would cause me to look away and change my course. I worried I would run into Sherry, and she would call me out not only for what I was doing, but why we hadn't spent time together in a couple weeks.

One afternoon I walked down Esplanade to Marc's house. If I ran into him on the street, I would act surprised as if I had no idea he lived in the area. I paced back and forth in front of the house a couple times. Screw it. I opened the gate, which was falling off its hinges, and went up the creaky steps to the front door. I knocked. No one answered. Sherry had mentioned Marc's bedroom was upstairs in the back. Maybe he didn't hear me. I walked along the side of the house to the backyard overgrown with weeds. In the center sat a dry fountain with a Roman goddess in the middle.

I stood at the bottom of the steps leading up to the second floor. A minute later, I was near the top before realizing what I was doing, the old force taking over, pushing me forward, making me try the door handle. It was open.

I looked down a hallway splashed with light coming in from each open doorway. I went into the first bedroom on the right. The classic Hawaiian shirt with palm trees and hula girls Marc had worn the day we went to the river hung on the closet door. He had worn it open, showing a trail of black hair from his chest down to his navel. My heart was pounding in the way it used to when I wandered around houses, not with the same intensity as being in Dr. B's house but strong.

I took the shirt in my hands and sat on the unmade bed. I looked around the room. He read books: *Dune, In Cold Blood, The Crying of Lot 49, Catch-22.* I was impressed. On the wall was a poster of Jimi Hendrix lighting his guitar on fire. A pair of well-worn cowboy boots sat in the corner, the right toppled over the left. A crystal hanging in the window caught the late afternoon sun, scattering rainbows dancing on the walls.

I saw some black-and-white photos on the dresser. I stood up and threw the shirt over my shoulder as I leafed through them. They were Ricky's photos from the day at the Pearl River. I looked at one of us in a circle, the water frothed by our kicking. Again, I felt Marc's hand on the back of my head. In another photo, our naked bodies were lined up on the blankets, Marc's hairy strong body on one end and my smooth, thin torso at the other, miles apart.

I heard a noise from another part of the house. I froze. If Marc caught me, I planned to confess, tell him why I was there, that I needed to see him in a bad way. I tossed the shirt on the bed and stepped into the hall. At the same moment, a young kid came out of one of the other bedrooms, bathed in golden sunlight, holding an embroidered bag from India. We stared bug-eyed at each other across a gap much larger than the ten feet between us, one of race, privilege, and economic opportunity. I doubted the bag was his, but I didn't want to jump to conclusions.

"Do you live here? I'm looking for Marc."

"He ain't here."

"How do you know?"

"Ain't nobody here. Just us."

"Just us."

"So, you don't live here neither?"

"No."

"Shit. Catch you later." He headed for the front stairs.

I went to the top of the stairs, watched him unlock the front door and run out, leaving it open. I descended the staircase, closed the door, and locked it. I walked through the dining room with its crystal chandelier and rose drapes to the kitchen. I left by the kitchen door and walked along the side of the house, trembling after the surreal thing that had happened. I hurried down the street, escaping into the chaos of the quarter.

When I returned to campus, I called Sherry.

"You've been avoiding me," she said.

"No. I've had a lot on my mind."

"Don't lie to me, honey child. Look, I've been thinking about the last time we were together. That was kind of shitty of me. I want you to be happy. I want you to find yourself. I really do. I know I can be pushy and act like I know everything. People have been telling me that all my life."

"I have to figure things out on my own."

"I know you do. I don't want to do anything that ruins our friendship. On that note, I want to share something with you. Marc and his friends went collecting mushrooms the other day."

"That's nice."

"I'm talking about magic mushrooms."

"Oh. What do you mean they went out collecting?"

"There are some pastures on the other side of Lake Pontchartrain where all you have to do is pick them. They found a whole bunch."

"People die eating bad mushrooms."

"These guys are experts. They do it all the time. You know, they're showing *2001: A Space Odyssey* at McAlister this Sunday. A bunch of us are going. You should join us."

"I don't know. I've never done psychedelics. I would probably jump out a window thinking I could fly."

"Art Linkletter's daughter was suicidal. Much easier to blame it on drugs. You will be surrounded by good people who will take care of you. Nothing bad is going to happen. Well, you might get a bit nauseous from the shrooms, but it goes away."

I agreed to join them in large part because Marc was going to be there. Considering all the drugs I had done, it was strange I was petrified of doing psychedelics. I had gone into Student Health Services the week before and gotten my prescription for Quaaludes. I felt like such a fake. I wrote down everything I was supposed to say to the doctor and memorized it. I figured if something went wrong with the mushroom trip, I could always pop a couple of Quaaludes to mellow things out.

Fifteen: An Odyssey

We all met at Ricky's apartment a couple of blocks from campus. Marc greeted me with a soul brother handshake and then leaned in to bump chests.

"Good to see you, brother," he said. I wondered if he remembered my name. He took my arm and pulled me aside. "Sherry told me it's your first time, and you had some worries. I'll take care of you, my man. If you're feeling anxious or paranoid or anything peculiar, come to me."

"Thanks, Marc. You're a good guy."

He grinned and arched his thick eyebrows up and down. "Let's see how Meredith is doing in the kitchen."

Meredith stood over a cutting board with a knife, chopping the mushrooms into small pieces. Marc picked up a whole one and showed it to me. It didn't look like the typical store-bought variety; it was less meaty but had similar characteristics of a head on a stem in a brownish color. A pot of water on the stove announced its boiling with a gentle rolling sound.

"I'm making tea," said Meredith. "Less chance of getting an upset stomach." She dumped the mushroom pieces into the bubbling water and stirred. "Double, double, toil and trouble." She cackled like a witch. "Now, we wait twenty minutes."

In the living room, the new Grateful Dead album was playing, and everybody sat on the floor, except Betsy who danced freeform to "Sugar Magnolia." I sat down next to Sherry. "This is going to be great," she said.

Meredith set the tray of teacups on the coffee table. "We need to hurry. We don't want to be late for the movie. The taste is weird, so best to drink it down as fast as you can."

A few minutes later, we walked down Pine Street in a blur of purple garments. Meredith had chosen the theme because of the color's association with magic and mystery. Marc was stunning in burgundy leather pants and a tuxedo shirt he had dyed purple. The others had found skirts, dresses, coats, and capes in various shades of purple and red. I came up with a purple Nehru shirt from a secondhand store, but I was underdressed compared to the rest of the entourage. Sherry had several necklaces, so she gave me one of irregular purple stones.

I had never seen McAlister Auditorium so festive. Balloons were everywhere, and many people blew bubbles through plastic hoops. Everyone stared at us walking down the aisle, making me feel self-conscious, the usual reluctance I had about traveling in cliques. At the same time, I appreciated being part of a group of people pushing limits. With each step, I had a greater sense of wonder and connection with my friends. I looked up at the ceiling and wondered why I had never noticed the rainbow halos around the lights.

"There's Kevin and Susan," said Sherry. "Looks like they have some seats in their row." A red balloon floated past at what seemed an extremely slow pace. I batted it and sent it in another direction, though its movement was in slow-motion frames.

Sherry took my hand as we went into the row. "Let it be. You'll be fine." She must have sensed my perceptions were altered. Sherry sat next to Kevin, and I was between Sherry and Marc.

Kevin leaned forward and gave me a smile that incorporated every muscle in his face. I could see each one working under the skin. "All good?"

I nodded. As my head went up and down, so did the room. When I breathed, the room did too, the walls closing in and out. Marc put his hand on my leg.

"Are you doing okay?"

A vibration from his hand warmed my leg from knee to hip. I stared at his hand as it pulsed with a palette of skin tones. The hairs on his knuckles moved as if swaying in a breeze.

I nodded again. If I opened my mouth, I wasn't sure what would come out. He squeezed my leg and took his hand away, the loss of contact sending my emotions tumbling down a spiraling slide into oblivion.

"Breathe, my friend," said Marc. "You'll feel better."

With each inhalation, I was aware we were all taking life from the same air. I was inhaling molecules of what others exhaled. As Marc sat next to me, I took in quantities of him and he of me.

The lights dimmed, and a collective gasp rose from the auditorium and filled the space as if it were a lung and then relaxed. My nose began to run, and I sniffled. A tissue magically appeared in my hand, and I was vaguely aware that it had come from Sherry's pocket.

The tissue came in handy as the opening music—the horns entering my ears and traveling through my body while the drums beat against my chest—teased my emotions, coaxed and shook them until water flowed from my eyes. "The Dawn of Man" section of the film followed with ape-men screeching assaulted my ears and made me feel sad the first tool produced by primates became a weapon.

It was difficult to watch. At times, I wanted to get up and run out of the theater, but after the first few minutes, I trusted the film enough to give myself over to it, letting it take me, through color and light, to ideas that seemed profound, though I couldn't always make the connections. I relinquished my tendency to analyze and only feel. My heart ached for the ape boned to death and the sad but necessary dismantling of the computer HAL. By the time we got to the "Stargate" sequence, I had completely lost myself, thrown back in my seat, Dave's eyes becoming my eyes as we traveled to Jupiter, transitioning to a new level of existence or awareness. At the end, the baby's eyes looked directly at me with a message I could feel but not process.

The lights came on, and I stared at the tissue in my hand as if the totality of what I'd experienced had been reduced to pulsating, damp, shredded paper. Sherry pulled another from her pocket with the flair of a magician, and it traveled through the air into my hand. I wiped my eyes and blew my nose. The room returned to normal respiration as if it had been holding its breath through the entire movie. Marc stood up and offered his hand. Once I was on my feet, he started to withdraw his hand, but I held on tight.

"Okay," he whispered. "That's cool." Sherry took my other hand. After the credits finished, they played over the sound system "The Blue Danube Waltz," one of the major pieces of music in the film. Instead of simply filing out of the auditorium like cattle, people waltzed, swirling about in capes and dresses like whirling dervishes.

Outside McAlister, people stood in small groups, lighting up cigarettes, sending curls of smoke upward, talking in subdued voices that sounded like the buzz of insects. Marc stepped to the center of their huddle. "We need a place to chill. I suggest my house."

"How do we get there?" said Meredith.

Marc pulled the keys out of his pocket as if it was a magic trick. "I have my car here."

"You can't drive, can you?" said Ricky.

"It wouldn't be the first time, no."

Sherry looked at me. "Are you cool with that?"

I nodded. I realized I hadn't spoken a word in three hours.

When we got to the car, Sherry indicated we should sit in the front seat. The idea frightened me, and I pointed to the back.

"Don't trust me, huh?" said Marc. He started laughing, and everyone joined in. Betsy couldn't stop giggling. The sober mood of the film lifted, and I let out a sigh of relief. Everyone noticed my protracted sigh, and a new round of sympathetic giggling took off. I ended up in the back seat behind Marc. I reached up and squeezed his shoulders. I didn't want him to think I didn't trust him.

Packed closely in the car, I detected a variety of human smells. If I closed my eyes, I could identify where each person sat by their distinct odor. Marc started the car, and the vibration of the motor entered my toes and traveled to the top of my head. I looked out the window and watched the street scenes dissipate as we drove by, appearing like fresh paintings someone sprayed with a power hose and scattered the paint behind us. Marc drove carefully along St. Charles, the big car swaying from side to side.

A myriad of sights and smells passed through my brain in what seemed like a whole lifetime before I sensed Marc put his foot on the brakes and smoothly pull to the curb in front of his house. He turned off the ignition, and it took forever for the motor to wind down, the crankshaft coming to a rest, the pistons relaxing. I could feel everything happening under the hood and had a visceral understanding of it, though I knew nothing about cars. We all sat quietly, amazed by the safe arrival.

Marc opened his door, giving us the go ahead to disembark. He led us along the side of the house to the back. The fountain goddess's gleaming whiteness stood out against the dark jungle yard. She turned her head to look at us and appeared to sigh.

We went in through the kitchen, and Meredith put on water for tea. Ricky cut up apples, peeled oranges, and piled all the pieces into a large bowl with grapes. Marc put on the Moody Blues's *On the Threshold of a Dream.*

Ricky lit several candles scattered around the living room. He took a piece of orange peel and squeezed it near the lighter, sending forth a multicolored flame.

He looked at me and smiled. "Do you want to try it?" I took the lighter and orange peel, creating my own fireworks.

Each piece of fruit had its own living light. The flavor exploded inside my mouth as I bit down on it. If I closed my eyes, I could watch the explosion on the back of my eyelids at the same time I tasted its sweetness. Between bites of fruit, I cradled a cup of mint tea in two hands and held my face above it, taking in the aroma and feeling the warmth. It helped soothe my sinuses. After giggling over the incredible sumptuousness of the fruit for some time, Betsy said she needed to lie down and was going up to her room. I didn't know she lived in the house, and I wondered if it had been her bag the boy had taken.

"Can I join you?" said Ricky. They floated from the room, leaving trails of happiness.

Meredith stretched out on the sofa. "That movie was exhausting." In a few minutes, she was asleep.

"I think she took a couple of Ludes," said Sherry.

Marc spread a blanket over her and motioned for Sherry and me to go upstairs. With each step I tried not to think about what we were doing, where we were going, and why. I was gradually coming down from my high, and old patterns of thought kept knocking on my mind's door, not letting me be in the moment, prodding me to worry about what would happen next.

In his room, the three of us fell on his bed, me in the middle. We lay on our backs, staring at the ceiling. "It feels like the bed is moving," said Sherry.

Marc waved his hands in the air. "It's the Earth. This bed is like a microcosm of the planet, spinning around, tilting toward and away from the sun, holding millions of people. It's a wonder we don't fall off as we move through space."

"The traveling through space scene was so intense in the movie," said Sherry. "I glanced at you, Nate, and you were not of this Earth. Gone, gone, gone."

"I know."

Marc rose on his elbow and looked at me. "He speaks."

I nodded.

"Oops, gone again."

Sherry got up to go to the bathroom.

"I think we better follow Meredith's example and take a Quaalude," said Marc.

I reached in my pocket and pulled out a couple of pills wrapped in a square of toilet paper.

"Well, look at you. You came prepared."

"I'm a Boy Scout."

He burst out laughing. "Me, I was too. Can you believe it?" He took one of the pills and fed it to me, his fingers touching my lips, smelling of oranges.

"Ick! It tastes horrible." I took the other and put it to his lips.

"I share in your suffering, me. Yes, it's bad, bad. Want I get some wada?"

"Too late now." I had swallowed, but the metallic taste kept popping around my tongue.

"Poor babies." Sherry was standing at the door watching us.

"There's one on the dresser for you. They're from Mexico, so I don't know if they're as good as what you high-class people get from the health service."

Sherry took the pill, but she had brought a glass of water from the bathroom to wash it down. "Water anyone?"

Marc reached for the glass. "Please." He took a sip and passed it to me.

Sherry lay back down. "You guys are too cute."

I passed the water glass to Sherry, and when my hand fell to the bed, it landed on Marc's. He moved his hand, but not to take it away. He rested it on top of mine and adjusted our fingers so that they were interlaced. "Your hands are cold, cold," said Marc.

Sherry let out a sound, something like, "Ah."

I was hyperaware of everything around me. I smelled the leather of his pants, the night coming in the open window, the soap Sherry had washed her hands with, the expectation of my own breath.

"Would you guys do something for me?" said Sherry.

Marc released my hand and again rose on his elbow, looking across me at her. "I'm inclined to say yes. Maybe you better tell us quick before we think about it too much."

"I want to see you guys kiss."

"Oh, that's easy." He leaned down and planted his lips on mine. It was only a moment, but the whiskers of his chin brushed mine. My heart bumped against my ribs.

"I mean a real kiss, damnit."

He tilted his head slightly as if asking my permission, and I nodded almost imperceptibly. He moved his body half on top of me, put his hand on the side of my face, and brushed his lips over mine before planting his mouth solidly. I put my arm around his back and pulled him close. I tasted the bitter Quaalude and the sweetness of the fruit he had eaten before. I tasted love and caring. My experience in kissing was limited. I imagined his was not. We let it happen, let tongues go where they wanted, let lips nibble without any sense of time or social constraints telling us what we could and couldn't do.

"Now that's more like it." We might have felt bad for Sherry except we knew intuitively she allowed us this indulgence, encouraged it. "I'm going to leave you two alone."

Marc disengaged long enough to say, "You don't have to. This is as far as I go on a first date, me." And then he dove back in, our legs now entangled. I loved touching his hair, pulling on a curl and letting it spring back into place. He ran his finger along the ridges of my ear. The drugs running through our bloodstreams loosened the inhibitions, but for my part, and I was inclined to believe on his, it was something we wanted. After a time, he pulled back again. "Air break."

Without looking, I knew Sherry was no longer in the room. "Is she all right?"

"Don't think she's *faché*." We glanced around the room. We had been oblivious to Sherry turning off the lamp and lighting a couple of candles. Shadows danced on the walls. "I'll go check." He stood up and became a giant figure on the wall, an image escaped from a nightmare.

"You look funny. Your shadow."

"I'll return in a sec." He was gone a minute and came back into the room. "She's in my roommate's room. He's away."

He took off his pants and shirt. "Me, I'm getting comfortable. You should too. Time to get under the covers."

I stripped down to my underwear and got in bed. The Quaalude was hitting strong. I was tired but craved touch. I wondered if our session was over.

"Turn on your side," he said. He pressed his body against mine and threw his arm over my chest.

"Like spoons. This is nice."

It was the first time I'd ever slept a full night in sweet contact with another human being. The sun streamed in the window and bathed us in its morning light as I lay on my side, watching Marc sleep. He was on his back with his hands crossed on his chest like a corpse. His nose formed a perfect angle, jutting out from his forehead and cutting back into his upper lip, a nose commonly found on Greek statues. Long eyelashes, fleshy lips, and a two-day stubble rounded out the face I had been smashed up against but couldn't appreciate. His eyes sprang open. They were hazel. I hadn't noticed the color.

"Hi," I said.

"You're awake." He didn't turn and look at me, give me a morning kiss. He patted my leg as he got up. "Really gotta make wada."

Time to go. I looked for a clock in the room. Back to a world controlled by time. I scrambled out of bed and put on my jeans.

Marc stumbled back into the room and fell on the bed. "Where's the fire, brother?"

"I have to write a paper this weekend. Can you believe it?"

He groaned and put his feet on the floor. "Me, I got to work later." He went to his closet and pulled out a pair of jeans. We still hadn't made eye contact, that simple acknowledgement so important when you've spent a night of intimacy.

Sherry was already in the kitchen. Ricky and Meredith had left early. "I can drive y'all home," said Marc. "Coffee first though."

I looked at Sherry. "We can get back on our own. Thanks."

"Suit yourself." He gave us both loose hugs. "See you soon?"

"Hope so," I said.

My legs felt leaden as we walked down the front steps, each step a letdown, a return to ground below sea level where I would be treading water instead of floating. I felt him standing at the door watching us. I didn't turn around. When I hit the street, a ray of sunlight shot through the trees and temporarily blinded me. I closed my eyes and saw a flash of geometric color instantly morphing into his hazel eyes, and then Dave's eyes as he passed through Kubrick's Stargate, and then the eyes of the man-baby at the end of the movie.

Sherry rubbed her stomach. "Let's get some breakfast in the quarter."

"I'm not as hungry as I should be, but yeah, that's cool."

"Oh, brother. Spill the beans. How was it?"

"The movie? The mushroom trip?"

"Ha ha. You and Marc."

"We didn't do any more than what you saw. But that was fine. Really...uh...nice."

"Nice?"

"We slept touching."

"You're happy with that?"

"Sure."

"You don't sound like it."

"This morning he was...I don't know...distant."

"Oh, lordy. What we have here is a case of post-trip letdown."

"I know. Reality strikes. What do I do? I've never been here before."

"You've got that love bug going on."

"Do you think it was only the drugs for him?"

"No, honey, I don't. But don't get your hopes up."

"Wait a minute. You got me into this."

"I did not have to twist either of your arms one little bit."

*

Only a few weeks of the semester remained, and I had papers to write and exams to study for. I had run out of Obetrol, but I found a source in the dorm for Dex, my least favorite of the uppers. I had promised myself I would end the semester with decent grades, more for my parents than me, and would do whatever I had to do to stay in school. My parents had enough to deal with. My mother had called me in tears a few weeks before, saying David was in Canada. As soon as he got his draft notice, he and

Lola had gotten married and left for Canada a few days later. They ended up in Montreal where David had a friend, another draft dodger.

"I thought you and Dad were against the war."

"That's not the point."

"What is the point?"

"If he tries to come back in the country, he could be arrested. He's an outlaw."

"But for good reason."

"We didn't even have a chance to see our son get married. And if they have kids, I won't be able to see my grandchildren."

"What are you talking about, Mom? You can go to Canada any time."

"I know, but it's not the same." She stopped to blow her nose. "Maybe we can take a trip up there next summer."

I talked her down and tentatively agreed to accompany them on a trip to Canada.

I became a hermit in the final weeks of the semester. I had not seen Marc since the night of the mushrooms. Sherry and I only got together a few times for meals. I spent a lot of time in the library and would come home with the hopes Marc might have left a message for me. I was pretty sure he had my number, but maybe he didn't. The person I saw most from the gang was Meredith. She was always in the library. In spite of her hippie façade, she was a dedicated student. I worried about Sherry, who seemed to care little about grades. She was more interested in wandering around the quarter and going to parties.

I had a bad crash after my last exam. I became depressed about going home for the holidays. David wouldn't be there, and Cindy told me she wasn't coming home because her mother was going to California to be with her. The only person I thought I could go visit was Danny's sister and her beautiful baby boy, but that might be awkward. I barely knew them. To brighten my mood, Sherry told me about Ricky's end-of-the-year party. On the morning of the party, I woke up with the excitement I would see Marc, who was sure to be there.

Sherry, Kevin, Susan, and I got to the party late, and it was already crowded. I scanned the living room for Marc.

"He's not here," I said to Sherry.

"You need to chill." She slipped a Quaalude into my hand.

He never showed up. No one knew why. For days after the party, I agonized about whether I should go to his house. I had to see him before I left. Two nights before my flight home, I showed up on Marc's doorstep. He wasn't in, but Betsy said I could wait since he would be home from work soon.

"What does he do by the way?"

"He works at his parents' electronics store in Metairie. He repairs radios, TVs, stereos, and shit. He's a technological genius. Who woulda thought?"

I heard the back door open, and boots pounded the old wood floors as he came into the living room. He gave me a big smile. "Now you're a sight for sore eyes, yeah."

"I am?" He gave me the soul shake and chest bump instead of a hug. He wore a work shirt from Theriot's Repair.

"I've been wondering if I'd see you. You going home for the holidays?"

"That's why I stopped by. I'm leaving in a couple of days."

"You want a beer?"

"Sure."

He got the beers and sat down next to me on the couch. "Merde, what a day! I felt tired, tired all day. I felt like a fish outta wada." I found it adorable how he threw French words into his speech, used double adjectives, and never pronounced the final *r* in words.

"Betsy told me you do repairs at your parents' electronics store."

"I've always liked fixing things. I'm not smart like you. I went to a vo-tech high school. Then I went into the service as soon as I turned eighteen, me. They said they'd send me to more training. Seemed like a good way to avoid Vietnam. Did my basic in Texas and spent a year in Germany. Over dere I worked on all kind a surveillance cameras and stuff like that. They called me the Ragin' Cajun Fixit Man."

"You finished your service already?"

"Yeah. I'm an old man. I just turned twenty-two."

"You've lived. I haven't even been out of the country." I thought about mentioning I would go to Canada the following summer to visit my draft dodger brother, but I wasn't sure how he would react as a vet.

"Talk to me, man. Whatcha been doing?"

"Been busting my butt, taking exams, writing papers. It's a relief to be finished. I thought I'd see you at Ricky's party."

He hesitated a minute, seeming to contemplate how to answer. "Yeah, I couldn't make it, no. Come see upstairs. I'm gonna get out of dese work clothes."

I sat on his bed while he changed. He sat down next to me and lit up a joint. We smoked and drank the beers in silence. I put my hand on his leg. He looked down at it.

"I like you, Nate. But I don't want you to get the wrong idea."

I took my hand back. "And what would the wrong idea be?"

"I got this girlfriend in Germany, you know, from when I was stationed dere."

"Of course you do."

"Don't be like that. I'm not freaked out about kissing a guy. I have absolutely no regrets about the other night. Regrets, hell, I passed a good, good time. You're a beautiful person."

"But?"

"It's all kind of new to me too."

"Was it so obvious it was new to me?"

"That's why it was so cool. We were like a couple of teenagers."

"Uh...technically I still am a teenager."

"You know what I mean. I'm trying to figure it all out. Okay, I'm going to be honest. I didn't go to Ricky's party 'cause I knew I'd see you, and dere would be expectations. People be all watching us to see what we was going to do."

"You're embarrassed people know we slept together?"

"I don't give a shit about that. I like things to be spontaneous."

I stood up. "I'd better go."

"Don't, Nate. Come on."

"You think this is easy for me. My whole life I've had these feelings that make me a freak. You have no idea. I keep finding people who I think might be like me, but they're not. I see people in the quarter who don't seem to give a shit about what people think. But I'm not like them either." I hated getting emotional. I always ended up in tears. I turned and started toward the door. He grabbed me from behind before I got there, turned me around, and held me, which made things worse, causing me to gasp and choke on my tears.

"The last thing I want is to hurt you. That's why I'm being honest."

"This is ridiculous." I pulled away from him. "I'm ridiculous."

"No, you're not. You feel things."

"I'm sorry." I walked out of his room and started down the hall.

"Call me when you get back."

"Thanks for the beer."

Sixteen: Off Campus

I started the spring semester with a supply of diet pills I had acquired while I was home for Christmas. I could always count on my hometown in that regard. When I wasn't running around trying to find old drug contacts, I sat home with my parents watching *All in the Family* on TV. They seemed pleased to have me home. We planned our trip to Montreal in the summer. My parents had never been outside the country, and Mom was particularly nervous.

"Thank God for your French. If I have to go to the bathroom somewhere, at least you can ask for me. I don't know what I'd do."

"Most people speak English there, at least in Montreal. It's not like going to France."

"How do you know?"

"When we started talking about the trip, I went to the library and looked at a guidebook. It also said Quebecois is different than French in France. I might not be able to understand them."

Mom kept obsessing about the trip, and Dad worried about driving outside the country. "Dad, Canada is just like the U.S. except they pronounce out like oot." It was the first time I got a hint of what my parents might be like in old age and was happy to return to New Orleans.

At Ricky's end-of-the-year party, he had mentioned he was looking for two roommates to replace the two who were moving out. Kevin and I made an on-the-spot decision to move off campus. Even though we had our separate lives, we remained close.

I had reason to be optimistic about my first experience living on my own despite the pain of having to cook for myself, pay rent and bills, and do all the things normal people did. It would be a new beginning. I had decided I was over Marc though I did spend an exorbitant amount of time thinking about all the casual nonchalant things I would say to him if I ran into him. I was sure I would never give him the power to bring me to tears again.

Sherry had also moved off campus into a small Creole cottage on Governor Nicholls Street in the French Quarter, only a few blocks away from Marc's. Her new roommate was named Lucius, a guy I hadn't met yet. The day of her housewarming party, I arrived at her door carrying a large plant. A man opened the door and I recognized him as Lucius from the description Sherry had given me. He was a light-skinned African American with freckles and a reddish-brown Afro. He wore a polyester shirt unbuttoned halfway down in a red-and-orange pattern that looked like it was on fire and white bell-bottoms that hugged his long legs.

"Goodness, it's a vision from the Garden of Eden bearing gifts." He took hold of the beads around his neck. "You must be Nate. I've seen pictures, and honey, I mean I've seen it all."

"Oh, Ricky's photos."

"Uh-huh. Come on in, sugar."

"Nate," Sherry screamed from across the room and came running over to give me a big kiss. "I see you've met Lucius. Isn't he fabulous?"

I looked around the crowded living room. The décor was all Spanish embroidered shawls, Japanese screens, and hand-painted fans. Flowers were everywhere, and the Stargazer lilies gave off a scent that was close to nauseating. I knew most of the women: Betsy, Meredith, and a couple of girls I had met at Ricky's party but forgot their names. Most of the attendees were men. The only man I recognized was Ricky. Despite his nonconventional outfits and not so masculine demeanor, he looked out of place. An older man in a sports coat and ascot was conversing with him, leaning inappropriately close. Ricky turned and gave me a nervous wave.

Lucius tucked his arm in mine and swept me away to make the rounds, introducing me to everyone. I felt a bit like fresh meat amongst the vultures and then immediately checked myself for thinking in those terms. Some of them were quite nice, and a few seemed to feel as awkward as I did. I talked to a guy in the military who had driven all the way from his base in Texas. I wondered if it was the same place Marc had been stationed and if they had known each other.

I met another guy, Manny, whose family had come from Cuba. He said he worked in a hospital. I noticed that nobody was specific about their job. Sherry later told me most of the men there had to hide their true selves at work and with their families. It struck a chord of fear in me and reminded me how Dr. B had been forced to live at home and how it had ended.

Ricky broke away from the older gentleman and came over to me. He slipped me a Quaalude. "Thought you might need this."

"Thanks. Not sure I'll be staying long. How are you doing?"

"All right."

"Sherry told me she invited Marc."

"Not surprised he didn't show up. Not his scene."

In a way, I was glad he hadn't shown up. He would have been uncomfortable. But I also wondered if he was avoiding me again.

After an interminable hour of trying to make polite conversation, always a struggle for me, I made my way through the crowd to tell Sherry I was going to leave.

"Aw, no," she pouted and hastily brightened up. "Marc might show up. He always comes late."

"If he does, give him my best."

When I got home, Marc was sitting on my front steps, head in hands. "Marc. Are you okay?"

He looked up with a drunken smile. "Me? Couldn't be better." He tried to stand up and would have fallen over if I hadn't grabbed his arm. I had seen him high on different drugs but never drunk. I got him inside, and we sat in the living room.

"Do you want some coffee or something?"

"Can I spend the night?" He punctuated his question with a loud burp. "Shit. I'm sorry. That was rude, rude." His speech was slurred. He was drunk and rude, but I was on the verge of doing anything he asked.

"I don't think that's a good idea."

"You're right." He lowered his eyes and pouted. "Might I would take a coffee and then be on my way, me."

We went in the kitchen. All I had was instant. I put water on to boil and stood at the stove, eyes glued to the water. He came up behind me and rested his chin on my shoulder. "Watched pot never boils say my nanny."

"Marc, don't. You can't..."

"What?" He moved back and fell into a chair.

"Why didn't you go to Sherry's party?"

"Don't care much for her roommate, no. I stopped by one day, and everything he said, he had to touch my arm, put his hand on my leg, make some stupid comment, tell me I should cut my hair some fag-ass way."

"So, you hate faggots. I get it."

"No, no. It's just...why he have to act dat way?"

"I know. Why can't fags act macho like you? Be real men?"

"You want me to go?"

I poured the water in the cup, put in a scoop of coffee, and slammed it down on the table in front of him, slopping half of it over the side. He grabbed my hand. "I wanted to see you. *Beaucoup*."

"You had to get drunk to do it?"

He pulled my hand to his lips and kissed it. "You once told me I was a good guy."

"That's what I thought at the time. Maybe I was only trying to get my faggot hands on you."

"Don't say that." His head rolled back like it wasn't properly attached. The jerk actually had tears in his eyes.

"You are one of the finest people I met in my life, yeah. I kissed and held you that night not because I was high. I wanted to be part of your goodness. I know you think I'm an asshole right now, but you have to know I like you beaucoup. Just not sure what to do with it."

"You could start by not tearing other people down for who they are."

"See what I mean? You're a better man than me." He still held my hand and grazed his lips over my knuckles. He took a sip of coffee with his other hand.

I let out a huff. "Honestly, I don't like him either."

He coughed and sprayed coffee all over the table. "You shit."

"But not for the same reasons." I stood up and he released my hand.

"Let me clean that up."

"I got it." I mopped it up with a kitchen cloth.

"What was that you said before about getting your hands on me?"

"You truly are an asshole."

"If you want me to go, say so."

"Go. Don't go. Go. It's all the same to me."

"If it's all the same, I'll stay." He got up and walked into a bedroom.

"That's not my bedroom."

"Oops." He came out and went into the right one and took off his clothes, all his clothes, and got into bed.

I brushed my teeth, took off my clothes, all my clothes, and joined him.

I was high from the Quaalude Ricky had given me, and he was drunk. Inhibitions were at a minimum. So was experience.

"I want to go all the way," he whispered.

"That sounds like high school. You want to fuck?"

"You done it with a guy?"

"Nope. And you?"

"I told you it's all new to me. I wasn't lying, no."

"I guess we'll figure it out."

"Jesus, come see and shut up."

We kissed for a while, but not with the same abandon as last time. Being high didn't stop us from feeling nervous. I thought of how I had seen Dr. B go down on James. It seemed like a good place to start. I burrowed under the covers. It took a while for him to get an erection, but as soon as he got hard, he started moaning. "Oh god. Oh god. *Ça c'est bon, bon, bon.*" A couple minutes later, "Stop, stop, stop, stop, stop."

"What?"

"I don't want to blow yet. I want to be inside you."

I repeated it with a German accent. "I vant to be inside you."

"Who the asshole now?"

"Funny you should mention asshole." I remembered how Sherry had gotten on top of me. His dick was slick with my saliva. It was bobbing ready. I straddled him, convinced it was going to hurt like hell. So be it. I had to do this. I eased myself down inch by inch.

"Aaaaaah," he screamed.

"Did you come?"

"God, no. I'm completely inside you, and it feels so fucking good. God damn. I never...I never... *Laissez les bon temps rouler*."

I couldn't believe it didn't hurt. I realized I was in control like Sherry had been. We moved our bodies. "Look at me," he said. I also remembered Sherry chastising me for closing my eyes. I opened them and wasn't afraid to let go. I gazed deep until I had memorized the pattern of his hazel eyes, where the green melted into brown, the tiny specks of yellow.

"This is great, fantastic, I love it," he said. "*Mais* can we try another...?"

It was his turn to take control. "Just do it." I rolled over and let him get on top of me. We didn't last long. He made a lot of noise when he came. I liked that. I started laughing. He rolled off me.

"Why you laughing?"

"It's a good kind of laughing. It's joy. Release. You have no idea how long I've wanted to do that."

"With me?"

"I didn't know you when I was twelve."

"Too bad, bad."

We lay side by side for a long time. He took my hand and held it.

"I'm going to tell you something. Don't hate me, no."

"I already hate you."

"It's a thin line between love and hate. I'm going away for a while."

"To Germany."

"Haven't seen her for about six months."

"And after having mind-blowing sex with me, you're still going to go?"

"Very funny."

"All this good stuff isn't going to be available forever."

"It is a risk, yeah."

"In all seriousness, I will miss you. I barely know you, but I like what I know. You need to figure out what you want."

"Do you know what you want?"

"You baby, you baby, you."

"Stop screwing around. You might not think so, but I do got feelings. I can only be what I can be. Maybe it's not exactly what you want."

"I don't know what I want. I've had sex with one woman, and now one man. It's not fair to compare, but it's inevitable that I will."

"You liked it with me better, no?"

"Way better. It feels more honest."

"It feels beaucoup more honest with you than most of the girls I've had sex with."

"Only most? Shit. I've got to get better at this."

"We can agree on something, no? No more of this feeling awkward or confused about each other."

"You were the one avoiding parties so you wouldn't have to run into me."

"Cher, whatever happens, I'm gonna always hold special the time I spent with you."

"That sounds like goodbye."

"*And* any time we spend together in the future unless you're a *couyon*."

"Couyon?"

"Asshole."

"Same goes for you."

He leaned over and kissed me. "Sealed with a kiss. A Cajun kiss is as solid as a handshake, yeah."

"You made that up."

Later, I was proud of myself for how cool I was in that conversation while inside my heart was breaking. The thought of him leaving so soon after we had met crushed me under its weight. I had a disturbing revelation. Did this mean I was over my obsession with Dr. B? How long can an obsession last if you don't know where that person is or if he is still alive? I had built this den in my head reserved exclusively for Dr. B, decorated with memories of his face and images of him naked. That room was beginning to feel a little chilly.

Dr. B aside, Marc was the first man I'd made love with, so it was inescapable—as long as the first isn't horrible, and sex with him was the farthest from horrible—that I would fall at least a little in love with him. Our bodies settled into each other, and the rest of the night we slept stuck together as if we had done it for years.

In the morning, Kevin was in the kitchen when we came out of my room. "Marc." The way he said it and the shock on his face told me he had heard us.

"Hey, where yat, Kevin?"

At the front door, Marc's eyes revealed a careful search for words. "I'm not leaving for a couple weeks, no."

"Aren't your parents going to miss you at the store?"

"Been training someone."

"In case you don't come back."

He shrugged. "I didn't learn much German over dere. Maybe it's time to learn a new language."

"We're learning a new language here."

"Sometimes the things you say give me the *frissons*. Chills."

"Will I see you before you go?"

"Fo' sure." He stuck out his hand.

"You can't give me a proper hug?"

"I thought maybe in front of Kevin..."

"Kevin's bedroom is the one next to mine. I think he knows all there is to know."

"I pass a good time with you, yeah." He hugged me tight and whispered in my ear. "Cher." His stubble tickled my neck, giving me frissons.

I whispered in return, "*Toujours*." Always.

In the kitchen, I faced Kevin.

"What the hell, Nate? You couldn't tell me, your supposed best friend?"

"What are you upset about?"

"You think I care if you're gay?"

"I thought you could always tell."

"I feel like a fool. The other day Meredith said she thought you might be gay. I assured her no, said I thought you and Sherry were having sex, and you had a girlfriend back home you write to all the time."

"Well, surprise. Lucky me. I don't have to worry about a girl pressuring me into marriage."

He hoisted himself up on the counter and took his coffee cup in his hands. I leaned on the perpendicular counter and stared at the dirty floor.

"Why didn't you tell me?"

"Truth is, that was my first time with a guy. I mean, Marc and I messed around the night of *2001*, high on mushrooms, but last night was the first time we went all the way as he put it."

"I had no idea Marc was gay."

"You should have seen the look on your face." I chuckled. "Well, he's not. He has a girlfriend in Germany. He's going over there in a couple of weeks."

"How do you feel about that?"

"Nothing I can do."

"You like him?"

"A lot."

He shook his head. "There's this nice guy in my ceramics class."

"No, Kevin. I mean, thanks, but no."

*

Two weeks went by without hearing from Marc. Not surprised. And then he called.

"I thought you left already."

"Sorry, cher. Don't be faché. Been busy getting ready for my trip."

"When do you leave?"

"Tomorrow. You can come see tonight and say goodbye."

"Hmm. You mean spend the night?"

"Me, I have to get up super early, I do."

"Okay, forget it."

"No. I mean I'm stressed, but I want to see you beaucoup."

I had to wait a long time for the streetcar, and the walk through the quarter had the quality of running in a dream and not getting anywhere. When I stepped into his room and saw the bags, it was a stab in my heart. The next second, I was heartened to see he still had things in his closet. "You didn't pack up all your stuff."

"Don't know what's gonna happen. If I stay, Betsy can do it, yeah."

We lay in bed in our underwear, talking about the day we met at the river. "You rubbed the back of my neck," I reminded him.

"You didn't try and stop me."

"But why did you do it?"

"I told you, I'm spontaneous. Or maybe you use some *gris-gris* on me."

"Why not Ricky or one of the girls? Why did you end up next to me in the water? Why did you kiss me the night of the mushrooms and come to see me the night you were drunk? Why did you make love to me and call me cher? Why to all of it?" My chest started to heave, and tears rolled down my cheeks.

"*Gardes don.* You got wada coming out a dose beautiful eyes." He held me and kissed my tears. "You make me sad, sad."

I sucked in air. "Sorry. I said I wasn't going to do that again."

"No need to apologize for feeling things."

We held each other in silence for a long time.

"Uh...we could...but I'm kind of nervous about my trip."

"I get it. You don't want to have the taste of me on you when you meet her."

"I got the taste of you in my head toujours. I won't forget, no."

"Frissons."

"Frissons."

From the front porch, I watched the taxi take him away. It wasn't light yet. The birds had no right to be singing so sweetly or the yard to smell so fresh. It had rained during the night, and water dripped from the trees like an IV to the earth. If only I could have something dripping in my veins to make me feel better. How could someone I had known for such a short time leave such a crater in my heart?

I trudged back into the house and entered the kitchen. Betsy had made coffee.

"You want some?"

"Yeah, thanks." It wasn't the drip I needed, but it was a start.

We sat across from each other at the table. The anguish in her face mirrored mine.

"I'm sure you don't know I was in love with him too. I moved in here thinking if I was around him every day, he might...but I realized I was better off being his friend.

He doesn't mean to hurt people. He's one of those rare persons who doesn't care who you are or where you're from, what you believe, whether you're a man or a woman. If he likes you, he takes you into his heart. I can tell you this, he took you into his heart in a big way. Beaucoup!" She laughed.

"And now he's gone."

"Yep. How are you doing, honey?"

"Okay. I honestly can't talk about it. I appreciate you telling me that." I stood up. "Do you mind if I use your phone to call Sherry?"

"It's kind of early."

"That's what friends are for, right?"

Sherry answered the phone with an utterance that sounded like a growl.

"Hi, it's Nate."

"What time is it?" she groaned.

"Six, six thirty. Not sure. I'm at Marc's. He just left, and I'm like…I don't know."

"Come over. We'll get breakfast."

We were the first customers in the café after they opened the doors.

We sat down, and I stared at the shiny menu. The glossy pictures and descriptions blurred. I felt dizzy and close to vomiting.

"He's gone?"

"Yeah. Germany. Girlfriend. You know the story."

"I'm still pissed at him for not coming to my party."

"He came to my house that night. He was drunk. We did it."

"Fuck and run. That's a real man for you."

"I'm not going to trash him, Sherry. Every moment I spent with him was something I'll treasure for the rest of my life."

"I'm sorry, honey." She reached for my hand across the table. "He's a charmer. That's for sure."

"It's been quite a year. My grandma died. One of my best friends from home OD'd. My brother fled to Canada to avoid the draft. I met you. I did psychedelics for the first time. And then that goddamn son of a bitch stole my heart."

"Okay, you don't want to talk dirt about Marc, but I've got to say guys like that are going to hurt you every time."

"*Now* you tell me."

"At least my friends at the party know what they want. And I think you're closer to knowing what you want now. I'm sorry you and Lucius got off to a bad start."

"He said that?"

"He thinks you hate him."

"I don't hate him. But outside of being your roommate, I have no interest in him whatsoever."

"That's a bit harsh. He's an accomplished dancer for the ballet."

"I'm not looking for a dance partner."

"He thinks you're real cute."

I held out my hands palms up. "In my right hand is Marc. In my left, Lucius. Do you see absolutely any similarity between these two people?"

"I still think you should talk to Lucius. If this is the life you choose, you need to know some things."

"Like not giving personal information in public, not telling people where you work, who your family is. I don't know if those people were telling me their real names. Better yet, we should all call each other Mary."

"You're upset. Your heart's broken. I get that. But don't take it out on people who are trying to live their lives and not end up in jail or beaten up on the street."

"Sorry. I know I've got a lot to learn. I need some time."

"Who knows? Marc might realize he can't live without you and come running back. I've never seen him look at another guy the way he looked at you."

"You're the one that told me not to get my hopes up."

"You're going to have a great life, and you don't need Marc Theriot." She squeezed my hand and released it.

Seventeen: Fat Tuesday

On a cool, rainy Sunday morning, I lingered in bed on sheets I hadn't washed since Marc had spent the night. Stupid, not to mention unsanitary. In such moments of loneliness, lying in bed, I caught a whiff of him, the oil of his hair or the tantalizing scent that only seemed to exist in the crevice where his neck met his shoulder blade. It was like a psychedelic trip flashback, an intense sense memory that shot me up into the sky only to dump me on the ground a moment later. In the depths of my self-imposed torture, I had spent an afternoon examining the sheets for a trace of him, coming up with a dark, curly pubic hair as if I had struck gold. A mind allowed to wallow is a dangerous thing.

The phone rang. Kevin called out my name. I was convinced it was Marc calling to say he was returning home. I jumped up and shivered as I threw on a robe. I took the receiver and infused my hello with all the carefree lightness I could muster. It was Cindy. Normally, her calls were the high point of the day, but this time the sound of her voice sent me tumbling into despair. It was day seven since Marc had left.

"I got your letter. Are you okay?"

"Sorry. It must have sounded suicidal." I knew I would regret the dismal, pathetic letter I wrote the day Marc left. "I'm better now."

"Like I told you before we both left for college, you're going to find someone wonderful. I feel it. You shouldn't settle for someone who is only half there."

"When he was there, he was a hundred percent there. At least I got a taste of the magic, the pinnacle of what you can feel with another person."

"And you will find that again. You don't have to answer, but I'm curious, does this mean that you've finally let go of Dr. B?"

"That hit me the other day. Since I met Marc, I've hardly thought of Dr. B. That realization made me feel sad and somehow weak. I never want to let go of people who have been so important in my life. I always want you to be part of my life."

"I missed seeing you at Christmas. Are you going to be home this summer?"

"At least for a while. My parents and I are going to visit David in Montreal. I need to find a job as well. My funds are running low. Mom and Dad are paying my tuition, but I have to cover rent and food." I didn't tell her, but I had looked into the cost of flights to Germany.

"Listen. I got a call from Roberta. She and Lonnie are thinking of going to Mardi Gras."

"Still together, huh? I guess some people find love."

"Transitioning from high school sweethearts to college lovers isn't always the easiest, but they're doing great, living together off campus. Anyway, she wants to contact you, and I thought I should ask you first. I think they're also looking for a place to stay. You can say no."

My first thought was that I wasn't up to it. Still in mourning. After a brief deliberation, I figured the distraction would be good. They were supportive when I was going through rough times in high school.

"Sure. As a matter of fact, one of my roommates hates Mardi Gras and is going out of town. They can have my room, and I can sleep in Ricky's. Guess I'll have to change the sheets." I laughed. "Why don't you come too? We could have a prom night reunion."

"I wish I could. But I definitely want to see you this summer. Let me know the dates you're going to Canada, and I'll try to plan around that. You're a sweetheart for letting them stay with you."

"It'll be fun."

*

Close to midnight, Roberta and Lonnie arrived at my house, traumatized after driving as an interracial couple through Arkansas, Tennessee, and Mississippi. Someone had told them they shouldn't drive at night, so they had gotten up early and driven the whole stretch in one day.

"We went in this restaurant in Arkansas, and if looks could kill, we'd be dead a thousand times. After that, Roberta went in a supermarket alone and bought a bunch of stuff we could eat in the car."

"Things are somewhat better here in New Orleans. I know a place that's open late if you're hungry."

"We're exhausted," said Roberta. "Mentally and physically."

"How about a beer? I've got some in the fridge."

"Now we're talking," said Lonnie.

On Saturday, we took the streetcar downtown as far as they were running and then walked the rest of the way to Lee's Circle to catch a parade. Parades had been going on since January, lots of them, and this was my second Mardi Gras, so I was bored with the floats that attempted to be original but blurred into variations on the same themes. It was, however, fun to see the festivities through a neophyte's eyes.

Roberta and Lonnie initiated the obligatory collection of Mardi Gras beads thrown from the floats. Lonnie kept saying he couldn't believe you could walk down the street drinking a beer in the middle of the day. Their childlike excitement was contagious, reminding me of the innocence of Midwesterners, my people. Despite all the scandals, big and small, on the street where I grew up, people at their core remained naïve. I had moved away from that since I had come to New Orleans. And yet, that was my core too.

I had read up on the history of the festivities, and as we passed through downtown toward the quarter, I explained the significance of the Mardi Gras colors. Purple meant justice, green faith, and gold power. When I first read it, it didn't sound right. Was justice the message we were trying to convey the night we all dressed in purple for *2001: A Space Odyssey*? And green is not the color I would have chosen to represent faith, but as a mere Midwesterner, it wasn't my place to criticize. I droned on about the krewes, the Mardi Gras social clubs that held balls and created floats, and for Lonnie's benefit, I pointed out how some of them like Zulu were mostly African American.

If I had seen Roberta and Lonnie go wide-eyed at their first parade, it was nothing compared to the surreal experience of crossing Canal Street and entering the French Quarter on Mardi Gras weekend. I was thankful my first impression of one of the truly unique neighborhoods in the country, its streets full of history, charm, and mystery, was *not* Bourbon Street during Mardi Gras. The antique grace of the quarter, its lush patios and Creole architecture, influenced by the many cultures to pass through the Bayou State, would be impossible for them to see, obscured by the crowds, debauchery, and noise of the holiday. But visitors who decided on coming to New Orleans for Mardi Gras weren't there for the subtle beauty of the city. I would throw them right in the middle of the party.

It was midafternoon, and Bourbon Street was already a sea of screaming faces—the kind of screaming fans do at huge sports events, letting out what has been bottled up all year. The revelers were so loaded with Mardi Gras beads, you couldn't see their necks. Music played from balconies and bars, giving people the nearly infeasible task of dancing and not spilling their drinks. Most of them had the jovial demeanor of afternoon drunks, but that could change by nightfall. After a whole day of being jostled, served watered-down drinks, and having their senses bombarded, some people would inevitably get testy.

The first thing Roberta and Lonnie wanted to do was get a Hurricane.

I made a face. "You're kidding." It was a horribly sweet drink of rum, passion fruit, orange juice, lime juice, and grenadine. I imagined a large quantity of the liquid served ended up as vomit on the street, but who was I to police tourist behavior?

"Is there something wrong with them?" asked Roberta.

"No, no. Whatever you guys want. Follow me." The lines at Pat O'Brien's would be horrendous, but I knew other places.

When I got them the drinks and Lonnie tasted his, I thought he was going to spit it out. "You should have told me."

"You've got to try it once."

"This will be the last." He laughed in a good-natured way.

"I kind of like it," said Roberta.

Halfway down Bourbon Street, a group of young ladies with massive quantities of dyed blonde hair that had obviously spent the night in orange juice can rollers approached us with saucer eyes and painted-on smiles.

"Hi. Where y'all from?"

"I am Johann from Germany." I put on a German accent. "I am wery happy to greet you." I bowed.

Lonnie stepped forward. "I am from Germany also." He tried to imitate my accent. "Ve all from Germany."

The girls looked at him in shock. "Really? We're from Alabama."

"Goot day, ladies." I led Lonnie and Roberta away. A few steps down the street we burst into laughter.

"You guys are terrible," said Roberta. "They were only trying to be friendly."

"You're right." I turned around. "Let's go back and find them."

"No, no, no," said Roberta. As Lonnie and I laughed again, it brought back memories of the fun we had at the prom, the innocence of those days before everything turned to shit.

Farther down the street where the crowd was most packed, a group of young women looked up at a balcony where a number of people had handfuls of beads. The women kept saying, "Throw me something, mister." And the ones on the balcony, mostly men, shouted, "Show us your tits." They bantered until one woman lifted her shirt and exposed her breasts. Everyone nearby screamed, and she was bombarded with beads. Now that the ice was broken, several of her friends exposed their breasts. Strands of beads rained down on the women.

"Don't women wear bras here?" said Lonnie.

I laughed. "They come prepared. Give it a try, Roberta."

"No way in hell."

"For my eyes only," said Lonnie.

We wandered up and down the street for as long as my nerves could take it.

"We'll have plenty of time to party later. Let's go see a different side of the city." I steered them toward Esplanade. "I want to show you one of my favorite streets, and it's not so crazy over there." They seemed willing to follow me anywhere.

I pointed out the live oak trees forming a canopy over Esplanade Street and the double-gallery architecture typical there.

"This street is so romantic," said Roberta.

Lonnie made a sound of disgust. "Did you see that? That guy's taking a piss on someone's front lawn in the middle of the day."

"People around here have to put up with a lot during Mardi Gras. I have some friends who live on this street. Let's stop in and see them."

We went up the steps of Marc's house and knocked on the door. Betsy answered in the harlequin outfit she wore the first time I saw her.

"Hi Betsy. Some friends from my hometown are here for Mardi Gras, and I'm showing them around. We were nearby, so I thought I'd say hello."

"Uh-huh." She gave me a look like she knew exactly why I was there. "A bunch of us just got back from a parade."

"We went to one too. These are my friends, Lonnie and Roberta." I could see several people sitting in the living room. They were listening to The Doors' *Morrison Hotel,* and the smell of weed was overpowering. Maybe this wasn't such a good idea.

"I'd invite you in, but I don't know if your friends..." She smiled at Roberta and Lonnie.

"Maybe we should come back another time."

"Look, if it's the weed, no problem," said Lonnie. "You remember prom night, don't you, Nate?" Roberta still held her half-full Hurricane glass, though Lonnie had discarded his.

Roberta took Lonnie's arm. "If I remember correctly, I provided the joint."

"Well, come on in. I need to talk to Nate, anyway." Betsy's words set my heart racing. Marilu from the house by the river and Meredith were in the living room with a couple of guys who looked like they'd stepped right off the record album cover. I'd seen them at parties but didn't know them. Betsy told Roberta and Lonnie to have a seat. Lonnie immediately struck up a conversation about the music while Betsy and I went into the kitchen.

"Sherry was supposed to meet us to go to the parade, but she didn't show up. I just called her. Something's happened to Lucius."

"What?"

"He was beat up last night. He's in the hospital."

"Is it bad?"

"I don't have the details. She's at home now. Maybe you should go over there. She's pretty upset."

"Yeah." The news was shocking but so far from the topic I expected, I was having a hard time adjusting. Betsy again read my thoughts.

"Sorry. I don't have any news about Marc."

"Sure. No problem. You're right. I should go over to Sherry's, but I have to figure out what to do with my friends. I guess they can go too."

In the living room Lonnie was in the middle of taking a toke, and Roberta sipped her drink. "Guys, sorry to break up the party," I said, "but there's an emergency, and we have to go to another friend's house. It's not far."

Sherry answered the door showing signs of lack of sleep, and her voice was pulled taut. She had been at the hospital since four in the morning and only came home to pick up some things for Lucius. I offered to go to the hospital with her and gave Lonnie and Roberta my key with specific directions how to get to my place. I wrote everything down.

Sherry said my friends should walk with us on the way to Charity Hospital as she knew where to catch a bus that would take them close to the apartment. After we had dropped Roberta and Lonnie at the bus stop, Sherry told me about Lucius's attack. He had been jumped coming home from a bar about two in the morning. He didn't know what happened. I guess people let him lie unconscious on the street for over an hour thinking he was passed out drunk.

The intensive care nurse told us we could go in but only for a short time. Lucius had multiple bruises on his face, one eye swollen closed, several broken ribs, a broken arm, and a concussion. He was awake when we went in.

"How are you doing, honey?" said Sherry.

"I'm so happy to see you guys. Nate, how sweet of you to come." It was obviously painful for him to talk.

"I should have brought some flowers. I know you like flowers." It sounded dumb, but I didn't know what to say. I felt horrible for the negative things I had said about him. Nobody deserved this, and we had a good idea why he was attacked. Not robbery. He still had his watch and his wallet when someone heard him moan and stopped to help.

"I hope they gave you some good pain medicine at least," said Sherry. "You don't have to say anything. We'll sit here with you until they kick us out."

Manny, in orderly scrubs, poked his head in the door a few minutes later. "I'm on break. I thought I'd stop in and check on you." I now knew where he worked and what he did.

"He seems to be doing a lot better," said Sherry. "The doctor will tell me little since I'm not family."

"You are family." Lucius was on the verge of tears.

"Is there anyone you want us to contact?" said Manny.

"No way."

Manny checked the IV. "I hear you."

"Do not call my mother unless they tell you I'm dying."

"You're not dying. You're too much of a mean bitch to die."

"Ow, ow. Don't make me laugh."

The nurse came in and said they were taking him out of intensive care. "We were afraid of the possibility of a punctured lung with the broken ribs, but things seem okay. We're going to move him to a regular room." She started out the door. "A few more minutes, then you have to go."

"See," said Manny. "You're not dying."

"Too bad for you." Lucius turned to us. "He's afraid I'm going to steal his gorgeous lover."

A look of panic distorted Manny's face, and he glanced up and down the hallway to see if anyone might have heard. "Jesus, Lucius. All right, guys. I've got to get back to work."

"I always did have a big mouth," said Lucius.

I looked at Sherry. "Was Manny's lover at your party?"

"No. He doesn't go to parties. A real mystery man. Manny rarely says anything about him except that they live together. Nobody knows where."

"Excuse me. I know. But I'm sworn to secrecy," said Lucius.

In my short life, I had seen a Scoutmaster who resorted to molesting boys, the deadly scandal that forced Dr. B out of town, Lucius getting beat up, and Manny's closeted life. The fantasy Marc and I could find true love and be together seemed absurd. And before that, my dream I could make Dr. B happy seemed doubly absurd. What examples did we have that showed us a path to happiness?

Sherry looked at me and sighed as if she understood my thoughts. "What a fucked-up society we live in."

"I never promised you a rose garden," said Lucius.

Sherry said she was going to stay a bit longer at the hospital, and I went home to my guests. Kevin and Susan were there, so the five of us went out for pizza.

Lonnie took a gulp of cold beer. "Aw. So much better than a Hurricane. Where's Sherry? I got the feeling you guys were dating." I wondered if he had forgotten the rumors about me in relation to the Dr. Baronian scandal, or if he just hoped I had found a normal life.

Roberta jumped in to change the conversation. "You have such interesting friends." Like that prom night in the motel room Roberta got me, like Cindy, like Sherry.

Lonnie laughed. "Toto, I don't think we're in Kansas anymore."

"Carbondale isn't the most interesting place in the world, but SIU isn't Squaresville either," said Roberta.

"What's SIU?" asked Kevin.

"Southern Illinois University. It's actually a cool place. The campus is right on a lake. Then again, it's not New Orleans. I don't know how you guys get any studying done."

"Sherry told me she's going to drop out," I said to Kevin.

"Not surprised. We're in a sociology class together, and she's failing."

*

Ash Wednesday brought a welcome relief to four days of partying and entertaining guests. I was sad to say goodbye to Lonnie and Roberta but glad to have that connection with my hometown. They were, like it or not, my people. At the same time, I was on a trajectory that would take me even farther away from my life in the Midwest. I was sure I'd never move back to Sangamon.

The spring semester dragged. No news from Marc. Lucius got better. I went by to help him with things he still had a hard time doing, running errands when Sherry couldn't do it. One day when I was there, Sherry came home and announced she was definitely dropping out of school. She would stay in New Orleans and find a job.

I was jealous of Sherry dropping out and unsure of my direction, but I knew I couldn't do the same. My parents would cut me off, and the draft would get me. My psychology courses were tedious, but I wasn't motivated to change my major after investing two years in it. I was a fake student, a fake hippie. Nothing seemed real.

Kevin and I liked to joke our major was Frisbee with a minor in Concert Attending. The January after Kevin and I went to West Palm Beach, a venue opened called The Warehouse, which took its name from the property's previous incarnation. It was an intimate space with a small stage, brick walls, and thick wooden beams along the ceiling. They booked some of the best groups of the time. Kevin and I went to the opening concert of The Grateful Dead, Fleetwood Mac, and The Flock. That night The Dead were busted in their French Quarter hotel room for drugs. From the spring of 1970 through the spring of 1971, we saw The Allman Brothers several times, Sly and the Family Stone, B.B. King, Pink Floyd, Dr. John, Small Faces, Cat Stevens, Elton John, and others. Tickets were four dollars.

Despite Frisbee, the concerts, drugs, and a hundred other distractions, I was again able to end the semester well, maintaining a GPA a little under 4.0. Of course, I had to give a lot of the credit to my "study buddies"—Obetrol and other uppers. But the emptiness in my heart remained.

Eighteen: And the Hits Keep Coming

I drove my parents' old '65 Ford Fairlane down St. Charles Avenue in the pouring rain with wipers struggling to clear the windshield. A car slowed down in front of me to make a turn, and I slammed on the brakes, coming within inches of smashing into the rear of it. I was sure the near accident had nothing to do with the couple of hits from a joint I had been offered at the last delivery stop. The near accident left me shaken with the all-encompassing body sensation of disaster.

I blamed it on the wiper blades I should have replaced when they gave me the car. It had performed well on our drive to Canada, but my parents had decided they needed a replacement. With both of them working, they could afford to splurge on a new car. Aside from the worn blades, the Ford was in great shape, used mostly by my mom to drive around town.

We had gone to Canada in June. Much to my mother's relief, people spoke English everywhere we went. My parents were pleased to see the stable life David and Lola had created in a short period of time—a nice apartment, Lola's job with IBM, and David's job at a local youth center where he supervised sports activities. Most of all, they enjoyed the hints David and Lola were thinking about having children.

By the time we got back, it was too late to get a summer job at home, so I set off with my new old car and headed for the sweltering heat of a New Orleans summer. Having my own transportation allowed for the fabulous job opportunity in the field of pizza delivery.

My friends called my car the Pizzamobile due to the odor of tomato sauce, cooked cheese, and spicy meat, which had permeated the interior since I had taken the job. A pizza box sat on the seat next to me, my last delivery.

I turned down Louisiana Avenue and found the address on Constance Street, a white Creole cottage with green shutters. Walking up to the house, I heard someone playing the piano. The playing stopped when I rang the doorbell. A man opened the door.

I squawked and dropped the pizza. For years I had imagined hundreds of scenarios for this event though never in the context of fulfilling someone's craving for pizza. We stared at each other across a doorway, unable to speak. I heard the steps of another person coming from inside the house. "What happened?"

A young man appeared in the doorway. "Manny?" I was in shock.

"Nate?"

The three of us looked at one another, and finally, the pizza on the ground.

"You two know each other?" Dr. B's voice was strained.

"We met through Sherry," said Manny.

I was hyperventilating. "I dr...dropped the pizza."

Manny looked at the ground. "Relax, man. No big deal."

"Oh, but...but it is. I mean, I won't charge you for it."

Dr. B picked up the pizza and opened the box.

"It's a little disordered, but I'm sure it'll taste the same. Of course I'll pay you for it." He handed the pizza to Manny. "Could you take it into the kitchen?" He took out his wallet. "I'll pay and join you in a minute. You have to leave soon, right?" He looked at me. "Manny's working graveyard shift tonight."

"See you around, Nate. What a coincidence, no? Wait until I tell Sherry. That's so weird."

Dr. B stepped out on the porch and spoke in a low voice, "How late do you work?"

I was still shaking inside, upheaval rolling through my body in waves. "You were my last. I have to return and cash out." My words came out between nervous gulps.

"There's a hotel on the corner of St. Charles and Josephine. We can meet in the bar in an hour." His voice was even, without emotion, matter of fact.

"Yes. In an hour." I stared at him in awe.

"Nate, everything's all right."

"Of course." I turned to go.

"Drive safely. See you in an hour."

I sat in the car looking at the streetlights through the raindrops on the windshield though the rain had stopped.

I rolled down the window to let out the overpowering odor of pizza, knowing that whatever happened, every time I caught that smell, I would think of Dr. B's pepperoni and mushroom tumbling from my shaky hands. I had an hour before the next phase of my life started. Or would it be only a blip on the screen? Dr. B had moved on. Of course he had. He was Manny's mysterious lover. I thought how that guy up there moved us around like pawns for his own entertainment. *If I promise to believe in you, will you stop screwing up my life?*

I started the car and drove back to turn in the cash from my last deliveries and take my cut. I raced to my house, worrying how I must have looked in my rain-splattered green military rain poncho, my hair in disarray, and my soggy tennis shoes. I ran inside and started throwing off my clothes. In my room I talked to myself, looking for the right shirt. "No, not that one. That one looks too hippie. Help! What do I wear? Oh, Christ, that looks like I'm going on a date."

I looked up and saw Kevin at my door. He must have heard me mumbling and opening and slamming my drawers.

"Are you okay?"

"Yeah. Yeah. I can't decide what to wear."

"You look like you've just seen a ghost."

"I sort of have."

"You going out?"

"I have to meet someone."

"Is it Marc?"

"No. Long story."

"Why don't you wear that gray retro shirt with the dark triangles over the buttonholes?"

"I forgot about that shirt. Thanks."

"Don't mention it."

I threw on my best pair of jeans and the shirt. I ran in the bathroom and brushed my teeth. I combed my hair. Back in my room I looked at the clock. Shit. I was going to be late. He wouldn't wait for me, thinking I stood him up.

I raced up St. Charles, running a few red lights. I parked the car and ran into the hotel bar. He wasn't there. I looked at a clock. An hour hadn't yet passed though it seemed like three. The bar wasn't crowded, and I stood in the middle of the room, feeling like an idiot. I turned around, and he walked in the door, wearing black jeans and a green golf shirt. He had changed as well. We awkwardly shook hands.

"What would you like to drink?" he said.

"A beer, I guess."

"Have a seat. I'll get the drinks."

I suffered the nervousness of being on an interview. He brought the beer I didn't want and his Coke to the table. We both took a sip of our drinks.

"You've changed. I always think of you as the paperboy who showed up at my door with a smile."

"Now I'm the pizza boy who showed up at your door with dropsy."

He chuckled. "But you've grown up."

"You're kind of the same. Maybe more handsome."

He smiled, but in the depths of the smile was a wince of pain as if he hoped I'd left behind such observations, a man telling another man he is handsome. "Manny doesn't know anything about my past."

"Is that why you wanted to meet with me? To make sure I don't tell him or tell someone who might leak it to him?"

"Living this way is constantly walking a fine line. We have neither pasts nor futures. We take each day as it comes."

"What do you get out of it?"

"Manny and I met at the hospital. We realized we had something in common besides running away from our pasts. His family came here after the revolution in Cuba. That's all I know. He never told me why he had to leave Miami in search of a more accepting place, but I can imagine."

"Why did you end up here?"

"I remembered a trip I took to New Orleans with some buddies in college. I saw people who were like me. I had imagined things might be much better than they actually are."

"You mean more open."

"I have to be extremely careful at work. I don't go out to bars, though Manny does. I can't go through again what happened at home. It would kill me."

"And now I show up like a stab out of the past. I bet you never in your wildest dreams imagined I was living here in the same city."

He pressed his lips together as if afraid of saying too much. "I want to be honest with you, Nathan. It wasn't a complete shock."

"What? Someone told you I was here?"

He looked down, put his hand to his forehead and rubbed it. "Our mothers are on the same hospital auxiliary. Of course they knew each other, but they avoided speaking because of...well, you know why. One day they were in a situation where, as ladies of a certain social class, it would have been odd not to have a polite exchange. My mother asked about you and your brother. Your mom said you were studying at Tulane."

"And it never occurred to you to look me up?"

"To accomplish what? Of course I wanted the best for you, but I hoped your course in life would be different."

"You still believe whether I see you or not is going to change my future? Who knows why we keep getting thrown together? Some may say it's a higher design and others it's purely random. But we can't deny it's happened. And of course, there's the fact that you saved my life."

"What are you talking about?"

"When I was seven, I came close to drowning in the country club pool. You dived in to save me."

"That was you? I had no idea."

"The hero jumps in to save the day and disappears, not waiting around to claim his just recognition."

"Anyone would have done it."

"But it wasn't anyone. It was you."

"I guess I could say you saved my life too. I wouldn't have done well in jail."

"And don't forget I tried to save you from eating that unhealthy pizza by dropping it on the ground."

"One thing I always liked about you was your sense of humor."

To hear him say he always liked something about me, anything, set off a patter in my heart. "It's a coping mechanism. I learned that term in one of my psychology classes."

"Is that your major?"

"Yep. I'm already doubtful it's going to unlock any mysteries, why we are the way we are or why certain people come in and out of our lives."

"I've started going to this new church called the Metropolitan Community Church. One of its central beliefs is we are equal in the eyes of God, including people who are considered deviants in other churches for who they love. I'm still skeptical, but it has given me some peace."

"Would you say you and Manny are in love the same way as any heterosexual couple?"

"Another thing I always liked about you was your fearlessness in asking the questions, usually questions I can't answer. Manny has provided me with the companionship I never thought possible. We have different needs. He needs to go out and be social. I'm happy staying at home. Living under the same roof as someone you care about and cares about you is nothing to speak lightly of."

"That's not exactly what I asked."

"Like I said before, we take each day as it comes."

"Let me try a more practical question. Now that we know we're in the same city, will we see each other?"

"You mean like the three of us going out to dinner? Or 'Hey, Manny, I invited the pizza boy over for a drink.'

I don't want him to know about my past. If I told him you were from my hometown, there would be too many things to explain, starting with why didn't we acknowledge each other at the door."

We heard a loud commotion in the lobby followed by a rowdy group of people entering the bar. Most likely they had just gotten back from Bourbon Street and wanted a nightcap. They laughed and spoke in elevated decibels as they passed by in a cloud of perfume and cologne. At the bar, they leaned on the counter or perched on stools, anything that would give them support.

One of the women turned around and surveyed the other patrons, eventually homing in on Dr. B. She tossed her mane over her shoulder and did a double take as if she had never seen a man so beautiful. She turned to her friend to make a comment, and the two of them attempted to correct their postures and engage in furtive glances at our table. One of the men kept asking the women what they wanted to drink, and they ignored him. The group was difficult to disregard if only for the comedy they provided, but I couldn't let distraction interfere with our conversation.

"And what about the two of us meeting as we're doing now?"

He glanced at the women and back at me. "I've finally gotten my life into calmer waters. It's not perfect by any means, but I don't want to jeopardize the relative peace."

"So, you don't give a shit what happens to me?"

"That is the farthest thing from the truth. I'm not saying I never want to see you. Give me some time. You as well. You need to focus on school."

I shook my head. "You're blowing me off." I stood up and pointed at the women. "I leave you to the vultures." I walked out of the bar but not too fast. My dramatic exit was calculated to get him to come after me, apologize for being insensitive, offer to get together again, suggest we get in the car and drive until we found another, kinder world.

I waited until I got to my car to turn around. The street was empty. So be it. I was desperate to get home so I could call Cindy. I was glad it was two hours earlier in California.

"Calm down, Nate. What is it?"

"He's here. Right here in fucking New Orleans. And he knew I was here, but he never tried to contact me."

"Okay. Back up. How did you find out?"

I told her the story of delivering the pizza to his house, how the guy he lived with is someone I had met. "I am absolutely convinced we are all men on a chessboard being played by a sadistic master."

"Did he tell you about going to visit Judy at her college?"

"We didn't talk about Judy. But wait. You talked to Judy? Please don't tell me you knew he was in New Orleans."

"I...I only found out a couple of months ago."

"That is fucked up, Cindy. That is totally fucked up." I slammed down the phone. A minute later it rang.

"Please don't hang up. I'm sorry. I agonized over whether to tell you or not. I felt like you had moved on. Even you said so. What's to be gained by dredging up the past?"

"Honesty, a world where people tell the truth. I'm so sick of people lying and hiding." I remembered my days as Mayor of Oak Street, all the secrets people kept, and all the other people who enabled them. Back then, I learned people had secrets, even in the most innocuous of places. What I had learned since was how destructive the hiding could be.

"Your sentiment is absolutely correct and high-minded, and then there is reality. Don't tell me you've never told a lie or hidden things in order not to hurt people. Have you communicated to your parents your feelings about men? Have you told your brother?"

If she only knew the secrets I held, the home invasions I had never told her or any living soul about—with the exception of Danny, no longer a living soul—the time I had spent in Dr. B's closet as a Peeping Tom, how recently I had snuck into Marc's apartment and spent time in his room. I felt ashamed.

"Point taken. I don't want to fight with you. I have so few people I can talk to. I only wonder why everyone is trying to protect me, as if knowing Dr. B was in the same city would make me hysterical."

"Uh…I'm not going to answer that."

"You think I'm hysterical?"

"I think you feel deeply. It is one of the best and worst things about you."

"What do you think I should do about Dr. B?"

"You can't force it, Nate. Write him a letter and tell him you're sorry you stormed out on him. Give him your phone number. Let him make a move. But you have to understand he might not. You also have to sit down and think long and hard about what you want if he does contact you. Don't pull out those tarnished fantasies you have about him and try to polish them. Think in a new way."

"Why can't you and I fall in love, get married, and live happily ever after?"

"Another thing I'm not going answer. You know why."

"People try it, at least the first part. Look at Dr. B and Jill."

"And look what happened. I would *not* shoot your secret lover. I would shoot you."

"That's not funny, and yet, it kind of is."

*

In the next week, I wrote Dr. B a letter as Cindy had suggested. No return address on the envelope in case Manny saw it. I made a great effort to follow the rest of her advice, but the flesh is weak. I drove by his house multiple times while I was out delivering pizzas. A few times I pulled over and watched the house. It was only the pizzas going cold that forced me to move on.

Near the end of September, Kevin and I went to an It's a Beautiful Day concert at the Warehouse. When we got home, there was a letter with simply my name on the wrinkled envelope. Ricky said Betsy had given it to him. I opened it with trembling hands.

Cher,

I'm sorry so much time passed and no letter from me. I told you I'm no good at letter writing. That doesn't mean I haven't thought about you and your blue eyes. Guess what? I'm learning German. Also my old army base referred some work to me as a private contractor repair technician. That way I won't starve to death. Ha ha.

I hope things are going well in school. Before you know it you will be a college graduate. Put me to shame.

Well, like I said I'm no good at letter writing. I just want to say hi and tell you I'm okay. At the bottom is my address. You can write me if you feel like it. Maybe you forgot me already. I don't forget you never, no.

Yours toujours,
Marc

Not a single word about the girlfriend. Nothing about his plans. No date, so I had no idea when it was written. He had barely said anything, and still it made me cry. Both the men I loved had thrown me crumbs in the last month, Dr. B telling me he liked something about me, and Marc saying he would never forget me. I wondered if it was better than nothing. I would show them. I would drop out of school and go live on the beaches of Mexico. Fuck them. I fell asleep holding the letter in my hands.

The next day before starting my delivery shift, I stopped by to talk to Betsy and see if she had any more information about Marc. A young man I had never seen answered the door. Betsy wasn't home. Right inside the door was a stack of boxes with Marc's name on them.

"Do you live here?"

"Yeah. I moved into Marc's room."

My heart sank. I had tested him, and he ran away. Now it seemed he had no intention of returning.

I had a couple of Obetrol in the glove compartment of my car. I took both. I was in free fall and needed to even myself out. I needed to emerge from the fuzziness, feel part of the world again. I needed to go out there and deliver those pizzas, make money, participate in the grand scheme of making the world go round. A short time later, I laughed at my notion of going to live on the beaches of Mexico. I chatted up my customers, smiled and made jokes. They gave me tips. Stuffing the money in the left front pocket of my jeans gave me a thrill beyond the simple value of the money.

Nineteen: Up Stairs

Sherry, Lucius, and I walked down Iberville Street toward Chartres. They had been trying for months to convince me to go to a gay bar, but I had a feeling if I crossed that threshold, there would be no turning back. They convinced me the Up Stairs Lounge was different from other bars, a safe space that catered more to blue-collar men and veterans, a few teachers and doctors and regular guys, instead of the effete clientele of some of the bars or the down and dirty of the sleaze bars. It was a community where everyone was welcome. I was buzzed and felt like I could handle any challenge. I felt pretty and witty and gay, as the song goes.

"Damn, girlfriend," Lucius said when I showed up at their place, "you didn't have to be looking so good. Nobody is going to even notice me." That afternoon I had put lemon juice on my hair and sat out in the sun. I bought a new, dark blue Mexican shirt with white and rust embroidery down the front and on the sleeves. I wore a pair of tight faded jeans that flared slightly over my lace-up, appropriately scuffed boots that added to my height.

Lucius took Sherry by the arm. "I just talked to Manny. He's going to be there tonight." Every time I was with Sherry, I had to bite my tongue not to say anything about Manny's lover, a word I hated, but it seemed to be the popular term for someone who was more than a trick. Perhaps I was only jealous someone could use that term referring to Dr. B. But I had promised Dr. B I wouldn't mention our previous connection, and I kept that promise.

We came to a dark awning with the words Up Stairs discreetly written on it in cursive. The door looked like a back entrance. We climbed up the old, creaky wooden stairs. The walls were lined with burlap, which didn't completely cover the pipes and electrical wiring against the brick walls. The dim lighting made me feel like I was entering the shadows. We heard music and laughter from above, and the smell of cigarette smoke was strong.

"Get ready," said Sherry. "The bartender, Buddy, keeps a microphone behind the bar and makes announcements of who's entering like we're going to a formal ball. It's fun, but it's also a way to keep track of who enters. It's a good thing you're going with us. Strangers are looked on with suspicion...until they're accepted, of course."

"Look, ladies and gentlemen," a voice rang out as we entered the bar. "It's Lucius back amongst the living, and the fabulous Sherry. And wait, who is this lovely vision? Welcome, sweetheart." Buddy stored the mic and came out from behind the bar to greet us.

Sherry put her hand on Nate's shoulder. "This is our good friend, Nate." And in a lower voice, "It's his first time."

"Here?" said Buddy.

"Anywhere."

"Ooooh. I guess we'll have to show him a good time."

"Humph," said Lucius. "Look, there's Manny. He's got a table."

The tawdry décor surprised me with its red fabric looped across the ceiling, red-flocked wallpaper, and red bar stools. How did all these normal-looking men, who were obviously not waiting to choose their dates from a lineup of scantily dressed women, end up in what looked like a French cathouse? I had expected a more flamboyant crowd, a room full of Luciuses. Instead, I might have been walking into a Tulane debate club meeting. But as the night wore on and the liquor flowed, the feathers came out, the hands danced in the air, and the laughter rose.

The music was kept low, so that people could converse. Eartha Kitt sang "C'est Si Bon," and I thought of Marc, but promptly tried to rid myself of the lump in my throat.

Sherry got drinks, and we sat down with Manny and a couple of his friends. Lucius and Manny started their usual bitch banter. "Manny, why so down in the mouth? Didn't get any last night? Trouble in paradise?"

I cringed, not only at the cattiness, but the fact he was talking about Dr. B, someone who would die at hearing his sex life talked about in public.

"And how are your relationships, my dear?" Manny said. "I heard you been entertaining all the boys at Cabrini Playground."

Sherry looked at me and shook her head. "You don't need to know."

A young man in horn-rimmed glasses and a sweater vest across the table leaned over to Sherry. "And where did you find this lovely creature?"

"He was my good friend at Tulane before I dropped out."

"You're not in a fraternity, are you?" Everyone at the table turned to me with concern on their faces.

I smiled. "Do I look like I'm in a fraternity?"

"Not really. You're much too cute."

"You're much too kind." The Obetrol was doing its magic, allowing me to flirt without realizing what I was doing.

Throughout the night, every time I said I was at Tulane, the next question was if I was in a fraternity. After a while I started saying, "I go to Tulane, but I'm *not* in a fraternity." I took Sherry aside and asked her what the deal was with Tulane and fraternities. She explained there had been incidents of frat boys luring guys out of gay bars while their buddies waited outside to beat up the victim in the old tradition of "rolling a queer." Sherry growled. "Can you believe that one time those motherfuckers beat a gay man to death and got off scot-free?"

Later, Buddy picked up the microphone and announced, "Our new Tulane guy is Nate. He is *not* in a fraternity." Laughter rolled through the bar. I laughed, but my laughter was immediately followed by a chill that flowed from head to toe. It was, in a sense, my coming out, my name announced in a room of homosexuals.

In line for the bathroom, I talked to a nice-looking man who said he was a lineman for the utility company. His friend jumped in. "Yeah, he likes to climb poles." He had an annoying snicker.

"Don't mind him." Jerry spoke with a Southern accent. "He's from West Texas, poor guy. I'm Jerry by the way."

"I'm Nate."

"And you're *not* in a fraternity."

I put my hand over my face as if blushing. "I'm embarrassed for my school."

"I can't imagine you hurting a flea."

"I once killed ten mosquitoes in a night. There was blood everywhere."

"I beat up a guy one time for calling me a fag. I was in the Marines." He wore a thermal Henley shirt that showed off his physique. "I'm not saying I'm violent, but I don't take any shit."

"I wish you had been around a couple years ago when a friend and I hitchhiked through the Florida panhandle. I thought these two rednecks were going to kill us. We managed to run away."

"Where were you hitching to?"

"West Palm Beach Pop Festival."

He tilted his head and winked at me. "You're kind of a hippie, huh?"

"I guess if I was a true hippie, I wouldn't be at Tulane."

"I've got some good weed at home."

"I'm here with some friends."

"A boyfriend?"

"This is all new to me."

"I screwed up, didn't I? Telling you I beat somebody up. That was stupid."

His friend had been listening to our conversation all along. "I can assure you Jerry is a gentleman, unless of course you don't want him to be."

"Shut up, Frank." And to me, "Sorry."

He had kind eyes. I wasn't necessarily afraid of him, but I felt awkward. Ending up in bed with Marc had been a logical conclusion to a series of organic events, as if the planets had lined up to bring us together. Going home with someone from a bar felt artificial. My mind flipped through the options, examining each from different angles. My body, on the other hand, was jumping up and down at the fact this person wanted to take me home for sex, or at least I assumed that was what was happening. Maybe he only wanted to smoke a joint with someone. Sherry, help!

He looked at me with a grin. "I can almost see your brain going like a pinball machine. No big deal, man."

"You seem like a good guy, and...uh...good-looking."

"You are so cute, and kind of a flirt." His friend came out of the stall. "My turn. See you later." And he was gone.

I returned to the table in an ornery mood. As far as I knew, Manny hadn't mentioned me showing up at their door as the pizza boy. I was ready for mischief. "Ordered any pizza lately?" I said to him. Both Sherry and Lucius were involved in other conversations.

He grinned and patted his stomach. "I think I need go on a diet. No more pizza."

"I don't know. That pepperoni and mushroom is one of our top sellers. Was that your choice or your...uh... roommate?"

He looked at me strangely. "We both like it. Why you say roommate?"

"I wasn't introduced. I didn't know if he was the famous mysterious lover or not."

"Well, he is."

"Okay. Piano player, huh? Very cultured. I'm guessing he's some kind of professional. Doctor maybe?"

Manny glanced at Sherry with a look pleading for help. She stopped the conversation with the person next to her and watched us instead.

"We have an agreement not to discuss our relationship outside the house."

"Not even with friends? I would think you'd be proud to have such a handsome and distinguished lover."

"Excuse me. I have to go to the bathroom." Manny got up and left the table.

"What was that all about? He looked freaked," said Sherry.

"Nothing."

"I saw you talking to that guy in line for the men's room."

"He's cute, isn't he?" I turned around to look for him. He was sitting a couple tables over. I smiled and gave him a half-interested wave.

"He's cruising you." In a short time, Sherry had become totally integrated into the community. She knew all the lingo.

"Nah. He's just being friendly."

"Here he comes."

I introduced Jerry to the others. He sat down in Manny's chair. Our knees touched. I leaned in close to him.

"Do you want to get out of here?" My crotch trumped my head. Surprise. Surprise. He put his hand on my leg in affirmation. We stood up. Sherry gave me a worried look. "We're going to catch a bite to eat," I said.

When we got outside, Jerry gave me a light punch on the arm. "A bite to eat?"

"In a manner of speaking."

We walked to his shotgun apartment on the other side of Esplanade in the Faubourg Marigny. He cleared clothes and newspapers off the couch and offered me a seat. He put on some Janis Joplin.

"I saw her at that festival I went to. A year later she was gone."

"The one in West Palm Beach?"

"You actually listen."

"I always listen to people I'm curious about." He rolled a joint, and we smoked it.

"You don't have to be a gentleman, you know."

He got up, took my hand, and led me into the bedroom. The musty smell of dirty laundry was in the air, and the bed was unmade. "I wasn't expecting company."

Less than an hour later, I walked down Rampart to where I had parked my car. I ruminated over my new persona, a person who had gone home with someone from a bar. I now knew I was capable of doing something I had always thought I was too shy to do. I also felt guilty I had used Jerry to prove a point. The sex was fine, not earth-shattering, though I wasn't sure what I was supposed to feel as it was only the second time to "go all the way," as Marc used to say.

When I said goodbye to Jerry at the door, I saw in his eyes he longed to know me better, an expression I would become quite familiar with over the next year. Overnight, I had become the hard one rather than the longing one. I wanted no phone numbers or second dates. The uppers helped me develop my ego strength, allowing me to harness my chaotic and unreasonable id. I was done with pining after someone, I told myself while driving down St. Charles Avenue in the mercurial hours of the night.

I hadn't heard anything from Dr. B, not even an acknowledgement of my letter. I had written close to twenty letters to Marc but torn them all to bits. Knowing I had a few friends I could count on was all that kept me from sliding into depression. I also now had a path to fulfilling my sexuality without experiencing emotional breakdowns. I was soon to learn my new persona came with an exorbitant price tag.

I occasionally went to Up Stairs with Sherry and Lucius, but not to hook up. Everything was too much in the spotlight. I preferred clubs where darkness reigned, where I didn't have to tell my name. I looked for new faces, out-of-towners. I still wasn't crazy about alcohol, so in order not to sit around for hours nursing drinks, I would work swiftly, spot my mark, and hone in. I didn't go for any particular type. It depended on my mood, the situation, availability. I never invited anyone to my house, both out of respect to my roommates and to avoid the awkwardness of having to kick someone out. Many of them wanted to fuck me, but some wanted me to do them or flip-flop. I learned how to do all of it.

I broke my promise to myself of primarily using uppers for studying. Every drug became a recreational drug. I couldn't always find Obetrol, so I would take Ritalin or Dexedrine. I would stay up for a couple days and then crash with barbiturates, Quaaludes, or Valium if that was all there was. I was aware of the dangers. Whenever I thought of Danny, or famous people who had OD'd, I put it out of my mind. I had always been able to control my habits, so much so that none of the people close to me knew I was a speed freak. Until they did.

My grades started slipping. I lost weight. People kept telling me I looked like I needed sleep. Cindy telephoned me.

"I've left several messages, but you didn't return my call. The last time I called, I had a long talk with Kevin."

"And?"

"He's worried about you."

"Kevin should mind his own business."

"Are you doing drugs?"

"Oh, I'm sorry. Have you joined the narc squad? Forgive me. I smoke marijuana, and I've tried hallucinogens. Why only yesterday I took an aspirin for a headache." I heard myself being an asshole to one of my oldest and dearest friends, and I didn't care.

"You don't sound like yourself. Please, Nate, if you've gotten yourself into something you can't control, get help."

"You know me, always in control. You're worrying for no reason. I'm sorry I was snippy before. I appreciate your concern, but it bugs me people are talking about me behind my back."

I had this creepy feeling Cindy might be worried enough she would call my parents. I couldn't let that happen. I had made up a bogus excuse for not going home for the holidays. As I knew my mom would be upset about my weight loss and the bags under my eyes, I told them I was working on a research project for one of my professors, and we were way behind schedule. But I had a feeling they didn't believe me.

"Kevin says he tries to talk to you, but you brush him off."

"Look, there's nothing to worry about. I'll talk to Kevin when he gets home tonight." By the end of the conversation, I had brought Cindy down from her cloud of concern.

Of course, I had no intention of talking to Kevin. We had grown distant. We hadn't gone to a concert together in months, my fault, and we rarely saw each other since he spent a lot of time at Susan's. Ricky liked to say we were the two best roommates he'd ever had—he never saw us.

The one thing in my life that ran like clockwork was my job delivering pizzas. I couldn't afford to screw that up. I needed the money for my "medications." One night, I delivered a vegetarian pizza to a man who looked vaguely familiar, maybe from one of the bars. He gave me a big tip and lingered at the door, staring at me like I was Michelangelo's *David*. "What time do you get off?"

I gave him a wry smile. "About the same time you do."

It took him a minute, but the light eventually went on behind his eyes. "Oooh."

"See you about ten thirty."

After that, I started getting a lot of deliveries for middle-aged men who had a lot more on their minds than pizza. Friends of the vegetarian? How efficient. Work and sex at the same time.

One night I went to the Hotel Monteleone with a man from St. Louis old enough to be my father. He had a flattop and glasses and wore a sports jacket over a golf shirt. He wanted me to talk dirty to him. After we did it, I had a sick feeling. When I put on my pants, I found two ten-dollar bills in my pocket.

"What's this?"

"Oh, I'm sorry. I should have asked you what your rate was. I can give you another ten."

I took the bills and threw them on the floor. "I don't want your money."

"But you must take it." He looked at me in astonishment. "You mean you're just in it for the sex? If I had known that, I never would have invited you to the hotel. That doesn't interest me."

"I'm not a prostitute," I protested.

"Oh, I see. You think you are so superior to someone who makes an exchange of money for sex. What a fine upstanding young man you are!"

I had one of those extremely rare moments in my life when I wanted to bust someone's jaw. My fist was clenched. It frightened me more than him. He might have liked it.

"Fuck you." I walked out the door.

Over the next few months, I lost track of how many men I had sex with. My tolerance for speed made me keep increasing the dose. I had to scramble to find more sources for drugs. It got so as every time I saw an overweight girl, I thought about asking her if she could score for me. Great pickup line. "Hi there. Have you thought about diet pills?"

I called one of my Obetrol sources back home to see if she could send me some. She told me that the biggest prescriber in town, Dr. Wahl, had been busted. Huge scandal. Things were dry, but she would see what she could do.

*

I sat at the bar. I was on my second vodka tonic, which was rare for me. My hands were shaking so much it was hard to hold the glass. The bottles behind the bar blurred. I had been having trouble with my vision. A guy at the other end of the bar seemed to be staring at me, but I wasn't sure.

I had run out of my meds. Fine, I thought. I would kick it. Get my life under control. I wasn't at the bar to pick someone up. I thought a few drinks would calm me down.

The man I thought had been staring now sat next to me. He wore a black motorcycle jacket and had a dark beard peppered with gray. "Looks like you could use a little something."

"I don't know what you mean."

"Uh-huh. I could see it from across the room. You can barely hold your glass."

"Just nervous. I'm new to this."

"You can't bullshit me. I know a freak when I see one. What do you do? Pills? Snort? Shoot?"

"Shoot? God, no. I take pills sometimes. Obetrol is my preferred."

"Got some of that."

"But I'm getting off it."

"You can't go cold turkey. You need a little bump to take the edge off."

A short time later, we were in his hotel room. He opened some capsules and crushed the tiny beads into a powder. He rolled up a dollar bill. "There you go."

I had never snorted before. It burned my nostrils like hell, and the taste in the back of my throat was nasty. But a minute later I was flying. After days sober, it was a gift from the gods. Not only was the effect nearly immediate, it was more intense. I jumped up and shouted, "Yowza!" I paced the room. "Yes, yes, yes."

"Slow down, partner." He grabbed me and threw me on the bed. He smashed his beard into my face in what I assumed was supposed to be a kiss. In my euphoric pacing. I hadn't noticed him taking off his jacket and T-shirt and didn't honestly care what he looked like. His entire torso was covered with hair, and with my heightened senses, his body odor had the power of a thousand men in a thousand locker rooms. I didn't want sex. I wanted to go out and conquer the world. I detached from what happened next as if looking from above.

How I got home was a blur. Nobody was in the apartment. In the bathroom I looked at my dilated pupils. There were bruise marks on my neck. I lifted my shirt. Bruises on my torso. Scenes of rough sex flashed in my head. That couldn't have been me. I turned out the light and left the house. I walked around the neighborhood. I half walked half ran to the twenty-four-hour market. I bought a Gatorade and drank it down.

On the way home, I flashed on the hairy beast shaking some pills into my hand, telling me I needed to chill.

I stuck my hand in my pocket to touch the Seconal, red dolls people liked to call them. My heart thumped wildly. I panicked I would keep spiraling up into the sky until I touched the moon. A man walked parallel with me on the other side of the street, and I was convinced he was going to rob me or attack me. I ran until I arrived home. At the kitchen sink, I popped all the pills in my mouth and drank a glass of water.

"Wada. Wada," I said out loud.

Twenty: Under

Muffled conversations surrounded me as if I was sinking to the bottom of a swimming pool.

"I think he said doctor. Should we call the doctor?"

"But what's the B? I'm sure I heard Dr. B. Over and over."

I'm drowning here. Can someone help me? It kept getting darker, no longer seeming like a pool, but the ocean, the Challenger Deep, its deepest part. *Somebody, please.*

Sometime later, I opened my eyes. A day? A week? A month? My first sensation was someone holding my hand.

Dr. B leaned over me. "Hey, there."

"I must be in heaven." My voice sounded hollow, weak.

"Do I look like I have wings?" With his other hand, he touched the top of my head. He opened my eyelids and looked at my pupils. A moment later, I was gone again.

The next time I woke up. Sherry was sitting by my bed. "Hi, Nate. So nice to see you." I must have looked at her strangely. "Were you expecting someone else?"

"I guess I dreamed it."

"You mean Dr. B?"

"Was he here?"

"For hours and hours."

"You know about Dr. B then?"

"The cat's out of the bag."

"Manny?"

"Everybody knows."

"He was here for...hours..." I couldn't finish the sentence. My chest heaved. Tears streamed down my cheeks. I lost myself in uncontrollable weeping.

Sherry took my hand and laid her head on top of mine. "Here, here, now. He'll be back."

"I was so stupid. I should have died." I choked out the words between gasps.

"A lot of people are glad you didn't. Kevin has been here a couple of times. Lucius, Ricky, Betsy, Meredith too. Some guy named Jerry who kind of looked familiar. Don't know how he found out. I talked to Cindy twice. She cried like a baby. The two of us were on the phone for about ten minutes, doing nothing but crying our pea-picking eyes out."

"I'm sorry."

"Dear heart, don't be sorry. We're the ones should be sorry. All this going on under our noses, and we didn't see it. You were screaming for help."

"More like whimpering. And my parents?"

"That was a tough decision. We left it up to Dr. B. He felt confident you were going to come out okay, so we didn't make the call."

"Thank you, Dr. B. You saved my life again. How much did he tell you?"

"Basically, that he was your neighbor, and he had to leave town due to a scandal—but it didn't involve you. No details. That was hilarious about you showing up as the pizza boy."

"You have no idea. Is Manny pissed?"

"Manny is having a hard time, especially since the doctor has barely been home in days."

"I'm so fucking weak."

Dr. B walked in the door. "I heard that. You are not weak, but maybe you weren't strong enough to handle the pain by yourself. We're not going to worry about that now. Today, we are celebrating that you're alive. Tomorrow we get to work." He came to my bedside and laid a hand on my arm.

"Work?"

"Detox clinic. But we're not talking about that now."

"Sherry told me I wasn't dreaming when I woke up and saw you there." My eyes welled up with tears again. I struggled to get out the words. "You don't know how important that was to me."

Sherry sniffled. "Damn it, Nate. Don't start again. You'll get me going."

He examined my pupils, checked the IV, and told me to open my mouth, a ploy to distract me more than anything. Though he wore a lab coat and a stethoscope around his neck, he wasn't the doctor attending me. I remembered he was a gynecologist. He touched my neck where it seemed I still had bruises since a pained look crossed his face. "As a matter of fact, you are strong. I'm expecting a full recovery."

"Then why do I feel so awful?" Every inch of my body ached, and the longer I was awake, the worse it got.

"It will pass. Are you hungry at all?"

"Can you stop doctoring and simply be my friend for a minute?"

"You know what?" said Sherry. "I'm going to step out and get a cup of coffee."

Dr. B fell into the chair, his eyes watery. "You scared the shit out of me." He sniffed and pulled the tears back in. "And another thing, I think it's time you started calling me Nick. The Dr. B thing takes me back there."

"I would love to call you Nick, as often as possible. Or maybe Nicholas since you always call me Nathan. You're like the only one except my mother when she's mad at me."

"Look who's getting sassy already. It's good to see."

"Thanks for not telling my parents. When I'm better, I'm going to see them. I have a lot to tell them."

"I think it best you leave my name out of it." He took my hand. "I have to go on rounds. I'll be back later." He turned around at the door. "Nathan, I'm so glad you're still with us. Things are going to be different."

The monstrous pain inside me became even more evident when they took me to the detox unit the next day. The tremors rattled me like I was nothing more than a bag of bones. I had pain from my crown to the soles of my feet, and the crying continued. Nightmares made me wake up screaming. They didn't allow me visitors, except Nick was able to get in. One day, he walked in when the untouched food tray sat by my bed.

"Will you take this fucking shit away? It's disgusting."

"Rage on, Macduff."

"What?"

"Macduff in *Macbeth*. Shakespeare."

"What the hell! You're so fucking corny. Shakespeare? At a time like this?"

A few minutes later, I was sobbing. "I'm sorry. So sorry. Forgive me." And when it was time for him to leave. "Don't leave me here alone, please." I wailed and ranted and knocked the food tray on the floor. The nurse came in with a needle.

It got better. I got stronger. They said I could go home after a week, but they recommended rehab. They took me out to Nick's car in a wheelchair. I was still weak. We got to my house, and Nick opened the door. There was a banner over the archway into the living room that said "Welcome home, Nate" along with a lot of familiar faces: Kevin, Susan, Sherry, Ricky, Betsy, Meredith, Lucius, and Marilu. I broke down crying, of course. They hugged me one by one and then put me in a chair and let me bawl. Sherry had made a lot of healthy food. Marilu brought wheatgrass juice.

When things calmed down, I motioned for Kevin to come over to my chair. "Can you forgive me?"

"Oh, shut up. I should be asking for forgiveness. We all fucked up. I miss my concert buddy. There are some great shows coming up at the Warehouse when you're feeling up to it."

"Soon, I hope."

After about an hour, everyone left except Ricky, Kevin, Sherry, and Nick. It looked too choreographed to be normal. Nick called us into the dining room, and everyone took a seat.

"Nathan, you've been doing great."

"Not sure the nurses in the detox unit would say that."

"They've seen much worse." He cleared his throat and looked around the room, making eye contact with everyone. "Sherry and I have done a lot of research. You could go to a structured rehab program, or you could try a plan we've come up with."

"What if I don't want to do either?"

"There's no do-it-on-your-own option. We have to be honest. Even in structured rehab programs, success rates are not stellar."

"That's why we've come up with our own plan," said Sherry. "All four people here today are committed to it. Please hear us out."

Dr. B continued. "You will live here, but one of us will be with you at all times. We have a schedule how things will work."

"For how long?"

"A month of twenty-four-hour attention. Another month with some down time."

"No way. You guys can't do that. It's not fair to you."

"We're all committed," said Kevin. "Ricky and I will take nights, logically."

"Betsy and Meredith have offered to fill in. Sherry will coordinate food, *healthy* food." She had started working at a vegetarian restaurant called Jerusalem Gardens and was studying nutrition on the side.

"Lots of walks, bike rides, picnics in the park," said Sherry. "It will be good for all of us."

I had always been independent, spent a lot of time by myself. Now I had a babysitter around the clock. I wasn't a particularly pleasant charge of my caretakers, often irritable. I had powerful cravings for the drug I had been taking since I was fifteen. Before the crash, I had discovered snorting, and I constantly thought about the super rush it gave me. I would dream about crushing the granules into powder. I had told my friends I was out of drugs, and it was true. I got angry with myself for not hiding some somewhere. I would also dream about opening a cabinet or a drawer and seeing a bottle of pills behind a can of tomato sauce or lifting up cushions of the sofa and finding a pill, which had fallen in the crack.

Sherry went to a lot of trouble making healthy food for me, which I would throw in the garbage after she left and beg Kevin to take me for a burger and fries. Fast food made me nauseous, but it tasted better going down. Marilu sometimes came by with shots of bitter, pungent wheatgrass juice and stood over me like a mental ward nurse until I drank it. I knew my friends were taking care of me out of love—not to mention a bit of guilt for not recognizing the signs—but reeducating an addict's body, mind, and spirit is the most difficult thing you can do, and success rates weren't great. I was bored to the point of tears and thinking about a future without the euphoria of speed sent me into bouts of depression.

The people who took the day shift tried to come up with ever more creative ways to get me out of bed in the morning. Sherry came over with a stack of books one day. She lined them up on my bed while I turned my face to the wall and burrowed deeper under the covers. She rested a book on my back. "You've got to read this one. You'll love it."

I shrugged my body, causing the book to slide off. She pulled back the covers and put it in front of my face. "Trust me on this one."

I opened my eyes and read the cover. E. M. Forster. *Maurice*. "Great, an Edwardian novel. I'm sure I can relate to that."

She retrieved the book. "Listen to this. 'In a highly structured society, Maurice is a conventional young man in every way, except that he is homosexual.' They couldn't publish it until after Forster's death it was so controversial. It's a love story between an upper-class rich kid and a groundskeeper."

"Do they commit suicide in the end?"

"The ending is hopeful. But you have to read it yourself."

I had tried reading recently, but it had been hard to concentrate. I would read a few pages and fall asleep. I seemed to be tired all the time. *Maurice* was the novel that got me back into reading, and reading was invaluable in getting me through that first month. Despite the stilted language, the story was moving. Tears? Many. And yes, I fantasized Marc crawling in my window in the middle of the night the way Scudder had in the book.

The therapist who tried to cure Maurice of his homosexuality by using hypnosis eventually admitted failure and suggested he move to a country that had adopted the Napoleonic code like France or Italy. In those places, homosexuality had been decriminalized. When Maurice asked if there might ever be a law like that in England, the therapist said that the British had always been reluctant to accept human nature.

The original plan for my education had been to study French and international business and possibly to live in France. I had gotten caught up in the *zeitgeist* of everyone wanting to understand human behavior and changed my major to psychology. If I ever went back to school, I thought I should return to my original plan. Life in France might be easier as I had little hope the United States was going to change.

The best thing about the surveillance schedule was spending time with Nick. I came to know him as a person, but getting to know someone I had idolized since I was a young teenager, someone who had sparked my sexual awakening, had its drawbacks. I was forced to recognize flaws: his propensity for settling for undeserving partners, his fear of exposure, his tendency to avoid what was difficult. He was like the rest of us.

We walked along a path in Audubon Park on a glorious sunny day as swans glided effortlessly on the pond beside us. I prodded him, with a mixture of mischief and real curiosity, about his relationship. "How is Manny doing?"

He raised his eyebrows and sighed. "He's fine. His work at the hospital is going well. He's thinking of going to nursing school."

"You know that's not what I mean. It can't be easy for him with you spending so much time with me."

"I told him it was something I had to do."

"Had to save me because you somehow felt responsible? I'm getting bored with you thinking every decision I make goes back to a teenage infatuation I may or may not have had for a doctor down the street. I'm responsible for everything I do, not you."

"When did you start taking diet pills?"

I let him change the subject. Too much gray area in the incidents that led to his tragic fall. I kept insisting that knowing him hadn't influenced me in any way, though I knew it had. I had come to believe the underlying attractions I had for men were innate. Those feelings sought a focus in the real world, and if the only one had been a horny scoutmaster, I might have kept them bottled up until I was better prepared to handle them. Some people keep their desires locked inside for years or even whole lifetimes. Being confronted with the image of a person of great stature in the community and of obvious physical beauty having sex with another man was something I couldn't unsee. It left its mark.

"I started when I was high school, sophomore year I think. A lot of kids were doing it. Did you know Judy was taking them?"

"Did she give them to you?"

I laughed. "She barely gave me the time of day. No. They were easily available." A few secrets like the fact that I stole my first Obetrol from Judy still had to be kept. In the recovery literature Sherry brought me, honesty and asking forgiveness of those I had wronged were important tenets. I struggled with that.

If my neighbors had been unaware I invaded their sacred space and discovered their secrets, was I obligated to ask for their forgiveness? Asking them for forgiveness would only cause more pain. Then I would have to ask them to forgive me for the new pain of bringing their secrets out by asking for forgiveness. Where would it end?

"I didn't know Judy was taking them at first. Her mother did. Keeping her weight down was so important for her to be on the cheerleading squad. I let the current thinking on the matter, that they were safe for weight control, sway me. You know I'm not Judy's natural father, right? Whenever I tried to take control over decisions regarding Judy, they would throw that in my face. Deep down, I knew diet pills were dangerous, but I did nothing."

"Cindy told me you went to see Judy at her college."

"I was cut off from her for a long time. Her grandparents hid or didn't forward the letters I wrote. Finally, I found out where she was going to school and showed up unannounced. Despite everything, we had a pretty good relationship when she was growing up. Those memories, though obscured by the tragedy, were still there, and little by little we were able to bring them to the light of day. We talk."

"I wish her well even though she tried to destroy me."

"We don't talk about those days. I suppose we should. She was a traumatized teenage girl. I know it's not an excuse."

"I've survived. You've survived. Time marches on."

Twenty-One: Wada

When my dreams weren't horrific, they teased me. An insistent voice said, "Cher, wake up. No more *fais do-do*. Come on, we're going on a big adventure." I wanted to stay in the dream, crawl deep into its arms. It felt divine. And then I sensed someone sitting on the bed. It was Sherry's day, and I wondered what scheme she had thought up to get me out of bed this time. A hand rubbed my head.

"Cher, I'm waiting, I am."

I rolled over. It was real. I sat up. I put my hands over my face. The waterworks commenced.

"You motherfucker," I croaked.

"I know." He took my arm and stood up, dragging me with him. "I'm taking you out." Once he got me up on my feet, he rubbed away my tears with his fingers.

I let my head fall against his chest. "I can't. I'm under house arrest."

"It's all cleared with Sherry, yeah." He put his arms around me.

"She knew you were in town? I'm going to kill her."

"It's only been a couple weeks, trying to get settled. I told her not to tell you. I wanted it to be a surprise."

"You might have given me a heart attack, you know."

"I thought you didn't care. You never wrote me, couyon." He stepped back and held me at arm's length. "They told me you looked like shit. You look pretty good to me, yeah."

"I hate you."

"I know. You hate me so much it made you cry like a petite. Now come on. Get dressed."

I grabbed a tissue and blew my nose. "Where are we going?"

"It's a surprise."

Kevin was in the kitchen making coffee and showed no surprise when Marc and I entered. "So, you knew he was in town too. Fuck you all."

"Oh, he's a nasty one today," said Kevin. "Sherry only told me a couple of days ago. And for the record, if I ever have a crisis like yours, I'm going to expect every goddamn important person in my life to show up. You're setting the standard, man." He handed me a cup of coffee.

I pointed at Marc with my thumb. "I wouldn't wish this on anyone. I mean, having to spend the day with this asshole."

"I'm sure you'll have a real boring time." Kevin winked at Marc.

"Me, I just wonder how long he's going to be punishing me. I'm a poor Cajun boy don't know no better."

"You want some coffee, Cajun boy?" said Kevin.

"Nah. Had some already. Bring that in the car, Nate. We got to get on the road."

Kevin shook his finger at them. "No crossing state lines."

We headed east in Marc's old LeSabre. I knew where we were going when we got on Chef Menteur Highway.

The sandbar beach, thankfully unoccupied, was the same as the last time we had been there though the green of the trees didn't seem so vibrant, the smells of the lazy river not so bold, the screech of blue jays not so fierce. My senses felt dulled. Marc spread a blanket and put the basket in a shady place. He took off his shirt and shoes. We lay back and watched the sun filtering through the cypress and oak trees.

"Are we going to talk about Germany?" I said.

"Not yet, no. Today we get to know each other again."

"Will you at least whisper sweet nothings to me in German?"

"Couyon! I think the old Nate is coming back stronger than ever."

"Where are you living?"

"At my parents for the time being. I'm going to start working at the store next week. We should go swimming. Take off your clothes."

"I do declare, sir, you are quite forceful."

He shook his head. "Yep, like I said."

"Seriously, I'm embarrassed."

"About what?"

"I lost a lot of weight. My body is ugly."

"I don't care about that."

"I do."

"The wada will do you good, good."

"God, how I missed you saying wada." Choking up again.

"Don't start."

"I cry all the time. It doesn't mean anything."

"It's nothing more than your emotions bouncing around trying to find level. Come on now. We're going in the wada and wash away dem tears for good." He got behind me and pulled my T-shirt over my head. "Stand up." He remained on his knees. He turned me around, undid the buttons of my baggy jeans, and pulled them down.

"Uh…while you're down there…"

He stood up and slapped my butt. "You got the devil in you, boy." He took my hand and led me to the water. We went in with our underwear on.

We waded out to the middle as the blue jays overhead made a racket. He splashed me, and we dove under. We came up at the same time. I stared at him while he wiped his eyes. With his beard and longish hair, he looked like Jesus in the pictures where he was baptized by John the Baptist.

"What are you looking at?" He dove under and swam upriver. He stood in the middle of the stream now looking like a river god, motioning for me to join him. What choice did I have?

Exercising my arms and legs felt good, but I was exhausted by the time I got to him. I was still weak. "I'll race you back," he said. I petered out about halfway to where we started. I walked the rest of the way, the mud squishing between my toes.

"Are you hungry?"

"Stomach has shrunk to the size of a pea."

"You've got to eat, cher."

"I know."

We got out of the water. Marc pulled off his underwear and hung them on a huckleberry bush. I did the same. "Why, we're as naked as Adam and Eve in the Garden of Eden."

Marc gave me a sidelong glance and grabbed the basket. "I made groceries, bought us a muffuletta to share."

I turned up my nose. "Muffuletta? And by the way, you don't *make* groceries."

"We're out in my country now, and that's how we say it. Am I gonna have to force feed you?"

I gave him an amused look. "I'd like to see you try."

"Got some fruit too. How 'bout I peel an orange?"

"I could eat some orange."

"Good boy."

The explosion of orange in my mouth took me back to the night of the mushrooms, the way I could taste the citrus in Marc's mouth when I kissed him. I wanted to kiss him so bad. *I must behave. I can't push.*

In the car, Marc asked me about Nick.

"What did Sherry tell you?"

"She said he was someone from your past, from where you grew up."

"He lived down the street. Was there something specific you wanted to know?"

"It seems weird how you ended up in the same city."

"The why of it I can't tell you. In the stars, I guess."

"It makes you happy, that, having him here?"

"Of course...on one hand. It's also confusing. When I met him, he was an adult, and I was a kid. Now we're getting to know each other as adults."

"Did he ever...no, don't have a right to ask you that, no."

It felt strangely like a boyfriend asking about a previous lover. But since I had never had a relationship, it was all speculation. "Seduce me? Is that what you're asking?"

"Sherry told me he's gay. Lives with some guy."

"And you think he couldn't have let a hot young thing like me right down the street go unmolested?"

"Grrr. Why you gotta twist everything around? Me, I'm trying to learn about things."

"Sorry. That wasn't fair. He was married with a daughter. I was the gawky kid who used to deliver the paper and mow their lawn. He would never lay a hand on me. But there was a guy in town who was willing and able. It caused a big scandal, and the doctor had to quit his job and leave. He came here thinking New Orleans was more open."

"Did you come here because he was here?"

"I didn't know. Cross my heart. I came here because I heard the Cajun boys were hot."

"You got one thing right."

"I don't know if it was the stars or simply the fickle finger of fate. After you left, I got a job delivering pizzas. One night he opened the door, and there we were."

"Life is crazy sometimes."

"All the time. I never thought I'd see you again."

"You have no faith, brother." He extended a hand to my leg. "I want to be part of your team. Do I have to ask him?"

"I don't know."

"You don't want me on your team?"

"It would put you in a different category."

"What category am I in now?"

"To be determined. I want you as a friend, not my babysitter."

"How am I different from your other friends on the team?"

"You're the only one I've had sex with."

He withdrew his hand. "Oh. Wait. I thought you had sex with Sherry."

"I did. I sort of forgot about that." I couldn't believe I had said that, as if having sex with Sherry hadn't meant anything. It had seemed such a big deal at the time. "I don't want to go straight home. Can we go to a movie?"

"Sure. You got one in mind?"

"I've been wanting to see *Cabaret*."

I guess he hadn't heard what it was about—a young man in a love triangle, struggling with his sexuality in Germany. He kept glancing at me during the film and shaking his head.

We walked in the door, and Sherry was in the kitchen with the latest healthy concoction she had created. "Where have you guys been?"

"We went to a movie."

"You should have called."

"God, Sherry. You sound like my mom. Actually, no. My mom gave me a lot more freedom."

"I'm sorry, Sherry. It was my fault," said Marc. "We had a great day."

I went in my room and slammed the door. Marc came in a minute later. "Go out there and apologize."

"You're going to tell me what to do too? Are you sure you want to be on my team? I'm a bastard sometimes."

"We all know this is hard for you, but Sherry is in there busting her butt for you. Come on."

"All right, I'll apologize. But do I have to eat that godawful food?"

"Couyon."

Marc stayed for dinner, and I forced down as much of the brown rice and vegetables as I could. I hugged Sherry at the door and thanked her for the food and for putting up with me. Ricky was on call for the night. Kevin was at Susan's.

Marc and I went in my room, and I put on some music. "Do you want to spend the night?"

I could see the wheels spinning in Marc's head, slowing down, going backward, speeding up again. His eyebrows came together, and then separated.

I put a hand on his shoulder. "I'm not talking about sex."

"You mean like the night we spent together before I left."

"Exactly like that. You were the last person I spent the night with."

"No way. What do you do for sex?"

"I mean sleeping in the same bed with someone for the whole night. Sex I've had. A lot."

"I don't want to know."

We stripped down to our underwear. "Shit. I think I've got sand in my crack." I opened the dresser and took out a couple of pairs of clean underwear and threw one to Marc. "I'm going to take a shower."

Marc looked at the underwear in his hand. "Don't know, cher. Wearing your underwear is like way too intimate."

"More intimate than…you're pulling my leg."

He laughed.

On the way to the shower, I stuck my head in Rickey's room. "Marc is spending the night."

"Uh…okay."

We lay side-by-side listening to It's a Beautiful Day. I felt at peace.

"*Bonne nuit*," I said.

"Good night, cher."

"Remember frissons?"

"Toujours."

*

My team sat around the dining room table. A meeting all about me. Marc had been invited since he told Sherry he wanted to be on the team. Marc and Nick in the same room, my long-time heartthrob and the first man I had sex with. And they were there because of me. Me. It was the first time they had met. I felt giddy and confused at the same time.

The recovery plan they had devised was impressive and seemed to be working. Kevin was in charge of the twenty-four-hour buddy schedule. Instead of having Obetrol as a study buddy, I now had watchdog buddies to keep the study buddy away.

Sherry researched information on rehab programs and distributed brochures and articles with underlined information appropriate for my situation. Nick gathered treatment suggestions from doctors who had dealt with drug addiction and communicated them to the group. Sherry also made menu suggestions to improve health and prepared meals when she could. Ricky was the entertainment director on the lookout for new movies, plays, art gallery openings, nature walks, lectures, anything to stave off the boredom, a big problem for people used to doing speed.

We had come to the one-month milestone, and three things were on the agenda for the day's meeting. Yes, we had meetings and agendas and goals and recorded notes. The first issue concerned whether Marc would be incorporated into the team or not. Nick opened the discussion, and I could tell he wasn't anxious to make changes in a team that had been successful so far. He asked Marc directly what his plans were for the immediate future and how difficult it would be to get there from Metairie at a moment's notice if need be. Sherry asked me what I thought.

"I want to see Marc. But if he's not on the team, would I need a chaperone?" I wondered if Nick knew about Marc spending the night.

"I personally have complete trust in Marc," said Sherry. "I know he has Nate's best interests at heart."

"Fo' sure that," said Marc.

"But I wonder if maybe we should look at the second item about free time," Sherry continued. The plan called for giving me some time when I could go out alone after the first month. "If you think you're ready for unaccompanied ventures out, maybe you could spend time with Marc then."

"Which brings up the question," said Nick, "about cravings for uppers. Still having them? How strong are they?"

"I have them. They're strong. Life seems incredibly dull sometimes. One thing I always felt when on amphetamines was that I was in charge of my life, that I owned myself. But it was pretty damn scary waking up in the hospital and seeing you, Nick. Oops, that didn't come out the way I meant."

Everybody chuckled in a much-needed release of tension. I saw Nick glance at Marc with a look of pride he had at least been there for me.

"I had all kinds of tubes and hookups to machines. I realized I could have died. I didn't want to die that night I ended up in the hospital, and I don't want to die now. Things had gotten out of hand." I returned to the moment I had popped all those Seconal in my mouth. *Could I honestly say I didn't think about bringing the pain to an end, a final solution? Was I so disgusted with the direction my life had taken I didn't want to live?*

"Of course you're going to have cravings. Everything I've read says you're going to have them for a long time," said Sherry. "We don't plan to do this for the rest of your life. We want to get you through the hard part. Right now, we're trying to get a sense of how likely it would be, on one of your solo outings, you would go looking for pills."

"I feel that it's not likely. We all know addicts can't be trusted, but I'm trying. I truly am. I want to finish my degree. That's going to be tough without my study buddy, but I have to do it. And I want to feel like I can negotiate this new world I've gotten into without uppers."

Sherry tsked. "New world? I think you can speak frankly here. You mean sex with men."

"I'm going to be honest, and I know this is going to make some of you uncomfortable. Things got out of control when I combined the drugs with prowling for sex. It sucks. Pun intended. What I mean is it's all freaky and fun while you're high, but then you have to come down. You have to face the fact you can't remember a sex partner's name, and you're not sure if you could pick him out of a crowd." I looked at Marc and saw the terror on his face.

"Let's move on to the third issue for today," said Nick. "We asked you to try a month completely sober, and you've done that. The question is whether you could use milder drugs like alcohol and marijuana. It might take the edge off some of the cravings."

"I never liked alcohol that much. I see smoking pot as fun to do with friends. Quaaludes are also nice." I glanced at Marc and saw a smirk on his face. "But none of those things were ever a problem. The pills, particularly Obetrol, started during those nerdy high school years and became associated with breaking out of my shyness, being able to sound witty and funny in social situations, participating. Not to mention it was super good for studying."

Marc lifted his hand like he was in class. "Can I say something, me?" His voice sounded nervous. "You were sober as hell when we spent the day together last week. But you were funny and witty and pretty much all those things I think you want to be. Seems to me like you don't need those pills, no."

Nick frowned. "I agree. I remember when you were our paper boy. I always thought of you as funny and smart and not particularly shy." *Do we have a third to tell me how wonderful and funny I am?*

"There's nothing wrong with being introverted," said Sherry. "But introverts sometimes feel like they're missing out on something, like everybody is having fun but them, everybody is having sex but them. How they perceive things isn't necessarily how the rest of the world sees them."

"Sherry, you should be the one going back to school," said Ricky. "I think you'd make a great therapist."

"If I return to school, it will be in nutrition. I'm going to change the world through healthy eating."

"Good luck with that," I said under my breath.

"I heard that, you ungrateful—"

"I'm kidding. You could serve me gourmet meals flown in from Paris, and I wouldn't eat them. Someday though, I'm going to get my appetite back. Marijuana is good for that, right?"

"Marijuana approved!" Nick pounded his fist on the table as if it was a gavel. He thought a moment. "Maybe as a doctor, I shouldn't say that."

The meeting concluded with a revised schedule where Kevin or Ricky would always be in the house during the night. Either Sherry or Nick would stop by during the day on weekdays, and Marc would come by on weekends. Marc wouldn't be an official member of the team in that he wouldn't have to come to meetings and make decisions. Afternoons during the week, I would have alone time. And smoking pot was okay. Ricky was happy about that so he wouldn't have to sneak out to light up in fear he would be tempting me.

The whole buddy schedule arrangement was bizarre, like I had arranged play dates. When I said goodbye to Marc at the door, I asked him if he was comfortable with the weekend hours. "I don't want you to feel obligated to see me."

"No problem as long as you behave." He cuffed me lightly on the chin. "No, cher, you know I like hanging out with you. This way it's guaranteed."

"I wonder what's going to happen after another month when I'm supposed to be on my own."

"Look around you, brother. People love you. Accept it, yeah."

We hugged, and he left. I turned around and caught Nick watching us. I smiled. He smiled. One big happy family.

"How do you feel about everything?" Nick said.

"Good. I know I'm incredibly lucky. After this next month, though, I have to go see my parents."

"Have you told them anything?"

"Nope. They don't know I dropped out of school. I got some 'splaining to do' as Ricky used to say to Lucy."

"Are you going to tell them everything?"

"You mean about being gay? I've got to. Gay. Drug addict. Dropout. That's going to be a fun conversation. Will you go with me?"

"You know I can't."

"I know. I don't feel like I can do it alone."

"You can. I'll call you every day. I am worried about one thing though. You have old drug contacts there."

"At some point, everybody has to trust me."

Twenty-Two: Triple Whammy

Everybody thought it was a good idea if I asked Cindy to meet me at home and be there to support me. She was more than happy to do it. I didn't fully trust myself to be on my own in my hometown where it all began and where I knew people who could supply me with pills. I kept thinking how much easier the conversation with my parents would be with a little bump. What I didn't realize at first was my parents had entirely different expectations when I told them I was coming home to talk to them about something important, and Cindy would also be in town. Before the fateful dinner conversation, Mom kept asking about Cindy and why she wouldn't be joining us.

While my parents were at work, I spent the day with Cindy.

"My mom is expecting an engagement announcement."

"You know moms, eternally hopeful."

"I don't know if I can bear seeing their faces when I hit them three times. I need chemical help."

"Drink some coffee. Don't be an idiot."

"Maybe I should only tell them about dropping out of school. Save the rest for another time."

"No. Boom. Boom. Boom. Get it over with. They'll recover. I know your parents."

"You know that day we met, I was high on a diet pill. It gave me the courage to talk to you. We might not be friends all these years later if it hadn't been for that pill. Drugs aren't all bad."

"You were taking them all through high school?"

"Yep. Not all the time. Not like I was this past year."

"I don't like the idea a stupid pill was responsible for our friendship. I had noticed you before we spoke that day and knew I wanted to get to know you. If we hadn't met then, it would have been another time. What made you start taking them all the time?"

"I felt like everyone abandoned me, Marc, Dr. B. He wants me to call him Nick now."

"You knew Marc for like five minutes, and Dr. B was in a relationship. Next."

"Kevin was always busy, and Sherry had found this new career as a fruit fly in the quarter."

She slapped my arm. "That's a terrible expression. I wouldn't want anybody calling me that. Anyway, you don't think you bear some of the responsibility for drifting away from Kevin and Sherry? Kevin said you were moody and hard to deal with at times."

"I was. It was a vicious circle. The more uppers I took, the more moody and irritable I became and the more I pushed people away. At the same time, I came to believe the way homosexual life worked was that you had to go out to bars and go home with guys until you found the right one. The more I did it, the more it looked like finding the right one was farther away. I took drugs to facilitate the greet, meet, and trick cycle. Another vicious circle."

"How are things with Marc and Nick now?"

"It's been great spending time with both of them, going out and doing things that don't involve drugs like movies, shows, museums. But it was also strange having your friends be the ones responsible for your recovery. It felt artificial."

"Did you and Marc have sex after he came back?"

"We slept together several times, only cuddled. We agreed it wouldn't be a good idea to have sex until I was 'a free man.' Most of the time I didn't feel that sexual anyway. But I loved sleeping with him, holding him. I know he loves me, but I'm not sure exactly in what way, and I'm not sure he knows either. I guess we'll figure it out in the next few months when we're not seeing each other because it's on the schedule."

"And Nick?"

"Sex?"

"I'm assuming that didn't happen or it would have been on the front page of *The New York Times*. I'm referring to getting along."

"I know his involvement in my recovery has put a lot of strain on his relationship with Manny. I'm not sure they had the greatest relationship regardless. I could say they're a mismatched couple, but what do I know? The concept of two men in a domestic living situation still seems odd to me. I can't say I haven't fantasized about it, but how does it work day-to-day?"

"I don't know. *The Odd Couple* with sex?"

Cindy dropped me off at home and wished me luck. I went into the old breezeway bedroom and turned it upside down looking for an Obetrol that might have fallen into a crack or gotten pushed to the back of a drawer. No luck. I had to face my parents sober though I did accept the martini they offered. We all toasted. They smiled in anticipation of a cause for celebration. I wondered which of the three things I had to tell them was the most devastating. Should I begin with the least troubling and work my way up or vice versa?

Mom called us to dinner, and in the center of the table, I saw the dish, which had been my favorite growing up, a pork chop and potato casserole topped with a creamy mushroom sauce. Sherry would have died. We did have a salad, though, of iceberg lettuce and tasteless tomatoes. Mom served our plates and sat down, still with an excited buzz about her. I tasted the pork chop and potatoes.

"Yum. Just like I remember it."

Mom was so excited she could barely sit still. "Oh, come on. Tell us. I can't wait any longer."

I force-swallowed the mouthful I was chewing. I took a sip of the martini. I contemplated running to the bathroom and vomiting. I chanced on an icebreaker of a different sort. "I ran into Dr. Baronian in New Orleans."

"What?" screamed my mother. I felt sorry for her, her face going through about fifteen emotions in two seconds. "That's the important news you wanted to tell us?"

"Not exactly."

"He lives there?" said Dad.

"He does."

Mom gripped the edges of the table as if she expected it to fly away.

"I've dropped out of school." Boom.

Mom's flat reaction surprised me as if she had expected worse. "Oh, honey, no."

"What do you mean?" Dad showed an uncharacteristic anger. "We sent your tuition for this semester. What did you do with it?"

"It's still in the bank." Lie.

"But what happened?" said Mom. "Was the pressure too much? I know that one professor worked you very hard, the one with the research project. You were doing so well."

"My grades last semester tanked."

"But why?"

"You should have told us. Your Mom and I were talking the other day about going to your graduation in a couple months."

"Not going to happen. Things in my life got out of control. I couldn't keep up with my courses."

Mom put her hand to her forehead. "That doesn't make sense. You're an excellent student."

"I'm a drug addict." Boom. That brought an end to any attempts to eat the food. I was sorry Mom had gone to so much trouble. Dad downed his martini and got up to make another.

Mom stared at the pork chop casserole. "What does that mean?" Her voice was unexpectedly calm.

Dad returned with a fresh cocktail. He was not calm at all. "Congratulations, son. We give you everything, and you drop out of school and take drugs. What are we talking about? Heroin? Dope?"

"Amphetamines. Diet pills. Mother's little helpers. A lot of the time it was to study for exams and write papers. I became dependent on them, built up a tolerance, so I had to increase the dosage. Later, you can't sleep, so you take something to bring you down. A cycle that can only end badly, and it did."

"What's happening with kids these days? You young people have had it too easy. You can't face responsibility. If there's a problem, you take drugs and go march in the streets or flee to another country like that's going to fix anything." Dad spoke with a bitterness that I had never heard as if for years he had kept it inside, and now it was leaking out.

"That's not helpful, Ben."

"Helpful? I always said we were too lenient with the boys, you and your Dr. Spock bullpucky. He's responsible for kids wanting instant gratification, running wild in the streets."

"Well, isn't this interesting? Putting the blame on me and Dr. Spock. And where have you been the last twenty years?" Funny how the focus had switched from me to their personal and, I imagined, long-repressed resentments about parenting decisions.

Dad shook his head. "One son out of the country and can't come home. The other, a college dropout with a drug problem. And you're trying to say it has something to do with me not being more involved."

"Hello, I'm still here. Apparently, you would prefer pointing fingers at each other than deal with the issues at hand."

Mom nodded in affirmation of what I said while Dad only growled in frustration.

"You said it ended badly," said Mom. "What happened?"

"Thank you for asking. I overdosed on barbiturates to bring me down from a binge of being high. I was in the hospital."

"My God, sweetie. People die of that. Please don't tell me you could have died."

I nodded my head, and she burst into tears. "And no one called us?" she wailed.

"I was out for a couple of days, but the doctors said things looked good for recovery. My friends made the decision not to call."

Dad now sat with his elbows on the table and his hands over his face.

"I went through detox and two months of rehab." I decided not to say it was a makeshift rehab organized by my friends.

"And all that time you didn't think to tell us anything?" said Dad.

Mom's crying sparked tears in me.

"I'm sorry. I didn't want to worry you. And I felt so embarrassed."

"Are you...are you okay now?" said Dad. "You look so thin."

"I'm off drugs. But like an alcoholic, your body has cravings. I'm gradually getting my appetite back. Every day is still a struggle." I blew my nose on the napkin.

"I want you to come home. You could finish your education here."

"I can't do that, Mom. I appreciate the offer. I have something else to tell you. I'm gay." Boom.

"This is ridiculous!" Dad yelled. He stood up as if to leave the room.

"Sit down!" Mom screamed. Dad crumpled into his chair.

"I know it isn't fair for me to lay all this on you at once. But it's all related in a way. I've been struggling with my feelings for a long time."

"But what about Cindy?" Mom moaned.

"Cindy is a dear friend who has been with me through everything. She came home this weekend to support me. I love her a lot. But not in that way."

Dad sat in a daze. Mom pushed her plate away and took a sip of her martini. She moved the glass to where the plate had been and wrapped her fingers around the base of the stem. The last revelation seemed to surprise her the least, though she had to play the mom. She drew a deep breath and let it out.

"It's not uncommon for young men to go through a phase."

"It's not a phase. I tried having sex with girls. It wasn't right."

"But if Cindy understands you and you say you love her, maybe you two can find some way..."

"No, Mom. It wouldn't be fair to her."

"I still think you should move home. There are too many bad influences in New Orleans. We never should have let you go there."

"None of it started in New Orleans. I started taking diet pills in high school. Lots of kids were doing it."

"Why diet pills? That doesn't make sense, especially for someone as thin as you."

"Diet pills are speed. They make you feel good, sometimes euphoric. And I had feelings for other boys since I was twelve." I looked at Dad. He sat comatose.

"That boy! What was his name? I knew that was not good."

"Danny. He died of an overdose, by the way. It was a warning I didn't heed."

"So, he got you started on drugs and...other things."

"It wasn't his fault. He never forced me to do anything."

I was scheduled to fly to New Orleans Sunday morning. Saturday was awkward to say the least. Dad barely spoke to me. Mom again tried to convince me I should live at home. Without going into details, I tried to explain how difficult it would be for me to live in the hometown now that I had acknowledged my homosexuality. In that conversation, Dr. Baronian was the elephant in the room neither of us acknowledged.

Before I left on Sunday, Dad pulled me aside and told me they wouldn't send me any more money. I was on my own. Mom made me promise to call every Sunday. Though I was going back to uncertainty, I couldn't wait to feel the moisture of New Orleans on my skin.

Twenty-Three: Downfall

My flight home had significantly depleted my resources, and with no more money coming from home, though Mom discreetly slipped me a couple of twenties at the door before Cindy drove me to the airport, my first order of business was to find a job. Sherry told me they were looking for a waiter at the restaurant.

"I'm not a vegetarian."

"It doesn't matter. I think you'd be great. Plus, you could learn from being around healthy food all day. And with that adorable face, you'd get a lot of tips."

It wouldn't be much money, but I was desperate. I also needed to fill my time. My ex-team checked in with me frequently, but it wasn't the same. As the days went by, my friends drifted back to their normal lives, and I became sole owner of mine. I sometimes found myself sitting in my room, staring at the four walls, bored out of my mind.

My dependence on drugs had been replaced with a dependence on guaranteed companionship. And the two most difficult to lose were Nick and Marc. Nick had checked in with me every day I was at home in Sangamon as he said he would. We had a specific time he would call, and I would sit by the phone to make sure I answered it. Back in New Orleans, he still called me nearly every day, though I didn't see him. I assumed he was trying to patch things up with Manny. Marc, on the other hand, didn't call. I missed our cuddle nights tremendously.

The first time I telephoned him after getting back, he acted surprised. "I thought you were still in the Midwest."

"No, Marc. I told you I was only going for the weekend." He seemed happy to talk about how things went with my parents and asked me about five times how I was doing. He signed off with, "I'll call you soon."

A couple weeks later, Sherry told me Marc had moved back into his old room on Esplanade after the guy who took his room left for New York. Since he hadn't bothered to mention that to me, I jumped to the conclusion he and Betsy were finally getting together. My stomach churned with jealousy.

At least my mind was occupied while I was at work. I didn't have to think about my life for a few hours. A number of times, I thought how much easier the job would be on Obetrol, remembering who ordered what, dealing with the pressure when the restaurant filled up, remembering each special request—vegetarians by nature seemed to have a lot. But working was much better than going home to an empty house.

Kevin spent most nights at Susan's, and Ricky was studying at the library when he wasn't partying. He had decided to go to med school and hoped to graduate with the best grades possible. I obviously wouldn't be graduating with my class, and with my parents cutting me off financially, I didn't know how I would save enough to return to school.

I saw Sherry at work, but she was the cook and barely left the kitchen. I did notice she had an affectionate friendship with a petite French woman who waited tables with me. I left it up to Sherry to broach the subject of lesbianism and was amazed when she didn't. In my reluctance to go home to an empty house, I sometimes stopped by Sherry's, and Ivette would often be there. Lucius would roll his eyes when Sherry and Ivette got on the floor to give each other massages or sat on the sofa reading each other's palms.

As the rising heat of late spring hit, and the sweet smell of jasmine and the fecund odor of Mississippi mud filled the air, my feelings of lust inevitably returned. My hormones had lit a bonfire and were dancing around it. I left work and walked up Esplanade. Marc's house was only a few blocks away. He would just be arriving home from his job.

Marc answered the door still in his uniform. "Nate, how are you doing, brother?" Even though he gave me a quick hug, I was crestfallen he didn't address me as cher.

"Good. I haven't seen you in a while. I wanted to talk."

"Sure. Come up to my room."

As soon as we got inside the room, I pulled him into a hug. I kissed his neck, moved up to his cheek and his mouth. He responded but without enthusiasm. I started undoing the buttons of his shirt. I was captivated by his smell after a day of work.

He pulled back. "Wait. I just got home, yeah. Not had time to shower my body."

"Please, Marc. I need you."

"I don't…" He looked away, trying to form words that wouldn't hurt me.

"You don't want me?" I dropped my hands and looked at the rainbows dancing on the walls from the prism. "You never wanted me. I was always a curiosity for you." My approach was completely wrong, but I couldn't stop myself.

"That's not true. Let's talk a minute. You said you wanted to talk."

"I lied."

I saw panic on his face. I was in crisis, and he didn't know what to do about it. He was afraid of doing the wrong thing. But as a person with a heart, he pulled me into an embrace and held me tight. It felt good, but it was too late for conciliatory hugs. I pushed him away.

"Forget it." I turned around and headed for the door.

"Nate, don't go. Sit and talk with me, yeah."

When I didn't stop, he followed me and grabbed my arm. I threw him off. I ran down the hall and down the stairs. "Cher," he called out. It was too late for that too.

I strode along Esplanade with a purpose. I went to a cottage in the Marigny on Frenchman Street where I had bought Obetrol a few times. He had some, but he charged me a ridiculous price because he said it was hard to get. I wanted to try snorting it again, and yet waiting until I got home seemed impossible. I went to the restaurant.

Ivette was there but not Sherry.

"Hi, Ivette," I said with a painful smile. "I badly need to use the restroom."

"*Pas de problème.*" She knew I spoke a little French.

"*Merci.*"

I locked the restroom door. I emptied a couple of capsules on the counter and crushed the beads with a spoon I had grabbed off the table. I rolled up a bill and snorted the powder. Burn. Gag. And then the universe opened. Why had I waited so long to do this again? I ignored the fact that it just about led to my death. I jumped up and down. "Damn. Damn. Damn." My blood raced through me like cars on a freeway. I heard the band Kraftwerk playing in my head. Beautiful. Smooth. Racing down the autobahn. Dopamine lifting me higher.

Someone knocked on the door. *I'm in the bathroom at work. I must leave.*

I unlocked the door and walked out. *"Au revoir, Ivette."*

"A bientôt."

I had heard about a bathhouse on Toulouse called Club Baths. The idea had never appealed to me before, but now it seemed like the perfect thing, a place to escape. I heard there were rooms that were completely dark. I didn't want to see anything, only feel. There were showers, a pool, a sauna, and private rooms, even a reading room. I headed for dark corners. Hands were all over my body. I felt I had descended into hell, but a glorious hell and exactly where I wanted to be.

What I remembered best hours later when I thrust my body out the door into the night were the sounds—the moaning, the slurping, the pounding of flesh on flesh, the shouts of ecstasy. I felt as empty as a cicada's abandoned shell. I walked over to the river and contemplated throwing myself in, to drift with the muddy current out to sea. Several people would be sad. One person would be furious.

I went to a pay phone near Jackson Square. By the time I dialed his number, I was weeping uncontrollably. "I'm sorry. I'm so sorry."

"Nathan, where are you?"

"Near Jackson Square."

"Sit in front of the cathedral. Stay there. Don't move."

Chartres Street was full of people. Partiers. Tourists wandering, not wanting to go back to their hotels and end the party. A man tap-danced and passed the hat. A woman noticed I was miserable and offered me the rest of her Hurricane.

It seemed to be taking forever for Nick to get there. I stood up and started walking away. He came up behind me, put his arm around my shoulder, walked me the several blocks to his car while holding on to me, not seeming to care what people thought, not saying a word. He drove me to his house. He sat me at the kitchen table and made chamomile tea.

"I suppose the tea won't do much, but it might feel good." He sat across from me. I couldn't bear to look at him.

"I'm such a fuckup."

"Drink your tea."

"Where's Manny?"

"He's staying with friends. You're supposed to call me before, not after."

"I know."

"I'm so glad you're okay. Do you want to tell me what happened?"

"I was upset that Marc has been ignoring me lately. I went by his house. I know I did the exact wrong thing. I tried to force myself on him. He couldn't handle it. And I couldn't handle that he couldn't handle it."

"I guess you realize you put Marc in a terribly uncomfortable position. You know he's not gay, right?"

"He's gay sometimes. I have a feeling you don't like him."

"I think Marc is a good guy, and he's obviously fond of you. I'm not sure if he's aware of the profound effect he has on you. That's why I was reluctant to have him on the team. Nothing we can do about that now."

I was ashamed to tell Nick I had gone to the bathhouse. Even if I had told him, he would have a hard time imagining the shameless things I had done. I told him I wandered around, afraid to go home. I did reveal I had snorted the drug though.

"Snorting is more dangerous and increases the chances of a relapse into addiction. You've worked so hard. We've all been proud of you. I'm not trying to make you feel bad, but this can't happen again."

"Please don't tell the others."

"I have to. That was the agreement we all signed. I want to bring everyone together tomorrow. Not Marc, of course."

"He's not to blame."

"I would like to hear what everyone else thinks."

One good thing about snorting is it goes through your system faster. My mind was still buzzed, but my body was exhausted, in part due to the sexual gymnastics of the bathhouse. I got flashes of what I had done and shuddered. Sleep tickled me with possibility. I yawned.

"I'll make you a bed on the sofa. You're going to feel awful tomorrow. Are you supposed to work?"

"Thankfully, no."

I lay awake on the couch, worrying that everyone was going to hate Marc and blame my relapse on him. At the same time, it wasn't lost on me that Nick lay in bed a few yards away. We were in his house alone, something I had fantasized about for years. I still felt filthy after what I had done a few hours before in dark rooms smelling of sweat and semen. I couldn't possibly force myself on Nick, even for a cuddle.

Twenty-Four: Fire

A customer at table four called me over. I braced myself, expecting a complaint. Still prone to irritability at the slightest provocation, I did the quick version of the visualization exercises Sherry had taught me. As I walked to the table, I took in six-count respirations and imagined my happy place. I didn't think Sherry would approve of my place, the Pearl River beach. In the exercise, I was supposed to be there alone, no group holding hands or Marc wiping the juice from an orange segment off my chin.

"I have a question," said the man, midthirties and balding. He was with a woman I assumed to be his wife or girlfriend.

"Be happy to answer if I can."

"I was skeptical about coming to a vegetarian restaurant, but my friend here insisted I try it. I have to say this lentil loaf is pretty good. What is the secret ingredient?"

I let out a sigh of relief and answered with a straight face. "Love."

He stared at me a moment. "You're fucking with me, right?"

I laughed. "Must be the peanut butter."

"Peanut butter? I kind of wish you hadn't told me that."

"Yeah. Sometimes the mystery is better than knowing."

Again, his stare exceeded the socially acceptable time by a few seconds. He had beautiful brown eyes. "I know exactly what you're saying. It's like that with people. My friend here likes to be mysterious, but I feel like I'm an open book."

"Books are good, open or closed."

"How about you? Are you open or closed?" His eyebrows bobbed up and down.

"Hank," said his companion. "Let the man get back to work." She smiled at me. "He doesn't get out much." We all laughed.

"Can I get you anything else?"

"Just the check," said the woman before Hank had a chance to embarrass himself further.

I walked to the counter to tally the bill. Sherry looked out from the kitchen and gave me a big smile. She called me to the window. "I love watching you with the customers. I'm so proud of you."

I shrugged. The last couple of months had been tough, but I had remained clean, at least as far as uppers. My friends rallied around once again. Everyone tried to spend as much time with me as possible. They told me it would be best if I didn't spend time with Marc. I knew they were right, but I wasn't always good at taking advice. I called Marc and apologized for trying to force myself on him. We took a walk in City Park and sat down on a bench near the old Langles Bridge. The oak trees and the green water reminded me of the Pearl River.

Marc threw his arm over the back of the bench. "Sherry was so mad at me. She dragged me up and down the bayou and left me for the crocodiles."

"I shouldn't have told them I went by your house."

"You know I care for you a lot. I hate myself for letting you go off that day. I was so confused."

"My emotions are all over the place, and it's not fair to other people."

"Me, I understand if you be needing not to see me. Anyway, you can do better than me."

"Don't give me that poor Cajun boy shit."

"This Cajun boy's got to figure some stuff out. If I don't call you, it doesn't mean I'm not thinking about you. If I don't respond in the way you want, it doesn't mean you aren't in my heart."

"You'd better shut up, or you'll get me going. Aren't I the weepiest person you've ever met?"

"You're 'bout the feelingest person I ever met, except maybe my mama, and I love her to death."

*

After my day shift in the restaurant, I sat in a corner, pen in hand, staring at a blank page of my journal. I sipped mint tea. After the relapse, Sherry had given me a bound notebook and told me writing down my feelings would be good therapy. I found it difficult to do at home but sitting in the restaurant as the early dinner crowd filtered in often inspired me. In a few weeks, I had filled half the book. Some of the entries were pure drivel, but others filled me with warmth. Expressing my thoughts in words on paper calmed me down. I could say anything I wanted since I would be the only one reading it.

A sad-looking young woman came in the restaurant by herself and sat at a table by the window. She watched the people walking by. It was the catalyst I needed, and my pen took off. It was after eight in the evening when the ideas stopped flowing. I packed up my things.

"Au revoir, Ivette."

"A bientôt."

I had been having trouble with my car and didn't have the money to get it fixed. But I enjoyed taking the streetcar, looking at the people, and I liked walking through the quarter to the St. Charles line. I strolled down Chartres Street past the cathedral, remembering the night Nick rescued me. Right around the cathedral, I smelled smoke. I looked up the street and saw plumes billowing into the sky. Fire engines screamed. Many of the buildings in the quarter were considered firetraps, and it wasn't surprising one of them had gone up in flames. Another block up Chartres, I noticed a peculiar quality to the smoke wafting down the street and hanging in the dense air of a New Orleans summer, perhaps a musty dampness in the old walls mixed with the burnt flesh of a barbecue.

I picked up my pace. The smoke thickened. A crowd blocked the intersection a couple of blocks away. Ladders of fire trucks rose into the air like cranes. *That's where the Up Stairs Lounge is.* I moved forward, but a part of me wanted to turn and run the opposite direction. The scene was utter chaos, people yelling, moaning, crying. The outside of the building was blackened, though flames were no longer evident. The head and torso of a man hung out a window, burned in his attempt to escape the security bars. A man sat on the sidewalk with a blanket around him, skin hanging from his singed arms.

The stench forced me to a find a place where the crowd was thinner so I could vomit. Drunken rubberneckers had wandered over from Bourbon Street, and businessmen in suits mixed in with firefighters and patrons who had escaped the bar, some of whom I recognized. Someone said dozens had died in the fire, another more than a hundred. Burned victims were rolled on stretchers to ambulances. A man in madras Bermuda shorts joked it was a fruit bar, and his companion retorted, "Yeah, a fruit fry."

I tried to push closer to see if any of the victims on the ground were people I knew, people dear to me: Sherry, Lucius, or Manny. It was Sherry's day off, and she and Lucius occasionally went to the Sunday beer bust, which drew a large crowd from five to seven, all you could drink for a dollar. I couldn't find anyone I knew to ask about Sherry. I ran as fast as I could down Chartres to Governor Nicholls Street. I banged on Sherry's door. No answer. I returned to the restaurant. Ivette was in the middle of taking an order. I waited until she came to the counter.

"Where is Sherry?" I gasped for air.

She gave me a look like she thought I had fucked up again, my wild eyes a sign that I was high. "I don't know."

"Did she say anything about going to the Up Stairs today?"

"I don't think so."

"Think, Ivette!"

"What's the matter with you?"

"There was a fire at the Up Stairs Lounge. Many people died."

"Mon dieu."

"I'm worried she and Lucius might have gone there. I went by their house. No one is home. Can you think of any other place she might be?"

"No." Her voice now sounded like a whimper. "What we can do?"

"I'm calling Nick. He has access to hospitals."

I pounded on the wall as the phone rang and rang. And then his steady voice said, "Hello."

"Thank god you're home. There was a horrific fire. People lying on the sidewalk badly burned." I stopped to take a breath. "Bodies hanging out windows. It's a nightmare."

"Slow down, Nathan. What are you talking about?"

"The Up Stairs. I just walked by there. Fire engines everywhere. I'm at the restaurant. I went by Sherry's. They're not home. I don't know what to do."

"Manny?" His voice faltered.

"I don't know. I didn't see him among the injured on the street."

His voice recovered, and he took control of himself. "I went to church service this morning, and Manny was there, but we didn't talk. Our pastor said a bunch of them were going to the Up Stairs beer bust to celebrate the new air conditioner someone had donated to the church. I declined, but I'm afraid Manny might have gone. I'll call the place Manny has been staying. Then I'll come and get you at the restaurant."

Ivette was having a hard time waiting on her tables, walking around in a daze. I helped her by serving plates and bussing dirty tables. It was nearly closing time, so we only had a few people left to serve, but it was a good distraction while we waited for Nick.

Nick and I returned to the scene of the fire while Ivette went to check Sherry's apartment again. The injured had all been taken away, but the spectators had increased threefold. Fire trucks lined up around the perimeter. One of the establishments down the street had set up a makeshift bar selling drinks on the sidewalk. Nick stared at the petrified man with the hair burned from his head and his right arm out the window, a singed mannequin.

"Mother of God! I think that's Bill Larson, pastor of the church." He shouted to a nearby fireman. "Are you going to leave him like that? Isn't there something you can do?"

He shrugged. "The inspectors are inside."

"Do you know how many died?"

"Can't say. A lot."

I thought I saw Buddy in the crowd. He would know if Sherry and Lucius had been there. But he disappeared before I could make my way over to him.

"We should go to the hospital," said Nick. "This is nothing but a crime scene."

"You mean someone did this deliberately?" The idea it was intentional hadn't entered my mind.

"The fireman said that the way it burned, starting on the stairway and moving up, sure looked like arson to him."

We got in the car and rushed over to Charity. Emergency was in pandemonium with burn victims, from minor to fifth and sixth degree lining the hallways. Nick was able to go in and survey the victims. He came out bug-eyed and clearly shaken. No Manny, Sherry, or Lucius, but he had seen others from his congregation. None of them were able to talk. Either our three loved ones hadn't gone to the bar, had escaped when the fire started, or their bodies were piled up in the inferno the bar had become. It was going to be a long night.

We drove to Sherry's house, and my heart leapt when I saw a light on. Lucius answered the door with a hand on his chest and tears in his eyes. Sherry and Ivette were curled up on the sofa, holding on to each other desperately as if they had barely avoided an apocalypse.

Sherry sat up. "Manny?"

"We don't know. Can I use your phone?" said Nick.

He called Manny's friends. Still no answer. He slumped into a chair.

"I have a bottle of scotch." I'd never seen Sherry drink hard liquor. She got the bottle and five glasses.

Nick hung his head. "I can't stop seeing Bill in the window."

We sipped the scotch without saying a word. When we finished, Nick said he should go home in case Manny went there.

"Do you want me to go with you?"

"Yes," he answered without hesitation.

Neither of us wanted to be alone, so we stayed up, talking some, but mostly sitting with our thoughts. No word from Manny. Several people called from the MCC congregation to talk about who was accounted for and who was missing. I could tell some of the people on the other end of the line choked up or openly wept over the loss of their pastor and possibly friends. At times Nick's voice wavered, but he never broke down.

Nick offered to drive me home about three in the morning, but I told him I didn't have to work the next two days, and if he didn't mind, I would like to sleep on the couch again. He seemed relieved he didn't have to go out or be alone. I thought he might tell me I could sleep in his bed, but he didn't. I admonished myself for the notion entering my head. Manny might be burned beyond recognition, his body piled up with the others that still hadn't been removed from inside the bar.

As I passed by his bedroom from the bathroom, he came into the hall to say goodnight. He hugged me and thanked me for being there. In the few moments I was in his arms, it dawned on me we had never hugged. In my mind, we'd had many embraces and much more, but in the real world, there had been nothing but an arm thrown over my shoulder when he picked me up that night in front of the cathedral.

In the morning paper the headline read, "29 Killed in Quarter Blaze." Inspectors were going through the bodies piled up in the bar, trying to identify them. Over the next two days, Nick and I made the rounds, looking for Manny. The people he was supposed to be staying with hadn't seen him since Sunday morning. We met with the remaining members of the MCC congregation, offering any help we could. As many as twelve members of the church were thought to have perished in the fire.

I watched Nick throw himself into efforts to help family and friends who had lost loved ones, hesitantly emerging from the bunker he had spent years building to hide his homosexuality. It was a struggle for him to associate his attraction to men with what was becoming a political movement in New Orleans.

I was admittedly unaware that a gay identity had begun to come to light in other parts of the country, political groups forming to further that identity. When the Stonewall riots happened, I had just finished a painful senior year in high school and moped around, feeling sorry for myself, anxious to leave for college. The rebellion wasn't even a blip on my radar.

But the antiwar movement was all around me in my formative years. My brother was a draft dodger. I went to demonstrations. And while we fought to end the war, we also battled to throw off the shackles of a restrictive society. I was ridiculed for my long hair and criticized for the way I dressed. I lamented that Black people still had to fight for full inclusion into our society. To see gay rights as an extension of those struggles was not a stretch for me.

The statements from local officials showed how much the public hated people like me. Identification of the bodies moved languidly, and they claimed it was because the victims carried false or no ID, implying criminal activity was part of what happened in places where homosexuals congregated. And the press, instead of focusing on how sad it was that law-abiding citizens were afraid to carry identification, they sensationalized the "seedy" atmosphere of the bars. They refused to acknowledge people were simply trying to be themselves and find love.

The people I spent time with during the week after the fire were stressed beyond belief as more bodies were identified and another burn victim in the hospital passed, bringing the death toll to thirty. But outside that circle, life went on as usual. On Monday evening, I had made it home to change clothes. Kevin was there. Yes, he had heard something about the fire. Beyond terrible.

"It didn't occur to you to check to make sure I was all right?"

"I called Sherry, and she said you were okay."

"I've been to that bar. So has Sherry. Maybe others you've met."

He hung his head. "I didn't think of that. Do you know anyone who died?"

"Nick's partner, Manny, is still missing."

"I'm sorry. Is there anything I can do?"

"Everybody goes about their business. Who cares about a bunch of faggots burnt to a crisp? A lot of people believe it was arson. Think of it. Someone deliberately started a fire that brought unimaginable pain and death to thirty people and their friends and family."

"I hope they find the guy. And tell Nick I hope they find Manny. I truly am sorry. Oh, by the way, Marc called. I left a message on your dresser."

"When did he call?"

"About an hour ago."

I wondered if I should call him immediately or let him stew in his not knowing, thinking that he might have lost me. I called him right back.

"I was so scared, cher, when I heard the news, me. I'm happy, happy to hear your voice."

"I was on my way home and walked by the bar shortly after the fire had been put out. It was like a bomb had exploded. There were charred bodies on the street, some dead, some alive, writhing in pain. Blood and other human fluids filled the gutter." I could have gone on with graphic details but stopped. At first, I wanted shove his nose in the pain we suffered until it occurred to me I might be frightening him, pushing him away. "I freaked out. Sherry and Lucius sometimes went there."

"*Dieu!* But they're okay?"

"They're okay. I have to go. I'm helping Nick look for his partner who is missing."

"Call me tomorrow, yeah?"

*

After I worked my Wednesday shift at the restaurant, I met up with Nick, and we went to a meeting about the upcoming memorial. A location hadn't been found. Several churches had declined. After the meeting, we went to Nick's. I told him I would stay with him until we found Manny, and he didn't try to discourage me. We entered the apartment, and Nick seemed to sniff the air, look around as if something was amiss. He walked down the hall.

"Oh, no," he said from the bedroom. I followed his voice to the back of the house. Manny's room had been emptied out. Drawers hung open, and the wastebasket was overloaded with discarded items. Nick held a note in his hand. He handed it to me as if I was his secretary, and he wanted it filed.

Dear Nick,

I can't live here more, this house or this town. So many friends are gone. They are killing us. I don't know what happen to you and me. I'm sorry for not tell you to your face. I'm going home. I think my mother didn't care. I call her and she cry. Tell me to come home.

Thank you for everything.
Manny

Nick collapsed onto the bed. He sat with his head in his hands. "I destroy everything I touch."

"That's not true. Manny's alive, Nick. He's going home." I sat down next to him and put my arm around his shoulders as he choked back tears. "From someone who has had a lot of experience, just let it go. You'll feel better."

He started slow and gradually worked his way to a full sob. I pulled his head to my chest. Such a strange feeling that someone was weeping, and it wasn't me. It felt good doing the comforting.

After a few minutes, propriety demanded Nick pull himself together as he always had. He stood up and wiped his eyes. "Thank you."

"You've always been there for me." Not exactly true. He had left town, and I had to suffer the consequences of the scandal through my senior year in high school. But I wouldn't begrudge him that. His suffering had been far greater than mine.

"I would like to be alone," said Nick. "Do you mind? You've been a great friend."

"Sure. I'll find my way home. I guess I'll see you at the memorial on Sunday."

"Yes. Please come."

"I will."

And as an afterthought, "Nathan, are you okay? You're not..."

"I'm fine, Nick." Nicholas Baronian. I thought of the first time I heard his name, the thrill that ran through me at the very sound of it. He was a doctor, a pianist, a tennis player, a man of great physical and inner beauty. He was caring and loyal. But he was human, and like the rest of us, he made bad decisions. He made mistakes. He had fears.

Twenty-Five: Love Game

I didn't go to any more meetings about the upcoming events to honor the victims, many of whom still hadn't been identified. Nick needed time to process the loss of friends as well as the loss of Manny, and I didn't want to be a distraction. I might have been fooling myself to imagine I was a distraction. I did my shifts at work and sometimes stopped by Sherry's to talk about the horrifying events, the lack of response from city officials, and the way the story had all but disappeared from the newspapers. We steered away from the topic of what Manny had done and what that meant.

My journal became my friend. I sat in my room and wrote about everything that had happened. I noticed both Ricky and Kevin were at home more than usual, perhaps feeling I needed the extra support.

On Saturday night, I was in my room listening to music and writing in my journal. Kevin had stuck his head in the door to say he was getting together with friends to play music. He had returned to the saxophone he played in high school and hoped to be part of a band.

"Ricky will be here if you need anything."

I frowned, looked up, and came close to questioning him what he thought I might need. Instead, I smiled. "Have fun."

Around ten p.m. the doorbell rang. Since I was sure it couldn't be for me, I let Ricky answer it. And then a knock on my door. "Somebody to see you."

I walked out of my room in baggy gym shorts and a dirty tank top. I should have changed, but I couldn't wait to see who it was. Nick stood in the middle of the living room, staring at the floor.

"Hi, Nick. I didn't think I'd see you until Sunday. Is everything okay?"

He looked up and forced a smile. "Yeah. Sure. Thought I'd stop by and say hello."

"Cool. Would you like some tea or something?"

"Am I disturbing you? Were you busy?"

"No, writing in my journal. I'll put on some hot water. Come in the kitchen."

"I feel bad about the other night."

"What do you mean?"

"I more or less told you to get lost. I didn't mean it like that."

"I didn't take it like that." Even though I did.

"Earlier this evening I was home. I played the piano, but I kept making mistakes. I tried reading, but I couldn't concentrate. To be honest, I felt so damn lonely, I didn't know what to do. I wanted company. And guess who I thought of?" I pressed my lips together, made a funny face, and raised my shoulders in a shrug. "My dear friend,

Nathan, who I've known far longer than any of the people here."

"We've been through a lot." Some of it he didn't know about.

"You know I never cried like that in front of anyone before."

"I guess what I've got is contagious."

"I like how you lighten a moment with your humor. Because I have to tell you, I'm nervous right now."

My heart flopped like a fish thrown on a dock on a summer's day. "Nervous about what?"

"I wanted to ask the secret recipe for the lentil loaf you serve in the restaurant."

I laughed. "Dr. B makes a funny. See, you can do it as well, lighten the moment." I walked across the room and wrapped my arms around him. He tensed at first. "It's difficult for you, isn't it?"

"What?"

"To feel like you have no control."

He settled into my arms and moved his hands up and down my back. "You were always someone I could look at but not touch."

"You're touching me now."

"And. It. Feels. Good."

"My place or yours?"

"Nathan. Nathan. Nathan. I'm not like you. I can't just jump into bed."

"Oh, you think I'm a slut." I dropped my arms and tried to pull away.

He held me tighter. "I only meant I'm not as free as you. But I'm not going to let you get frustrated with me and run away."

I hugged him anew. "All right by me. What if we tried sleeping together with no sex? I know it would be hard to resist all this fabulousness."

"Is that a word?"

"It's perfectly okay for us to create our own words, our own language, our own way of being together. There are no rules for people like us."

He rested his chin on my head. "You're so fucking smart."

"I know. And funny. And an emotional mess."

"Not the last part." He moved his head to press his lips to mine, a kiss not quite like a friend, but a far cry from being a lover.

"Who taught you to kiss?"

"We're working into this...gently. And yes, I would like to spend the night with you."

"Back to my original question, my place or yours?"

"I have clean sheets."

"Good call. Mine are filthy."

I went in my room and got a change of clothes for the memorial the following day. I picked up my toothbrush from the bathroom. I knocked on Ricky's door. "I'm going out with Nick."

"Okay."

*

Nick and I met Sherry, Ivette, and Lucius in front of St. Marc's United Methodist Church on Rampart Street, the only house of worship willing to hold a memorial service for the fallen victims of the Up Stairs Lounge fire. Over two hundred people filled the pews.

"Nice turnout," said Nick.

Sherry shook her head. "I don't know. With all the thousands and thousands of gays in New Orleans, this is all who showed up? The church isn't even full."

The mood was somber, and organ music played. Flowers filled the front of the church, and several pastors from MCC churches in other cities had made the journey to honor those who had died. Word on the street was that they were pretty sure who started the fire, a disgruntled drunk and part-time hustler who many remembered causing a scene and being kicked out of the bar that evening.

As I sat in the pew between Nick and Sherry, I found myself tuning out the speeches and instead replaying the conversation Nick and I had had lying close together on the clean sheets while a ceiling fan spun above us.

Nick admitted that he and Manny had been little more than roommates the last six months.

"Was he hooking up with other guys?"

"I don't know. I suspect he was."

"What a fool not to come home to you."

"You think I'm worth coming home to?"

"If you made me an offer, I might give it a go."

"I thought you were still in love with Marc."

"Let's be honest. Marc was the first man I had sex with, I mean real sex. Gay or not, he made it the most beautiful first. In those circumstances, did I have any choice but to fall in love? But I can't wait around for years for him to decide what he wants. Most likely he'll find a girl, marry her, and make her miserable. Do you know what you want?"

"I've never thought in terms of what I want, only what I can get."

I turned on my side and rose on my elbow, chin to palm. "You amaze me. With all your education, you're pretty dumb. Have you looked in the mirror?" I thought of the poster that had hung in the Up Stairs Lounge, now reduced to ashes, of the *Cosmopolitan* centerfold of Burt Reynolds lying naked on a bearskin rug. Burt Reynolds had nothing on my Dr. B.

"You're talking about physical attractiveness."

"Well then, look in the mirror again, but this time look into your soul." I pointed to his chest, an excuse to let my hand fall on the bed of curly hair I had longed to touch that first time I had seen him naked in the country club locker room. I stared at the perky brown nipples nearly lost in a sea of curls.

"I see my damaged soul."

"Okay, so the outer casing has a few scars. But look beyond that, the true wonderful essence of you."

"Sometimes I don't know if you're brilliant or full of shit." He looked down at my hand, now plowing gently through his body hair from stomach to chest.

"I'm brilliantly full of shit."

He took my hand in his. "That feels wonderful although a tad distracting. Let's talk about you, your plans."

I giggled, dying to reach down and see if he had an erection, but I controlled myself. Unlike with Marc, I felt what we had going didn't have an expiration date, that we could take our time. "I want to go back to school. I want to learn French fluently and study international business. Later I'll get a job in Paris or Lyon or Toulouse-Lautrec."

"Toulouse-Lautrec was an artist."

"Right. The point is I want somebody to love. I don't want to hang around in bars or have anonymous sex or hop from bed to bed. Look where that got me." He raised my hand to his lips and kissed it.

"I thought your point was you were going to France and leaving me behind."

"I guess I left out a part. To complete my studies, I need to work a while and make some money. Once I've finished my degree, maybe I'll go on to get a master's. That's going to take time and emotional support. I don't plan to go anywhere for a while. I've got kind of a family here."

He groaned. "Did you have to say the family word? It was all sounding so nice. I can imagine you telling your parents about the plans for the future. Oh, and by the way, I'm moving in with Dr. Baronian, my lover."

"Are you my lover? We haven't had sex yet."

"We're speculating, doing exploratory research."

"Did you say moving in with? It's not nice to play with a young man's heart."

"Or an old man's."

True, Nick was fourteen years older than me but still young.

"Can I kiss you?" I said. "I mean a real kiss?"

"Yes, and I'll try to do better this time."

I rolled on top of him and pressed my lips to his. One thing I didn't have to speculate about now was whether he had an erection or not. I cupped it in my hand and broke away from the exploratory research of each other's mouths. "Not bad for an old man."

He roared and flipped me over, his full weight on top of me. "I'll show you."

"Please do."

Despite his roar and pinning me to the bed, he was at times hesitant, slowing his heaving, loosening his vice grip on my hand, which he held above my head while he probed the scent of my armpits. "Nice," he said.

"I'm not a gentle flower, you know."

"Meaning?"

"You still seem a bit unsure."

"I have to keep reminding myself you are no longer a boy, but a full-grown man...and I do mean full grown."

"You're going to make me blush."

"I love your smart-alecky shyness, your selective fearlessness, your audacity in keeping me in your thoughts all these years. And your goddamn mesmerizing eyes aren't bad either. I guess I've always been a little afraid of you."

"Bullshit. You're afraid of yourself, what you want to do with me."

He shut me up with an aggressive kiss, putting his hand at the back of my head to press us closer.

I was shaken from my reverie by the rousing voice of MCC founder Troy Perry from the podium, building with emotion, encouraging gay men and women to hold their heads high. During the next speech by another visiting pastor, Perry interrupted and returned to the podium, informing us television and press cameras were set up outside. Anyone who was afraid of losing his job or being outed to his family could exit by a side door. All the attendees set to murmuring, discussing, and arguing. My friends and I looked at each other. Nick had the most to lose.

"You think I'm worried about someone discovering I'm a homosexual," said Lucius. "Pa-lease."

"We have the blessing of our boss to be here," said Sherry. "No way we're getting fired."

"I'm in the same boat," I said. "I suppose if the footage goes national, my parents might see it, but they already know."

Nick let out a big breath and took my hand. "I'm leaving with all of you, out the front door."

He held my hand, and I squeezed tightly as we crossed the threshold. The crowd spilled out onto the sidewalk in front of the church, greeting and hugging while passengers in cars gawked as they rolled by. I was holding Nicholas Baronian's hand, walking out into daylight where cameras might be broadcasting it to the world, surrounded by loved ones and sexual deviants becoming aware we had to expose ourselves to the light and fight for what we wanted.

As I stood huddled with my peers, fortified by Nick's hand still clasped in mine, I saw a glimmer of hope we could change people's hearts about same-sex love just as the antiwar movement had turned the majority against the war in Vietnam. But as much as I wanted to focus on changing the world, I couldn't stop smiling about finding my place in it. I was in the thrill of, at long last, finding somebody to love, and he seemed to feel the same. Sherry stood apart, talking with Lucius and a couple of his friends, but she kept looking in our direction, grinning as if witnessing a miracle.

"I have an idea," said Nick.

"Hop on a plane and go to Paris right now?"

"Nothing that crazy. There are some tennis courts near my house. I remember seeing you play with your brother."

"I haven't played for a long time."

"Me neither. After...well, I thought I might not play again."

"When I was fourteen, I started taking lessons with the idea you and I might play some day...tennis, that is."

He laughed. "I welcome your humor in my life."

"I'm sure I could provide you with lots of humor on the tennis court after not playing for so long."

Nick looked up at the sky. "Perhaps the rain will hold off long enough.

An hour later, we were across the net from each other. He had power and technique while I had the pleasure of not taking the game too seriously. Knowing it was highly unlikely I could beat him, I was completely at ease. We pounded the ball back and forth, increasing the pace with each stroke. I saw it as a physical display of affection we could do in public, taking on sexual overtones. The service was his, I the receiver. He hit deep, topspin. White fuzzy balls back and forth. Grinding. In. Out. Approach shot. Follow through. Overhead. Slam. Ace. Moonball. Passing shot. Nice touch. Drop shot. Love game.

The sky darkened, and the first drops of rain fell. A thunderstorm stood ready to rock the afternoon. We would not be walking into a sunset, but instead, I would seek shelter from the storm in a house, in a bedroom, in the arms of Nicholas Baronian. The journey had been painful and glorious and frustrating and adventurous and mind-blowing and beautiful and nearly deadly and lovely, and, the best part, it would continue.

Acknowledgements

I owe a debt of gratitude to my editor, Ashley Kingsbury, who took a chance on me and worked tirelessly to bring this work to fruition. I also want to thank the rest of the team at NineStar Press for the work on this book. Early readers Jerry Wheeler, Jim Provenzano, Louis Flint Ceci, and Mary Hardcastle made invaluable suggestions in the editing process.

Thanks to Lou Ann Alsip who helped get the French phrases in order. Robert Fieseler's award-winning book, *Tinderbox: The Untold Story of the Up Stairs Lounge Fire and the Rise of Gay Liberation,* was vastly important in getting the parts about the tragedy correct. Frank Perez and Jeffery Palmquist's book, *In Exile,* was also helpful in providing details about New Orleans gay culture in the time this story is set. A large number of friends and my five siblings have been supportive of my work, but most important was the love and support I received from my husband, Robert Green, to make this book a reality.

About Vincent Traughber Meis

Vincent Traughber Meis is a member of the San Francisco Bay Area writing community. He has been a community college teacher, an editor, and a world traveler. His writings include novels, short stories, and travel articles. He was a co-creator of the imprint Fallen Bros Press where he has published his five previous novels. Three of these novels have received Rainbow Awards. His writings have appeared in magazines and short story collections. He lives in San Leandro, California with his husband.

Email
vtmeis@sbcglobal.net

Facebook
www.facebook.com/Vincent.meis

Twitter
@convince415

Website
www.vincentmeis.com

Also from NineStar Press

Give Way by Valentine Wheeler

Kevin McNamara's life after retirement is...fine. He has friends, a few consulting gigs, and an ex-wife he's finally on good terms with. But when he meets an intriguing stranger—a rarity in close-knit Swanley, Massachusetts—in his apartment lobby, he can't stop thinking about him or about the unexpected attraction that knocked him flat.

Awais Siddiqui never thought he'd want to come back to his childhood hometown, but when his grandmother falls ill, he's the only one who can move back to help. Awais figures he'll be back in a big city soon enough—but then a silver fox on his route catches his eye.

It's never too late to accept a second chance at love.

First Impressions by C. Koehler

When Henry Hughes and Cameron Jameson meet for the first time at a Coming Out Day party, it's anything but love at first sight. In fact, it's an unmitigated disaster, despite a scorching physical attraction.

Henry, whose social anxiety gets the better of him, humiliates Cameron, and when Cameron finds out about Henry's past in adult films, he assumes he dodged a disease-covered bullet. Yet as Henry runs into Cameron again and again, he realizes he might have misjudged the younger man. He also realizes that Cameron won't let go of his own initial view and thinks Henry is an unmitigated ass. First impressions are lasting impressions, and Cameron seems to misinterpret all of Henry's words and deeds.

It's not until Henry confronts Cameron that Cameron realizes just how wrong he's been, but he thinks he's lost his chance. Yet when disaster strikes Cameron and his friends, Henry rides to the rescue. Will Cameron be able to put aside his pride and shame to accept Henry's help and his heart?

The Q by Rick R. Reed

Step out for a Saturday night at *The Q*—the small town gay bar in Appalachia where the locals congregate. Whose secret love is revealed? What long-term relationship comes to a crossroad? What revelations come to light? The DJ mixes a soundtrack to inspire dancing, drinking, singing, and falling in (or out) of love.

This pivotal Saturday night at *The Q* is one its regulars will never forget. Lives irrevocably change. Laugh, shed a tear, and root for folks you'll come to love and remember long after the last page.

Connect with NineStar Press

www.ninestarpress.com

www.facebook.com/ninestarpress

www.facebook.com/groups/NineStarNiche

www.twitter.com/ninestarpress

www.instagram.com/ninestarpress

9 781648 902758